emerge

A FORTUNA NERA NOVEL

BOOK 1

SAGE ST. CLAIRE

Cover design: Susan Renee at Jack'd Up Book Covers
Editing: Bobbi Hailey

Print ISBN: 979-8-9955299-0-3

lets stay connected!

Scan here for Spotify playlists and Social Media for Sage St. Claire!

To those who have been convinced your darkness is the ugliest part of you...

To love someone unconditionally is to face someone's darkness and still choose to see their light playlist

Prison - The River

Sam Tinnesz - Play With Fire (feat. Yacht Money)

Jessie Murph - I'm Not There For You

Tame Impala - The Less I Know The Better

Magnolia Park - SHALLOW

Spiritbox - Sun Killer

Sleep Token - Emergence

Tate McRae - Miss possessive

Sleep Theory - Static

Bring Me The Horizon - Follow You

Sleep Token - Give

Taylor Swift - The Fate of Ophelia

Sleep Token - Granite

Dayseeker - Pale Moonlight

Olivia Dean - Ok Love You Bye

Olivia Dean - Let Alone The One You Love

PRESIDENT - Conclave

Olivia Dean - Echo

Taylor Swift - Wi$h Li$t

"I am terrified by this dark thing
that sleeps in me..."

-Sylvia Plath

author's note

Content intended for a mature audience only. Due to explicit language, graphic sex, detailed depictions of violence, and other possible triggers, reader discretion is advised. For a detailed list of triggers, please refer to:

https://www.sagestclaire.com/content-warnings

prologue

Sebastian

"YOU HAVE to get the fuck out of here. There's no other way to spin it. There is a fucking fox in this hen house, Sebastian. I will not watch them pluck away your feathers one by one until you're dead. We will find out who is behind this fucking treachery, but you have to go somewhere you can lie low." Matteo, my second in command and most trusted confidant, says.

"I hear you, but this is my empire. It is mine to rule, Teo. Mine to defend, and mine to watch crumble if that's what is to come." I reply.

"I understand, but you can't do any of that if you're fucking dead, Bash!" He barks back at me, using the nickname he's called me since we were children.

Teo is the only person in this world who speaks to me with so much familiarity and gets away with it. Even my own mother, God rest her soul, spoke to me with a formality you don't usually hear between mother and son. Then again, she knew from the moment she saw two pink lines, she was bringing the heir to Fortuna Nera into this world. Not her child, but the future head of The Family.

"I will not tuck my tail between my legs and run like a scared dog just because of a few death threats, Matteo. I'm not a fucking child." I tell him, throwing the papers he brought me across my desk.

The humidity in Florida is suffocating. Of all my business hubs around the world, this is my least favorite. I fucking hate the sand and the fake, spray-tanned women. I miss my home. Italy is where my soul belongs, and it's been far too long since I've set foot on my home soil. As much as my mother wanted me to love Spain the way her family has for generations, I never truly felt comfortable there. I have always felt as though the devil was chasing me, and I could never truly be at peace. But in Italy, my mind finds solace.

I scroll through my phone until I find the contact I'm looking for, Beckett Hayes. Together with his associates, he has been looking into who the mole in Fortuna Nera could be. As much as I trust Teo with the very air I breathe, one can never be too careful in this line of work. It's gone by many names over the years.

Mafia. Mob. Gangsters. The Family.

To me, I just call it what it is. Business.

"Mr. Hayes, I'm getting a little impatient with this

cat-and-mouse game. I know you and Mr. Negan have been working to find the holes in my operation, but my patience has run out. I need names." I demand, leaving the phone on speakerphone as I throw a few bundles of cash to Matteo and he shoves them into a duffel bag.

He tells me the information he has for me could implode my organization. As if I didn't already know that.

Fuck.

Matteo is right. I need to leave Florida, there's no other choice. Alarms ring out on the exterior of the club, drawing Matteo's attention away from my phone call.

"Seb, get the fuck out of here NOW!" He whisper-shouts, dialing the helicopter pilot who is always on standby on the roof.

Beckett's voice comes through my phone in the middle of the chaos rising around me.

"Seb, can you meet me at my house this weekend? I think I might have an idea." He asks.

"Of course, I can be there in less than forty-eight hours." I reply, pulling my pistols from my shoulder holsters and making sure they both have a round in the chamber before I hang up, sliding my phone into my pocket.

I'm too fucking old for this shit. When my father took control of this organization at only twenty-two, he ruled with little opposition. No one dared to speak out against his commands. Those brave enough to try met the end of a .45 with no mercy. I thought by thirty-nine, I would have a tight grip on my reign over Fortuna Nera the same way he did. I do not show leniency. I do not allow excuses. You pay for mistakes in blood under my rule. But there have always been those who believed I should never have been given the helm. My father may have been born and raised Italian, but my mother was the Spanish mistake he was never supposed to have made. He was already promised to a nice Italian girl from a wealthy allied family. Meeting my mother and having me blew those plans all to shit.

Machine gun fire sounds downstairs and Matteo jumps into action, locking down the office door while barking orders into his cell.

"Go, NOW!" he says, throwing the duffle bag in my direction. I have no choice but to listen to him. If I stay here, we will all die. If I leave, we will have the chance to fight another day.

one

Vanessa

"IS your friend gonna be here some time today, Helo? Because I really need to get back downstairs. Rory doesn't actually work for me anymore, ya know." I ask him, leaning against the small kitchen island, absent-mindedly spinning the keys around my finger.

I've known Helo for at least half a decade, so I know I can trust his word. But I'm getting sick of waiting for this guy, who supposedly will make a great new tenant.

"Sebastian will be here, Ness. He's usually very... prompt. Annoyingly so, really. Something must've delayed him." Helo texts furiously on his phone, his brows pinched together.

"Yeah, no shit, Sherlock." I tell him as I push off the counter. "Listen, I'll be downstairs. He can check things out and let me know if it's a good fit. You've got the contracts already drawn up, right?"

He nods without looking away from his phone screen.

"Cool, come find me when he's ready to sign." Dropping the keys on the table next to the front door, I let myself out.

The stairs at the back of the building stop right in front of the back door to Mug Life, the coffee shop I run here in Grovewood, South Carolina. My life here is slow and simple, the way I always imagined it would be. Growing up in the burbs of Miami, I'm accustomed to a constant stream of noise. I've gotten used to the serenity of Grovewood, and I hope I never have to go back.

At only twenty-four, I never dreamed in a million years I would be where I am. A business owner? Well... kind of. Living on my own, hundreds of miles away from the only family I've ever known? Never thought it was even possible. If you ask my mother, it's the ultimate betrayal. I should be home, taking care of my parents and popping out babies like my older sister has for years and years before me. My baby brother was the only one of us allowed to go wherever his heart or his dick took him. It was supposed to be my turn to enter into the *family business*. If you consider running coke for a drug syndicate and never getting to have any dreams of your own a business.

The second I turned eighteen, the pressure of that potential responsibility wrapped around my throat like a noose, squeezing until spots danced across my vision.

I'd already worked every single day after school to pay for my car and the several lines of credit my parents had already taken out in my name. I couldn't imagine continuing to bust my ass for the rest of my life just to give it all away to someone else because of a misguided sense of responsibility. I cared about my parents, but they weren't good people by any stretch of the word. Hell, they weren't even morally questionable people who were decent parents. That I could've handled. They were apathetic at best and deceitful at worst. I got the hell out of Florida as fast as I could and never looked back.

Pulling open the back door, I see Rory, my closest friend and former barista, leaning over the front counter, locking lips with her husband. You'd think after you marry someone, you'd get tired of being around them all the time, but with these two, you never get that vibe.

"Gross! Not around the danishes!" I say, covering my eyes.

Rory laughs, untying her apron and handing it to me as she rounds the front counter.

"Aww, what are you gonna do? Fire me?" She bumps her hip against mine.

"Didn't I already do that?" I laugh, and she just rolls her eyes. Most days I miss her terribly. But I'm so proud of her for finally fulfilling her dream and opening a dance studio here in Grovewood.

"Thank you for covering. I really appreciate it. Ended up being a colossal waste of time, but still. I appreciate you always helping me out when I need it," I hug her tightly, knowing she absolutely isn't a hugger but not giving her the chance to escape my affection.

"I'm always here, Ness. Don't hesitate to reach out. This early in the morning, I can't even open the studio, so I'm happy to help," she tells me with a warm smile.

"Yeah, and I love free shit." Breaker says, holding up his cup and scone. She smacks his arm, and he just shrugs.

"Oh, don't act like you don't get free shit here all the time!" I tell him. Breaker does all the IT work for everyone in this building. This coffee shop, the tattoo studio next door, and the jewelry shop on the corner are all his domain when it comes to our internet or cybersecurity needs. Digitally, I'm pretty much useless, so I'm grateful to have him.

"Thanks, Ness. See you later!" He calls out as the bell over the front door signals their exit.

Two girls in workout clothes come in, and the routine of my morning begins. The flurry of iced macchiato's and venti cold foams is almost enough to make me lose track of the fact Helo's friend is supposed to be stopping by at some point to sign this rental agreement.

I'll admit, I was surprised when he suggested he knew someone who could sublet the apartment above the coffee shop. Helo has been my accountant for about a year now. Apart from his coffee order and love for his wife, Willow, I know relatively nothing about him or who he associates with. But I trust he would never suggest someone who would destroy the place or leave me in a bind.

When I moved to Grovewood, the universe brought me to this coffee shop. I'm a firm believer in being in just the right place at just the right time, and that's exactly what happened when I met April.

Technically, it's April who owns Mug Life and the apartment upstairs, on paper. But she's living it up, retired, tan, and drunk in the Bahamas or Italy or wherever her heart has taken her this month. She trusts me to make all the decisions here because I've proven to her I can handle these responsibilities. And I know one day, when I can afford it, all this will be mine. To some, it may seem like a small dream. Like pennies in a wishing well. But to me, it's everything I've ever wanted. It's the chance to live the life I want to live, not under someone else's thumb or expectations.

The bell over the door rings, and a man crosses the threshold. I swear all the air leaves the building. Is that shit even possible?? I read about things like this happening in the smutty books Rory and her friends recommend to me all the time, but I've never actually experienced it for myself until this very moment. He's the epitome of tall, dark, and handsome. He's every single thing my intuition tells me I should run the fuck away from as fast as I can, and never ever look back.

But for some reason, I can't drag my eyes away from him. He looks refined, elegant almost. Which feels like such a weird statement to make about a man. He's over six feet of flawless olive skin in an Armani button-down. It's not something you see every day in a small town in South Carolina. I've definitely never seen a man with a neck tattoo that wasn't Satan in a fucking Sunday hat.

My favorite alternative metal singer's rich voice pulls me back to reality as the band's music plays through the speakers around the shop. The two girls at the counter talk back and forth about the daily specials before they both order venti iced skinny lattes. I watch Satan's gaze trail down their bodies from where he stands behind them in line.

First ick.

He steps up to the counter, his eyes meeting mine as I work to finish their drinks. They widen slightly, honing in on my chest before coming back up to meet my unamused stare.

Second ick.

I've always been a curvier woman with a big chest. Men have had full-blown conversations with my tits before, but I'll be dead and buried before that happens to me in my fucking place of business.

"Welcome to Mug Life. Can I help you?" I ask, doing my best to mask the disdain in my voice.

I finish one iced latte, sliding it across the bar to one of the girls while starting the other. The man stands there, silent and unmoving. Just watching me work. It's completely unnerving.

He may be the most gorgeous man I've ever seen in my entire life, but the silent, predatory way he's watching me is fucking creepy.

"Sir, are you going to order?" I ask again, and he smirks.

"Depends, *Bambina*. Are you on the menu?" He asks with the confidence of a man who is used to getting exactly what he wants, when he wants it.

My jaw drops. Iced caramel latte flies through the air before my mind has time to compute what I'm doing. The Latina in me has always reacted before thinking.

The bell over the door chimes, but this man and I are caught in a stare down, a battle of wills, and neither of us is willing to be the first to break. He's furious, dangerously so. The twitch in his jaw and the murderous glare in his eyes tell me so. But he should learn to watch his mouth before speaking to a lady he's just met.

I see Helo walk up behind the man out of the corner of my eye, his face ashen.

"Oh. Great. I see you've met Sebastian."

two

Sebastian

THE SUGARY LIQUID drips from the collar of my black silk shirt. I don't blame her, I deserved it. In my defense, the moment I saw her flawless caramel skin and crimson red lips, I was aching to feel them wrapped around my cock. Her wild curls frame her face, pulled back in a way that keeps them out of her eyes but barely tamed. Damn, this woman is a fucking stunner. It's a shock to find a woman so uninterested in crawling on her knees the moment she sees my face.

I've spent decades with women kneeling at my feet, begging for a taste of the Arsenio Empire and everything it offers. They don't want me. Not the real me, at least. Hell, they don't even know me. They just want the money, the cars, the expensive clothes, and the jewelry. And of course, the drugs. They all want the drugs.

But here, no one knows my name. For once in my

life, there are no sycophants lining up to kiss my ass. I'm really not sure how to handle it. There have always been those who criticized my father for marrying my mother and naming me as his heir, however, no one dared cross the man. He ruled with an iron fist until the day we laid him into the ground. He would be ashamed to see what I've made of this family.

Don't get me wrong, I've generated billions for Fortuna Nera. I've grown our reach far beyond the borders of Italy. Yet there are plenty of those, mainly my uncles, who don't believe the Arsenio line should ever have mixed with the Spanish. That I simply shouldn't exist. My own flesh and blood believe I shouldn't be alive, but in this business, it's not something one would find surprising.

Yet here I am, standing in this fucking coffee shop in some backwater town in South Carolina. Covered in iced coffee because I can't control my mouth.

"This fucking guy?!" she screeches. "I think the fuck not."

The coffee shop cleared out quickly, leaving Helo, the irate barista, and myself here alone.

"Well, she certainly has a mouth on her, doesn't she?" I smirk, not helping my case at all.

"If you want somewhere to live, you'll shut the fuck up while you're behind." Helo says out of the corner of his mouth.

He grabs a few napkins from the counter, shoving

them in my direction before whispering something to the fuming barista. She gestures wildly back at him, obviously not happy with whatever he's telling her. She is glaring daggers at me over his shoulder, making my cock twitch in my pants.

Fuck, I love a feisty woman.

This is *not* the reason I'm here. I need to focus on regrouping. On figuring out what the hell is going on inside Fortuna Nera and eliminating the cancer inside my operation. Just thinking about it makes me want to put a fucking bullet in my skull, but I know it must be done. As my father always taught me, like all things in life, there is no end until death.

"Please, allow me to start again. I apologize for my behavior. I have travelled a long distance, and I am quite tired. But I make no excuses. I am Sebastian. It's very nice to meet you, miss...?" I ask, interrupting Helo and stepping around him to offer her my hand.

She crosses her arms over her chest, pushing her tits up. It takes a ridiculous amount of self-control to keep my eyes trained on her amber ones, but I manage. Her expression doesn't budge.

"This is Vanessa Diaz. She is the woman kind enough to offer to rent the apartment above the coffee shop to you, so play nice, please?" Helo says, glaring back at me.

I give him a short nod before retracting my hand and sliding it into my pocket. The tiny gold hoop in her nose glints against the light as her nose twitches, and I stifle a smile.

"Well, I would appreciate the space. However, I'm happy to have anywhere to change out of this shirt at the moment." I smirk.

Her eyes gleam, something devilish banked there, but she doesn't apologize.

"You're welcome to change in the bathroom over there after you clean up this mess off my floor. I'll grab the rental agreement if you two want to have a seat at the table by the window. We can go over a few things." She doesn't ask, she demands. I've never cleaned a floor in my fucking life, but for this woman, I'm actually considering it.

She throws a towel across the counter at my chest, and I catch it, completely speechless. Helo stands next to us, watching the exchange with an expression that is equal parts amused and concerned. I'm sure, for her safety. He's seen me cut off a man's finger for pointing it in my direction. Yet here I am, crouching to the floor to clean the disaster of ice and coffee she threw my way, and I almost want to laugh about it.

"She has a...commanding presence, doesn't she?" I scoff, and Helo just laughs.

"I'll make sure the paperwork is in order, you just change into something a little less dark roasted." he says, sitting at a table by the window.

I drop the wet towel into the sink behind the counter

as she watches me like a hawk out of the corner of her eye. She really is a beautiful woman. How a woman like that ended up in this town is a mystery to me. But hell. I'm stuck here, too.

Walking to my car, I grab a clean shirt out of the bag I quickly threw in the trunk in my hurry to leave Florida. Bundled underneath the minimal amount of clothes I was able to bring along is the one possession I refuse to travel without. I shove it back down to the bottom of the bag, refusing to think about it right now. There are definitely more pressing matters at hand.

Not bothering to change inside, I strip the wet shirt off, tossing it in the trunk and slipping on a clean one. I opt for white this time, hoping to make me look less like the devil as a dry laugh sounds behind me.

"You really should be more careful doing that in broad daylight, you know. The old biddies would probably have heart attacks. It's not every day a tattooed Italian adonis strips in front of a coffee shop in this town, Seb." A soft, feminine voice says from the storefront behind me.

"Ah, Miss Willow. How lovely to see you this morning. I would apologize, but I'm not sorry. I would rather you be able to see all of this than have to see only your husband for the rest of your life." I smirk, dragging the t-shirt down my abdomen slowly. Willow, Helo's wife, is the manager of the tattoo shop next door, and over the years of our business connections, I've come to know her well.

"I'm good. One cocky, dominating man in my life is more than enough, thanks." She laughs, waving as she walks back into the shop.

Pushing open the door to the coffee shop, I find Vanessa and Helo sitting at the front table, looking through the contract together. She glares at me but says nothing as I pull out the remaining chair next to them and sit down.

"Contracts are nothing new to me, so shall we begin?" I suggest, and Vanessa rolls her eyes.

"Listen here, Mr. Fancy Pants. This is my circus and these are my monkeys. So how about you chill the fuck out and answer the same questions I ask every potential tenant, and then we'll see where it goes from there, okay?" Vanessa straightens her spine, posturing herself to show she's the boss in this situation. If that's what she needs to move this encounter along, then so be it.

"Very well, Ms. Diaz. I will answer any question I can. Within reason, of course." I responded, giving Helo a pointed look. Surely he's given her some insight as to why I'm here, right?

"Look, maybe we've all gotten off on the wrong foot here. Sebastian won't be able to disclose all the information you typically request, but I can vouch for him. He won't be a problem, Ness, I promise you that," Helo states, and I nod.

"You'll barely know I'm here, Ms. Diaz. And the rent won't be an issue. I have some...problems to sort out with my business, and once that is settled, I will be on my way." I tell her. She narrows her eyes at me, unsure if I can be trusted, I'm sure.

"How long should I expect these problems to take to get sorted out? It takes time to list the space and advertise. Should I be expecting you to leave in the middle of the night a week from now? Or will you give me at least thirty day's notice?" she asks, sarcasm evident in her tone.

"I will pay six months in advance, regardless of how long I'm here. In cash. At the end of six months, we can reevaluate. Sound fair?" I suggest.

Her brows raise in surprise, and I smile internally, glad I finally feel like I've gotten the upper hand on her. I may manipulate people to get what I want from them, but I've never cheated any hard working coffee shop owners out of their money, and I don't intend to start with Vanessa.

Besides, the amount I would pay in six months for rent is nothing compared to the thousands it would cost to pay someone to get rid of her body.

"Fine, but you bring a prostitute to my rental and you're paying an additional cleaning fee." She snaps, scrawling her name across the contract and pushing her chair back with more force than necessary. She clearly doesn't care for me. Helo drops his head back in exasperation, but I can only laugh.

"I'm not sure how you pissed her off so quickly, but I'd play nicely, Sebastian. You might need her help." He suggests, and I scoff.

"I think I'll survive without a venti cappuccino, but thanks for the advice. Now, I believe you and I have some more important business to discuss?" I sign my name on all the necessary lines that seem like little more than a formality to rent the four walls upstairs. Moving on to my business, I push the contract away and listen as Helo slowly dismantles the world I've worked since birth to build.

three

Vanessa

"OKAY, but is he hot? Objectively speaking, please don't give me details because I don't roll that way." My sister Aria asks.

She's the closest to my age and the only one of my sisters still willing to speak to me after I left. We'd both been branded the black sheep in our own ways, me for daring to live my own life, and her for deciding men weren't in any way appealing to her.

"Completely missing the point," I reply, wiping the counters down as I close up for the night.

"I don't know, Ness. Kinda feels like the point. Hot guy literally living at your mercy? Many a jealous bitch would be willing to fight you for this opportunity." She laughs, the familiar tick of the cash counter in the background.

"They can have him, he's an asshole." I tell her as I dump the last of the espresso grounds out of the press.

"Are you working at mom and dad's?" She doesn't have to answer me. I already know she is.

"Don't judge. I need the money. The restaurant isn't doing great right now." She replies, huffing out a breath.

"I would never judge you, Aria. You do what you've gotta do, I understand completely." I rinse the pieces of the machine, setting them to dry. The contrast between my life and my sister's is not lost on me.

Right now, hundreds of miles away, she's counting and banding thousands of dollars in drug money for a syndicate that's brought nothing but pain and suffering to my family for generations. As much as I'd like to say I left them behind without a second thought, I can't. Leaving my home, my family, the only life I'd ever known, was the hardest thing I've ever done. Starting over on the right side of the law, for once in my life, left me feeling more confused and lost than I care to admit. Luckily for me, I made friends who painted in shades of morally grey, rather than just black and white.

"I don't know, Aria. He's not the dark, broody, 'give me love because I'm so damaged' kind of bad boy. He's just the gross, misogynistic kind of man-boy who sets women back decades every time he speaks." Rinsing out the drip trays from the espresso machines, I leave them to dry on a rack near the sink. Her husky laugh comes through the phone, warming my heart.

God, I miss her. I miss her wit. I miss her jasmine perfume. I miss the way she could wrap an arm around my shoulder and make any hard day feel just a little less heavy. She was more of a mom to me than anyone else, including our actual mother.

The hair on the back of my neck rises, and suddenly I feel as if I'm being watched. It's after 9 pm. There's a faint sound of tattoo guns buzzing from the shop next door, but when I turn around, no one is there. The street outside the front window is silent. Not a single car passes by. Still, I can't shake the feeling that someone's eyes are on me right now.

"Ness? Helloooo? Earth to Vanessa?" Aria shouts through the phone.

"Huh? Oh, yeah, I'm here. Sorry." I reply, still searching for the source of my paranoia,

"Did something cute walk by?" she jokes, and I scoff. I know she means well, but she doesn't take anything seriously. You'd think with our upbringing she would have a better sense of security. Or at least self-preservation.

"No, Aria. There is nothing cute in this town. Well, unless you include Doug. He's the most handsome man on the planet, obviously." I tell her, finishing up my final cleaning duties so I can get the hell out of here. "I gotta go. I'll call you tomorrow. I love you."

"I love you too, sis. Doug doesn't count as a man, by

the way. Be careful!" The line clicks, and I toss my phone across the counter.

Usually, Grovewood is never a scary place to be after dark. I'm never afraid of much, knowing I have some well-armed and very protective men right next door, should I need help. But tonight, something just feels off.

Maybe it's the new energy radiating from the upstairs apartment.

After signing all the paperwork today, I left his keys with Helo and got back to work. I saw him for only a moment when he moved his fancy car somewhere other than the front of my shop, but nothing since then. Come to think of it, where did he park his car? I haven't heard a peep from upstairs all day. I figured he might ask for help or maybe need directions working the stacked washer and dryer. I can spot a man who's never done his own laundry before when I see one. But nothing, not a single word. Usually, I leave my contact information available for every tenant, just in case of emergencies.

This is the first time I've felt that decision was a mistake. I'd rather he use Helo as an intermediary or, better yet, I'd rather he die in a horrible fire than contact me directly.

Unfortunately, that would mean I would also lose my business. And that means far more to me than his life. I'm just finishing reloading the juice cooler to be ready for the morning when the light above the front door flickers out.

"What in the horror movie bullshit is going on?" I say, my voice echoing across the empty room. I grab the nearest object, moving slowly toward the front door.

How a plastic travel coffee tumbler is going to protect me from Michael Myers, I have no idea. But it's all I've got going for me.

"Great, all I need now is a thunderstorm outside and some masked serial killer chasing my ass down the street. That would really be the cherry on top of this perfect fucking day."

"Would it?" A dark voice sounds from a dark corner behind me, and I screech.

My body jumps two feet into the air, arms and legs flailing in every direction, the coffee tumbler flying towards the corner where the voice came from. Something inside me *knows* who it is, but I can't tell my fight-or-flight instincts I'm not about to be killed.

Who knows? Maybe I am.

"Gesù Cristo, sei una pazza stronza!" The voice shouts charging towards me.

I attempt to turn and run and bump straight into a table, knocking the air from my lungs. Way to fucking go, Vanessa.

Strong arms wrap around me from behind, preventing me from escaping. I kick and flail, but I'm lifted off the ground with ease.

"Let me go! I swear to God I'll fucking kill you! Let. Me. GO!" I shriek, but a hand clamps over my mouth.

"Will you knock it off? I'm not going to hurt you! It's me, Ms. Diaz." I finally recognize the sound of Sebastian's voice, and fury builds inside my chest.

"I'm going to remove my hand from your mouth, but I need you to compose yourself with some modicum of decorum, please? I don't think either of us needs the police called here in the middle of the night over a woman screaming her fucking head off for no reason, hm?" His mouth is close enough to my face, I can feel the heat of his breath fanning across my cheek.

Being held like this, one arm banded across my waist, one hand tightly across my mouth, shouldn't turn me on. But...

As soon as he moves his hand away from my lips, I bite into the fleshy part of his palm. He howls in pain as I jerk my head to the side, and he pulls his hand away.

"Estás loca!" he growls, and I shove him backwards. He holds his hand up to the light, and blood trickles down his wrist. I can't help but smirk, knowing I'd never go down without a fight.

"I'm crazy?! You broke into my store in the middle of the night! How am I the crazy one, asshole?" I say, shocked he would dare try to blame this on me.

"And could you try to stick to English, please? My Spanish is a little rusty and I don't even speak whatever the hell you were yelling at me before."

"Italian," he replies through gritted teeth. "I came down here because the water is not working upstairs. I know you assume me to be some kind of barbarian, but I do like to brush my teeth and wash my hands."

The fight leaves my body at the venom in his tone. I've never been a bad landlord. Not like the kind of slum-lords my parents always had to deal with in Miami. Knowing he's been dealing with this problem all day and didn't say anything makes me feel like shit. But I haven't exactly made myself very approachable. My muscles slacken, and he lets me go.

Stepping out of his hold, I almost miss the warmth of his body. Almost.

"I'm sorry. I didn't know it was out. My brother didn't...never mind. I'll contact the plumber tomorrow and have it taken care of. Until then, you're welcome to use the bathroom here in the shop. The spare key is usually tucked behind the downspout outside the back door." I reply, my mind finally connecting the dots.

"Wait, how did you even get in here? I always keep the doors locked when I'm closing up." I cut my gaze to his, and he just smirks.

"I have a great many skills, Ms. Diaz." He shrugs, leaning against the table.

I can't help but choke out a laugh. The audacity of this man kills me.

"I'm going home. Lock the door behind you when you leave, please. This is my livelihood. I know a man like yourself, someone who keeps an excess of Armani in the trunk of his car, probably doesn't understand the importance of that. But when you're sleeping in that car because I've evicted your ass, you might." I shove past him, grabbing my purse from behind the counter and walking toward the back door.

"Oh, and the next time you feel like committing felony breaking and entering, let me know in advance. The sheriff has a thing for me, and I'd love to see you in cuffs."

four

Sebastian

THREE WEEKS IN THIS TOWN. Three weeks of near radio silence from Matteo as to what's going on within my organization. Last night I received a text.

Folly Beach Pier. 6 AM.

Nothing else, no number, no name. Outside of the associates I have in this town, no one but Teo knows I'm in South Carolina. Maneuvering my black Lexus through the back roads towards the beach, I force myself to believe it will be him meeting me this morning.

I tried to choose my least ostentatious car when I left, but this is still a two door, luxury sports car. I may be the most business minded Arsenio to lead the family in decades, but we've all had our vices.

My great-grandfather's was the drink. He couldn't

stay sober long enough to form a business alliance or make a decision that moved the family forward. My grandfather's downfall was gambling. He did a decent job hiding it for a long time, spending his personal fortune before dipping into the organization's money to pay off his debts. That behavior eventually led to his demise. My father, arguably the biggest traitor of them all depending on who you ask, his indulgence was beautiful women.

Even after he met my mother, there were still dozens of women. He would call it *an appreciation for the beauty in this life*. I just call it whoring. Out of the four children he fathered, only I am legitimate, and none of us are purely Italian, the way Fortuna Nera would've preferred it. Ultimately, what can you expect from an organization whose name literally means black luck?

I pull into the barren parking lot and see Teo's Ducati parked at the edge of the pier. Glancing down the boardwalk, I see him standing at the end, where the ledge extends high over the water. Waves crash against the posts below, their ferocity foreshadowing what's to come during the impending conversation.

Parking, I walk down to him, the railings and benches along the edges showing weathered wood, the exposure to salt air and time wearing them down. Sometimes, I feel as though my soul looks the same on the inside. I'm far from elderly, but my mind and body have lived a thousand lives in my nearly forty years. The sky ahead blends softly between blues and pinks, the sun barely rising over the sea.

"Teo," I say, clasping him on the shoulder.

He turns, his stern expression breaking when he sees me. Matteo is my oldest and most trusted friend. He pulls me into a one-armed hug, and I notice the yellowish-purple bruise healing under his left eye and the torn skin on his knuckles.

"Damn, it's good to see you." He blows out a breath, falling onto a bench nearby, dropping a folder next to him. "I brought you Illy Coffee. It's the best I could do right now. I haven't been home yet, but I should be going back in a few weeks. I'll see what I can do."

"I'm not worried about fucking coffee, Teo," I grumble, dropping onto the bench next to him. "What happened to your face?"

He lights a cigarette, pulling a deep drag into his lungs, letting it linger, and then exhaling.

"Don't worry about it. Wasn't related to Fortuna business." He smirks, and I glare at him.

"I thought you agreed to stop the fights?" I questioned.

"They're more necessary now than ever. There's so much tension in the ranks. The boys are restless. Everyone is waiting for orders, Bash. They need some way to channel that energy, or they'll take it elsewhere. You need to give them something to do. I'm just keeping them busy." Matteo flicks the cherry off the end of his cigarette and shoves the butt into his pocket.

"What's in the folder?" I ask, not taking my eyes off the sunrise.

"Helo said it was a close family member who organized the Miami attack. It wasn't hard to figure out which ones had access to all the right bank accounts, all the right safe houses. I've narrowed it down to three options." he says, flipping through the information he's gathered.

"Tell me. I can tell you which one has the balls it takes to take a shot at me." I close my eyes, an ache already building in the space behind my eyes.

"Well, there's Massimo. He's definitely close enough. He's got access to every accou-" he says, and I scoff.

"Definitely not. Massimo is still afraid to look me in the fucking eyes at family dinner, Teo. He calls me Mr. Arsenio, and I'm his first cousin. He didn't do this. Who's the next option?" Leaning my head back against the worn wood, I let the cool ocean breeze glide over my skin. Part of me wishes I could jump off the end of this pier and let the waves carry my body out to sea.

Maybe someone would find me, maybe they wouldn't. Either way, maybe I don't fucking care anymore.

"Nico. He's got the means. He had the opportunity. I know he's got the fucking ambition. But does he have the balls? That I don't know. I mean, he's just a kid, but kids these days don't have the kind of respect we did." He suggests, cocking his head to the side.

"He's barely 19, Teo. I know his father wishes he had been the oldest Arsenio brother and held the reins in this family. But he wasn't, and that was never an option for him," I remind him. Beginning to raise my voice, I continue, "There's an order to things. They've been done this way for a hundred years. I didn't create this hierarchy, Matteo. I didn't ask for this responsibility." I pound my fist against the wood to punctuate every sentence until my knuckles crack.

Matteo doesn't respond, knowing my fury is already balancing on a knifes edge.

"It's not Nico. While Uncle Gio may not have the respect for me he should, he respects the family, the legacy. My father's legacy. He would never tempt the fates that way, and his son would never make such a brash move without his permission and funding. Who does that leave?"

He says nothing, looking out over the horizon with his jaw clenched tightly. I don't have to ask. We both know the truth. If I'm honest, I've known for years.

Luca. My closest cousin in age. His father is younger than mine by less than one year, and my father never let him forget it. Luca and I have been in constant competition since birth. He was beyond livid when I named Teo as my underboss, despite the fact Teo's father had been my father's underboss before him. Luca felt the position belonged to him simply by birthright. But I don't play that game. In my world, you earn what you're given. Luca had his eye on my throne from the time we were old enough to know what power was.

If anything were to happen to me now, with no heir or named successor, the empire would be in his hands. I don't know why I didn't immediately assume he was behind this. Maybe I knew, and I just didn't want to admit it. Because admitting such things means a war is on the horizon. His father will not yield, should I bring these betrayals to light. He will go to his grave arguing his son is the rightful heir because he is purely Italian, and I am not. The concept is so archaic, but it's no mystery why he feels that way.

"You know what this will mean." He lights another cigarette, the smoke billowing through the air around us.

"You know those things will kill you long before I let Luca fucking Arsenio destroy what we've built, Teo." Leaning back, I cross my arms over my chest.

"The men need direction. You need to make some decisions before we leave here today." He ashes his cigarette, flipping open the file and getting down to business. "The New York office is hemorrhaging money. The Irish have been encroaching on our territory in several areas, pushing the limits, I believe. Trying to find a weak spot. We've got options for dealing with it. I can tell you what I'd prefer, but it's your choice."

“Send extra men, the ones who favor the fights, to New York. We will not pay them for the territory that already belongs to us. They will remember their place, or they will never see their mothers or their precious whiskey again. If the boys meet any resistance, burn the pubs on West and on 67th. I’ve been too cordial with Ronan Murphy. If I need to remind him in blood, I will.” Cracking my neck, the pain behind my eyes grows. It’s always something in this fucking world.

“I’ll make sure it’s done. And you? How are you down here?” Matteo cuts his eyes to mine, and I look away, knowing my expression will give away how fucking miserable I am.

“It’s fine. I’m just ready for this to be sorted so I can go home.” I lie, knowing the repeated frigid cold showers are getting old very fast. “I need a favor from you, though.”

“Name it, boss.” He stands, shaking out his sleeves.

“I need you to give me everything you can find on Vanessa Diaz, my new landlord.” I smirk.

“We talking just the basics or blackmail material?” He asks, flicking his lighter open and setting the folder he brought on fire.

He holds it by one corner, watching the flames devour the pages. His eyes glaze over slightly, fixated on the orange and red flickering between us. Fucking pyro, he always has been.

“Everything you can find, Teo. Don’t burn down the

pier in the meantime." I slap him on the shoulder, and he drops the folder into the metal trash bin next to us.

The bin goes up in flames as we make our way back to the parking lot. Seems to be a metaphor for the way my shitshow of a life is going these days.

"Take care of yourself. I fucking hate leaving the city. I'd rather this shit be over soon." He shakes my hand, swinging a leg over his Ducati and pulling his helmet down over his face.

"We shall see."

five

Vanessa

A COLD DRAFT blows across my legs. October in South Carolina isn't usually chilly, but it has its moments. I know I shouldn't sleep with my windows open. All the guys at Grovewood Ink have told me repeatedly how much of a safety hazard it is. But they don't know the life I grew up in. The kind with real hazards you find outside of Hallmark towns like this one. I've lived in houses where *lock your door* meant the one leading to my bedroom to keep the local dealer from crawling into my bed after my parents passed out when I was fifteen. Aria was the only person who made sure I could always take care of myself. She taught me how to fight and who to trust...*no one.*

What I could never admit to her were the dark desires I have always harbored, the ones that grew harder and harder to deny the older I got. The ones that told me a masked stranger slipping into my room in the middle of the night, watching me sleep, completely and unknowingly at his mercy, lit a fire deep inside me that burns to this day, hotter than anything ever has before.

Just as the thought crosses my mind for the hundredth time, the floorboards creak in the living room, and I gasp, sitting straight up in my bed. Doug raises his head from the end of the bed, a low growl building in his throat. I pull my heavy black duvet up to my chin. The weight of it has always been so calming to me, but not tonight. I've never been scared living alone, never until this very moment.

"Don't be stupid, Vanessa. There's nothing there." I tell myself, petting Doug's back. "It's fine, baby. Just an old house."

He looks back at me, his expression telling me he thinks I'm a dumb bitch. But I keep him in kibble so he won't argue. Kicking the blankets on top of him, I climb out of bed, closing my bedroom window and making my way across the cool wood floor into the living room. All is quiet, nothing at all disturbed. The windows and doors are shut and locked, which might be a first for me. The half-empty glass of water I always leave next to the kitchen sink still sits untouched. Dust particles float through the dim light shining over the back door. Breathing deeply, I close my eyes. Doug nudges my hand, and I stroke his soft ears. It's such a simple gesture, but it's given me peace since the day I brought him home.

"We're okay. Everything's fine, boy. Let's just go back to bed." I tell him, patting his side as I walk back towards the bedroom.

He makes a lap of the small living room before following me back to the bedroom and curling back into a ball at the foot of the bed. When I found Doug at the shelter here in Grovewood, he was skin and bones with a stupid name like Curtis or Travis or something like that. Doug felt like a name fit for the gentleman he really is. They told me he was rescued from a dogfighting ring where he'd been used as bait because he wasn't much of a fighter, even though he's such a big boy. He's a purebred Doberman, so anyone who came to the shelter looking for a family pet had been scared to adopt him. His size and general willingness to avoid most people were instant red flags. But not to me. I took one look at his beautiful chocolate brown eyes and knew he was just waiting there for me to find him. We've been inseparable ever since. I've heard it said sometimes pets find a person when you need them most, and that always felt like bullshit to me before I found Doug. Now I can't imagine my life without him in it.

I try to go back to sleep, staring a hole through the ceiling for what feels like an eternity. Do I want there to be some unknown intruder in my house? Of course not. But does the idea of a masked man breaking in, finding me here, and bending me to his mercy turn me on? Way more than it should. Civilized society would be appalled by the thoughts constantly circling in my mind, but I can't help them. I never could.

My eyes finally begin drifting closed, my lashes like heavy weights sinking, dragging my body back into the depths of the deepest sleep. My dreams beckon me back, as inviting and safe as they've always been.

"Così bella, diavolina. So fucking beautiful." His deep voice says.

I'm paralyzed, completely frozen. Maybe in fear, maybe from something much more sinister. His fingertips drag from my ankle to the hollow behind my knee, and goosebumps spread across my skin like wildfire. Where the hell is my dog and why isn't he eating this man right now?

I try to speak, but nothing comes out. My heart pounds in my chest, the sound echoing in my ears so loudly I'm sure the man can hear it where he stands. I don't want to face him, afraid seeing him will make this dream a reality.

"Look at me. Show me those beautiful eyes." He demands, and a shiver runs down my spine. The defiant part of me wants to bury my face in the mattress and never give him what he wants, but my body betrays me. I turn to face him, and I'm filled with equal parts horror and intrigue. I want to scream, to cry out for help, but I don't.

He's wearing an ornate mask, concealing most of his face. t's white with a bold black sunburst symbol on the forehead, looking almost ceremonial. The lower portion is adorned with intricate gold filigree, accented with small, blood red jewels. His mouth is visible beneath the gold, showing his wide grin and straight white teeth. His skin is inky black, as if it's painted. Surely he must be the devil himself, come to drag me to hell. A dark hood is pulled over his head, covering any distinguishing features.

His hand skims higher, dragging across the cotton fabric of my panties and up my ribcage. My breathing picks up, my heart racing inside my chest. Why haven't I screamed? Fought back? Heat builds in my core as his hand grazes the side of my breast, a gasp escaping my lips.

His eyes flick to mine. Even though they're sunken into the mask, the deep dark brown feels so familiar. His slender fingers find their way around my neck, resting there but not squeezing. My pulse thrums against his skin and he smirks, the white of his teeth a deadly contrast against his black skin.

"Do I make you nervous?" He flexes his fingers, and I swallow instinctively. I move to shake my head, but he grips my chin tightly.

"Do not lie to me, diavolina. I can feel it in your blood. I can smell it on your skin." He brings his face closer to mine, fear and madness warring for control over my emotions.

I want to reach out and touch him. I want him to touch me. I want him to leave this place and never darken my fucking doorstep again. I can't let this dance go on any longer, the emotions inside me crashing like waves against a lighthouse in a turbulent storm. I want out.

Jerking my head from his grasp, I move to sit up,

wondering once again where the hell Doug is. If he were at the end of my bed where he usually sleeps, the intruder wouldn't have stood a chance.

"Get the fuck out of my house!" I scoot back on the bed out of his reach, but he just laughs, standing to his full height and towering over me.

"There's nowhere you can go that I cannot reach you." He flashes that wicked grin one last time before lunging toward me. The scream I've been holding finally rips free.

My body slams onto the hardwood floor, blankets tangled around my legs. Doug barks loudly outside my bedroom door, scratching and pawing at the frame frantically. How the hell did that door get closed in the first place? I would never shut him out of the bedroom. He whines louder and louder as I stumble to my feet, rubbing my sore hip bone.

"Hold on, boy. I'm coming." As soon as I turn the handle, Doug bursts into the room, sniffing every inch of the floor, the bed, my body, not stopping until he's covered every surface of the room.

"What the hell happened last night, Dougy? I never have dreams *that* crazy." I ask him, rubbing his favorite spot just behind his ears before walking into the kitchen. I stop short, my blood turning to ice in my veins.

The cup that always sits half empty next to my kitchen sink has been cleaned and sits upside down in the drying rack.

six

Sebastian

I HAVE three laptops set up on the small island in my kitchen, all tracking different shipments leaving different warehouses under my control. I should be worried having this many devices tunneled into the backend of our security feeds, but Breaker assures me there's no way my security team will know I'm watching. That in and of itself is concerning. I aim to employ the best in the world in all avenues, and I may need to reconsider using the men here in Grovewood on a more permanent basis.

"These two, they're following the correct routes. But that one? This isn't the plan. He's at least 20 miles off course already," I tell Breaker, watching over his shoulder as he tracks the trucks in question.

"Do you know who should be on that route? If you have an idea, I can access their phones." His features are set in stone, his gaze laser focused on the screen in front of him as he types line after line of code into some satellite tracking program.

"For this route? Should be my cousins, Angelo and Vicente. There's no telling who they brought with them. It could be any of a few hundred men. They are supposed to be heading towards this route," I point towards the normal path they would take from one warehouse to another to drop off their regular delivery. "But they're taking a huge detour. Can you see any reason why?"

"I don't see any road construction or delays, nothing that would create a need for them to go this way." Breaker replies, pounding away on his keyboard.

Endless lines of code stream across the screen before a crackling sound echoes through the speakers of his laptop, followed by the sound of Italian curse words. I recognize Angelo's voice instantly, having grown up with both him and Vicente nearly my entire life. At first, they're not talking about much. The weather, the drive, the woman Angelo fucked last night. But then the conversation turns to something much more interesting.

"I really don't think this is a good idea, Vince," Angelo says, sighing heavily. Breaker and I watch as their truck takes another turn further away from their designated route, and my jaw tenses.

"Luckily, Luca doesn't pay us to fucking think." Vince replies, and the betrayal burns deep in my veins.

Breaker's hands hover over the keyboard for only a moment before he continues typing, running a program that begins recording everything they're saying. It's always been a possibility in this life that things could turn out this way. People can always betray you. But there is typically too much fear present for that to be a factor. Evidently, I have failed to instill that kind of terror in the men at my mercy.

"I don't know, Vince. This isn't the way things are supposed to go. The family isn't meant to undermine each other this way. I don't have a good feeling about it. Makes me feel sick," Angelo groans, and I find a small comfort knowing he doesn't want to be put in this position.

"Stop bitching, Ange. The job is almost done. I won't ask you to help with this shit again if this is how you feel, but we're already in it now. Let's just finish this delivery and move on." Vince replies, the sound of papers rustling coming through the speakers.

"And what do you suggest we tell the boss, Vince? What exactly do we tell Sebastian when he asks why half of this fucking shipment is missing?" The fact it's taken nearly half an hour for one of them to mention my fucking name is infuriating as fuck. I've done nothing but take care of every member of this family my entire life, and this is how they repay me? By stabbing me in the fucking back and stealing from me? They will pay in blood for the betrayals they have committed today.

Before my mind can wander too far down the rabbit hole on the many ways I will seek my revenge, a knock sounds on the door to my apartment.

Who the hell could be knocking for me? Breaker and I exchange a confused look, both knowing that pretty much everyone I speak to in this town is currently in this room or calls before showing up at my door. Grabbing my pistol from the edge of the island, I brace my shoulder against the door, peeking through the small peephole. The very last person I expect to see on the other side is also the one haunting my dreams since the moment I stepped foot in this town. I slide the gun into the small of my back, releasing the chain on the door and cracking it slightly before smirking down at her.

"Ms. Diaz, to what do I owe this great pleasure?" I ask, my eyes unable to stop from sliding down the length of her perfectly curvaceous body.

She scoffs, rolling her eyes and planting a hand on her hip. That only serves to accentuate her full waist and the flare of her hips even more, making my mouth water. She is fucking delectable. The things I would do with this woman, if only given half a chance.

"I'm not here to talk to you, Sebastard. Is Breaker here?" She cocks her head to the side and tries to peek around my shoulder. I pull the door into my body, preventing her from seeing into the room behind me.

"Maybe I can help you. I have a great number of skills, Vanessa." I drag out her name, watching her eyes rake over the ink lining my skin. I know she finds me physically attractive, that much is too fucking obvious. But I also know she hates my guts. It's an intoxicating combination, making me want her even more.

"I wouldn't accept help from you if you begged on your damn knees, fuck boy. Can I speak to Breaker, please?" She crosses her arms, pushing her perfect tits up and drawing my eyes directly to them. A smirk paints her lips, and I realize she's fucking with me on purpose. Never in my life have I ever been told I can't have something I want. Until now.

"Wait here." I say, attempting to close the door behind me and leave her standing in the hall. But the woman is persistent. And annoying as fuck. She pushes her way in behind me, not bothering to listen.

"Or come on in, Ms. Diaz. Un-fucking-invited." I grumble. Slamming the door behind me as she walks ahead of me into the living room.

Breaker hits a few keys on his computer, and all the screens go dark. He understands without question how important the need for discretion is when it comes to my business, for her protection more than anything else. In my world, the more you know, the more disposable you become.

"What the hell are you two into? Why do you need this many computers? Is this like some kind of extreme gamer weirdo thing? Are you using poor Break to organize a vast network of online girlfriends because no one else wants to sleep with you, Sebastian? Are you the Tinder Swindler?!" she asks, raising an eyebrow, and Breaker suppresses a laugh.

"Definitely not. What's going on, Ness?" He asks, turning to face her. His concern for her is genuine and touching, but I really don't fucking care or have time for their Hallmark family moment right now.

"Yes. Please tell us the crisis. Dark roast shortage, is it?" I cross my arms over my chest, leaning against the island. I can't begin to imagine what could be so important she would barge her way into my space like this.

"I need a security system in my home." she says, and the room is silent. Breaker gives her a confused look, and I can't help but laugh.

"That's it? That's the big problem? You need a doorbell camera to check on your package deliveries or some shit? That could've been a text message. We are doing serious business here, Ms. Diaz. Maybe you've heard of that? And you interrupt to ask this man about security systems?" My tone comes across condescending, and I mean for it to.

If looks could kill, my enemies would be rejoicing today. She's pissed, but I don't give a fuck. She's wasting my time.

"Did something happen, Ness?" Breaker asks, concern for her evident in the way he speaks. I roll my eyes, unable to contain my annoyance with this bullshit.

"I think...I mean, I don't really know for sure but...I

think somebody…" she stumbles around her words and I'm done with this.

I cross the space, squaring my shoulders in front of her, my presence dominating. Gripping her chin between my thumb and forefinger, I watch Breaker tense out of the corner of my eye, but he doesn't move to stop me.

"Spit it out, Vanessa." I command.

"Someone was in my home last night." She replies, her head tilted back to meet my gaze, eyes soft and mesmerized by the control I can command over her so easily.

"How do you know this?" I ask, not releasing my grasp on her.

"Things were moved. And Doug, he was locked out of my room." She speaks almost as if she's in a trance. I look back at Breaker, his brow furrowed in concern.

"Who the fuck is Doug?" I refuse to release her, something in me loving this power.

"Her dog." he says, turning back to his computer without another word.

He pulls up a dozen different security feeds around town, scanning through each one looking for some kind of clue as to who could've been in her home last night. Breaking eye contact with her brings her back to reality, and she smacks my hand away, stepping out of my hold.

"Excuse you. Don't you dare manhandle me! I don't know where your hands have been! Gross!" she says, wiping at the spot on her face where my hand had just been. Fucking drama queen.

"Trust me, Bambina. If I were to manhandle you, you wouldn't be complaining." I smirk, and she steps forward sharply, her expression tight with frustration. Her hand arcs through the air in a quick, decisive motion, connecting with my cheek in a sharp slap. My head jerks slightly to the side from the impact, my eyes widening more from surprise than anything else. This woman never ceases to amaze me with her audacity. For a moment, the room hangs in silence, the tension between us louder than the sound itself. Breaker doesn't dare say a word. She rears back to swing on me again, and I catch her wrist in the air.

"Listen to me very carefully," I say, my voice dropping several octaves and dripping with disdain. "This will be the final time you take liberties with disrespect in my presence, Ms. Diaz. You do not understand exactly who you are fucking with. I have removed a man's tongue for far less than the bullshit you've spewed from your toxic mouth."

We're locked in a battle of wills, my grip on her wrist tightening the longer she stares me down. I could snap it easily. I won't, but she will fucking back down. I won't have her barging into my house like she owns the place. Especially because my sources have already confirmed that she does not. I squeeze tighter, and she winces, her eyes squinting into sharp slits before she turns her head away. Releasing her, I give her a small shove backward, wanting to put as much space between us as possible.

"I'm going for a drive. Get her out of here, Mr. Negan. I will return within the hour." I grab my keys from the bar, not bothering to look her way as she rubs her wrist while scowling my direction.

"What do you want to do about-" Breaker starts, but I hold up a hand. I don't want her to know a fucking thing about my business.

"I will call Matteo now. We'll have a plan when I return." Leaving the apartment, I don't bother softening the blow of the hard slam of the front door.

Fuck, I can't wait to get out of this place and back to my life.

seven

Vanessa

I'VE BEEN MINDLESSLY WIPING the same spot on the counter for the last ten minutes. I know if I don't stop, I'm gonna fuck up the countertop and I can't afford to fix something like that right now.

"Earth to Nessa. Helloooo?" Rory waves her hand in front of my face, and I blink, snapping back to reality.

"Huh? Were you saying something?" I ask, tossing the rag onto the back counter.

"Nothing Earth-shattering. What's up with you?" She leans both elbows on the counter, dropping her face into her hands.

When Rory left my shop to open her own dance studio, I was sad to see her go but so happy to watch her follow her heart to where it truly belonged. Now, most days she spends more time here than she ever did when she was employed at Mug Life.

"Can I ask you something?" I busy myself with clearing pastry plates and coffee cups off tables as she watches me intently.

"Of course." She takes the dishes from me, placing them into the sink behind the counter.

"It's kind of...personal. Feel free to tell me to fuck off." I joke, knowing she keeps most of her personal life to herself when it comes to the business side of Breaker's world.

"How much do you know about Sebastian?" I ask, and she stops walking, propping her hip against the counter.

"More than a little, less than a lot. What kind of information are you looking for, Ness?" She raises an eyebrow at me, and I fall into a chair across from her, resting my head on my palm.

"He said something the other day. It just made me wonder," I tell her. I'm not sure how much I should really say, if anything at all. Maybe Breaker keeps Rory completely in the dark about the things he does.

"Are you asking me about the man? Or about his business?" She sits in the chair across from me, a smirk painting her lips.

"I'm not interested in him." My expression is unfazed. I mean it with every ounce of my being, I am not at all interested in fucking Sebastian.

"Uh huh. And the six foot asshole warming my bed every night wasn't interested in me at all either.

ANYWAYS, if you're asking me for specifics, I can't give them to you. But if you're asking me if he's a good man, I can tell you he is. He's protected my family and people I love in ways I can't even begin to explain." There's a sincerity in her eyes that's unmistakable.

"Good men don't cut people's tongues out, Rory." I scoff, thinking she'll be appalled. But she doesn't even flinch.

For a moment, she just stares back at me as if she's wondering if I'm being serious. Standing with a shrug, she walks over to the cooler and places a five dollar bill down before taking a water bottle out and twisting off the top. She takes a long drink, leaving me swimming in my own thoughts. Just before I feel like I might drown, she clears her throat, crossing her arms and narrowing her eyes at me.

"You of all people know this world isn't black and white, Vanessa. People aren't always just good and evil. Do you think my husband is a bad man?" She asks, and I jerk back.

"What? No! Of course not!" I exclaim. Breaker is one of the most caring, selfless people I've ever met. Rigid and a bit of an asshole if you cross him? Maybe. But never an evil man.

"Yet you would be shocked by the number of lives he's taken in my defense. In the defense of others he loves. There are skeletons in his closet stacked so high they'd bury him alive. But I choose to see him for who he is, Vanessa. Who he really is." She has so much faith in the man he is, it makes me jealous.

"Sebastian is different. I can feel it. He's not...he's just not the same kind of man Breaker is, Aurora. He's colder." I stare out the front windows, watching the cars driving by at a snail's pace. This town is always so slow, so safe.

"Cut him some slack. The world he lives in isn't like ours. Some things just require you to be more detached. More...dickhead-like. Sometimes bad people do good things for the right reasons, Ness." Her sly smile makes my head swim. What the hell does that even mean?

Is Sebastian a bad guy? A good guy who does bad things? A fucking vigilante? Who the hell knows? I feel way more confused than I did at the beginning of this conversation. All I wanted was a simple yes or no, and she gave me fifty shades of fucking confusion.

"I'm trying to ask you if I'm safe around him. Normal people don't cut people's body parts off, Aurora. But evidently Sebastian has." I roll my eyes, wondering even more now if his threat was a gross exaggeration or something far more sinister. But I don't have to think too hard. I know he meant it. I've seen the truth in his eyes when he spoke. The man has no need to lie or place empty threats at my feet. His real experiences are scary enough.

"I'll put it this way. Would I leave him alone to babysit Jasper? No, but *only* because I'd worry more for

Sebastian's sanity than Jasper's safety." She laughs softly, and in all of her unspoken words, I have my answers. There is nothing in this world she holds more dearly than the safety of her son. If she would trust Sebastian to protect him, then he can't really be all that bad. Can he?

Not wanting this man to occupy any more space in my mind than he already has, I force him from my thoughts.

"New subject. I missed you in class this week. Are you cheating on me with a different yoga class?" I joke, lightening the mood.

A small smile teases across her lips, and she avoids my eyes. Rory isn't ever one to beat around the bush in telling me things how they are, so her avoidance is odd behavior.

"Something you want to share with the class, Mrs. Negan?" I cock a brow at her, and she drops her head back, staring up at the ceiling as if she's contemplating giving me the codes for nuclear launch.

"If I tell you, you absolutely can not tell my husband that you know. He's so sensitive, Ness. I know he doesn't seem like it, but he is, and he wants to be careful...," she trails off, looking out the front window, completely lost in her thoughts.

"Cross my heart, hope to...well, let's not have anybody dying around here, okay?" I take her hand in mine, pulling her attention back to me. "Whatever it is, you can tell me."

"I'm pregnant again. I was at a doctor's appointment, that's why I missed Wednesday morning yoga." Her voice is soft and quiet, her smile so warm and full of excitement.

My eyes burn with unshed tears. Since the day I moved to this town, Rory has embraced me wholeheartedly. She never judged a single part of my past, my family, or any sordid detail I ever shared with her about where I came from. I could never begin to express my gratitude to her for making this place feel like a real home. The thought of their family growing again is such an incredible joy.

"Oh, Aurora," my words are watery and choked, "I'm so excited for you guys!"

Tears fall, streaming down my cheeks freely until I'm a full-blown raccoon. But I don't care. I can't imagine two better or more deserving parents than Rory and Breaker. They're the kind of people I wish would've raised me as a kid, but we all play the hand we're dealt.

"Thank you, we're really excited. Nervous, terrified, but so excited." She responds, and I get it. I can't even imagine the amount of responsibility of caring for another human. I'm barely hanging on, just taking care of Doug.

Now more than ever I feel the need to keep my problems as far away from her as possible. Whoever is creeping around my house in the middle of the night, if this ghost even exists, it can't touch her and her family.

Later that night, I find myself staring at the crooked shiplap ceiling in my bedroom. Doug snores quietly at my feet as my mind races through a thousand different thoughts.

Jealousy...

As happy as I am for Rory and Break, I envy the love they share and the security their family provides for them both.

Loneliness...

I lie here every night in my own home surrounded by a life I built with my own hands, but at what cost? My family, my friends, nearly everyone I grew up loving feels like nothing but a memory I've long outgrown. I don't regret the decisions I made that led me to Grovewood, but sometimes I wonder if I will ever have the kind of life my friends do. Will I ever have a man who truly loves me for me? Who knows the depths of my soul and accepts the darkness he finds there?

Wind blows hard against the side of the house, making the trees rustle nervously against the siding. That sound never used to unnerve me, but lately it has been. I tell myself there's nothing to be afraid of. The house is old, so is the town, and nothing here is going to harm me.

Popping a sleeping pill into my mouth, I chug half a glass of water, leaving the rest on my nightstand before wrapping my blanket around me and forcing my eyes closed.

"Oh, diavolina. Might as well have left the door unlocked for me with a sign that said free buffet. You are mouth watering. And all for me?" My masked stranger runs his hand down my thigh. I'm frozen in place, my limbs like lead, completely incapable of escaping his touch.

"How...did...you..." I try to speak, but my words are whispered and slurred, like I've had an entire bottle of whiskey and finished it off with a joint.

"How did I what? How did I manage to find my way into your mind again when you've tried so desperately to keep me out?" He asks, and my confusion only deepens.

Is that what this is? Is it all a vivid dream? No, I know the glass was moved last time. I know Doug was locked out of my room. Doug. Where is my dog?

"W-wh....my dog..." I force the words from my mouth, and he grins, his smile vicious and sharp.

Panic floods through me, goosebumps spreading across my skin where his fingers trail. I listen for the familiar sound of his collar, but all I hear is the sound of blood rushing in my ears. Searching the man's face for any scrap of reason, any semblance of reality in the room with us, but I'm met with the same beautiful but terrifying mask from before. The moonlight reflects off the white surface, illuminating his dark features. Now, even more than the first time, I am more convinced than ever he is truly the devil. But why is he haunting me this way? What have I done to deserve this?

"Deserve? You think I'm here because you deserve this? No, diavolina. I'm here because I cannot stay away from you. Because I'm drawn to you like a moth to the flame. Because from the moment I laid eyes on you, you felt like mine. And I take what's mine, Vanessa." His voice is cool silk, sliding across my skin smoother than anything ever has before. The way he says my name, with such familiarity, it's like he's known me my entire life.

As much as I want to fight him, to fight back against his far too presumptuous words, I can't. Because some sick part of me agrees with him. Since the moment he first touched my skin, I felt like he claimed me as his, like I can't get the thought of him out of my mind, even though I have no idea who hides behind his false face. He has consumed my every dream, and fears of who he could be have taken nearly all my waking moments as well.

"D-don't..." I do the best I can to shake his hand from my body, but it's no use. I can hardly move a muscle. Surely he's drugged me in some way. Sleep paralysis maybe? I've never experienced such a complete disconnect between my mind and body, but as desperate as I am to escape this room right now, it feels impossible.

His hand glides higher up my thigh, palm skating easily across my skin. Electricity buzzes in his wake, heat blazing across my skin, warming me straight to my core. I shouldn't be turned on by this entire experience, but I can't make my body not want it. Any rational woman would say fear is the biggest turn off but apparently not me.

"Don't what, diavolina? Don't give you exactly what you want? You think I can't feel the heat from your body? Smell the sweat from your skin? I know you want this just as badly as I do." He lowers his mouth to the shell of my ear, his voice a rough whisper. "I will give you everything, Vanessa. Everything you dream. Everything you desire, but are too scared to admit out loud. I will give it all to you."

His black fingers wrap around my throat, squeezing until I see stars. But I don't resist. I let him drag me into oblivion. Wherever he wants to take me, I want to go. It has to be better than this lonely existence.

"I will live and die for you, diavolina. All I ask is for you to do the same." His grip shifts, turning my head toward his. I can't see his eyes, but I know they're boring into mine. I can feel them.

"Will you? Will you die for me?" He asks so simply.

That's the last thing I hear before my vision blurs and fades to complete darkness.

eight

Sebastian

BANG

Bang

Bang

My hand instinctively finds my pistol on the nightstand as I sit straight up in bed. Ragged breaths escape my lungs as I try to shake the sleep from my mind. It's rare sleep finds me at all these days, so I'm not sure if the sound came from my dreams or not.

Bang

Bang

Bang

Bang

No, not a fucking dream at all. I climb out of bed, my gun trained on the doorway. This apartment is so small, it's not as if there are many places for an intruder to hide. And most intruders don't knock on the fucking door at two in the morning. Leaning my shoulder against the door, I glance through the peephole and see the object of my every nightmare. The vixen who haunts my mind. What the hell is she doing here?

Dropping my pistol on the kitchen island, I crack the door open only enough to push my head through. She stands in the small hallway, one hand white-knuckling a bag slung over her shoulder and a large black dog on a leash in the other. Vanessa is always a large presence, her energy encompassing any space she enters. She is the most unwelcome distraction, especially at this time of night.

We both stare silently at each other for several long seconds. Her face a mixture of discomfort and trepidation, mine one of indifference. She looks down at her dog, a tall black Doberman whose eyes are laser focused on me. He looks mean as hell, but it's been decades since I was afraid of beasts.

"Was there a fire?" I ask, my tone flat and unamused.

Her eyes narrow into slits, anger boiling deep within her dark irises. Her fist clenches around the leather of the dog leash, which only makes me smirk. There's just something about riling her up. It's more entertainment than I've had in years.

"No, asshole. There wasn't a fire. Despite my better judgement, I need help. Even though every single intelligent bone in my body screamed at me to stay the fuck away from you, I clearly didn't listen. Because I don't want to bring trouble into my friend's lives or into their homes. Especially near their families. Rory trusts you, so some stupid, fucked up part of me felt like maybe I could too. But obviously that was a wasted brain cell." She tugs the leash, turning on her heel to leave.

Something squeezes in my chest. Something like... empathy? No. I don't fucking care about her. But I do care about Rory and Breaker, and I can't deny they have done so much for me. Between Breaker and Helo deep diving into the shitshow that is currently my family business, and Rory's constant comedic relief making the worst days feel a little bit lighter, I almost feel like I have friends here.

"Wait. Come in." I hold the door open, and she hesitates for only a moment before ducking under my arm, her dog trailing inside behind her.

Staring into the hallway, I take a deep breath and wonder what the fuck I'm doing. I can't afford to bring her into the mess that is my life right now. Hell, I can barely keep my shit straight, much less help anyone else. I don't even like her enough to offer my help willingly.

Shutting the door, I watch her taking in my space for the first time. There's very little here. It's not as if I really had time to pack for a lavish vacation. I threw my essentials into a bag, took what Matteo had already prepared for me, and got the fuck out of town while I still could.

"I really love what you've done with the place," she says, her tone flat and sarcastic.

"If you're going to be a bitch, allow me to show you back to the door." I gesture, and her shoulders tighten.

"No, I'm sorry. It's just...it's been a long night. Really, I...appreciate you letting me in." She acts as if it's almost painful for her to choke out those words, and I smirk. Fucking drama queen.

"Who is this?" I ask, taking a step towards her dog.

She backs up a little, putting her body between him and I protectively. He leans around her, just as curious about me as I am about him. Call me soft, but I love animals. He stretches his neck, sniffing the air in my direction, and I reach out towards him.

"He's very skittish around strangers. Especially *strange* men." She hammers home the last part, making sure I know how she feels about me.

"Really? Doesn't seem like it." I tell her, leaning against the kitchen island, letting her hold him back. He whines, looking up at her. "You don't have to keep him leashed. There's nothing in this apartment he can damage."

She seems shocked by that response. As if she expected me to tell her to keep her mutt chained up in the basement or something. I may be cruel to those who deserve it, but never to an animal. She looks at me unsure, down at him, and back to me again. But my features don't change. I'm reluctant to welcome her into my space, but him? He's welcome anytime.

"If you're sure," she says softly, unclipping his leash slowly.

He shakes his full body, walking towards me tentatively. Stopping about a foot away, he stretches his neck as far as he can, sniffing my hand as if he's deciding if I'm worthy or not. He looks up at me, dark brown eyes buried in a sea of inky black fur, and his eyes narrow. Mutual recognition ignites in us both, predator sensing predator. He takes another step forward, and I stand to my full height.

"Sit," I command, and he obeys. Vanessa makes a squeaking sound behind us, but she doesn't comment.

"Down." He lies all the way down, and Vanessa's brows raise in surprise.

"He never listens to anyone. Me, occasionally. When he feels like it, maybe. But never anyone else. What did you do to my dog?" She crosses her arms over her chest, pushing her perfect tits up, and I shrug.

"He recognizes who the alpha is in this house." I reply, and she rolls her eyes. "What's his name?"

"Doug," she says with a smile, and I look at her like she's fucking insane. Because she is. Who names their dog Doug?

"I swear you get weirder the more I learn about you." I turn to walk into the kitchen, and Doug stands, following behind me.

"Thank you, I take that as a compliment!" She shouts across the small room, dropping onto the tan leather couch. She laughs for a moment, then suddenly looks around, confused.

"Wait, where did this come from? This unit was fully furnished! This isn't my couch! What happened to the black linen couch that was here? And the side tables! What the hell?" She jumps up, rushing around the space, looking at all the furniture I've replaced over the past few weeks. "This dining table is completely different! I had a cute little white one! This is so...dark and... modern..."

She sneers, walking back towards the bedroom, but I don't stop her. Instead, I stand in the kitchen, petting Doug and chugging a glass of water. She was bound to find out at some point. I was hoping it would be after I left, but here we are.

"What have you done?! There wasn't anything wrong with my furniture, you pompous assface! I just bought some of this stuff!" She charges back into the kitchen, stopping inches from my face. Her spicy scent, a mixture of cinnamon, vanilla, and coffee, surrounds me, clouding my mind for only a moment, but I shake it away.

"That shit was old. It needed replacing." I don't feel it needs more explanation than that, but the anger in her eyes says otherwise. "The couch smelled like weed, the bed frame was broken in three places, and two of the dining chairs didn't match. I am accustomed to a certain lifestyle, Ms. Diaz. I wasn't going to live beneath that because of your pride."

"That *shit* was mine, Sebastard! You don't get to just decide someone else's belongings are garbage and throw them out!" Her voice gets higher and higher, almost a screech, as she points her black manicured nail in my direction.

"Are you forgetting whose home you're standing in right now, little girl? Get your fucking hands out of my face, Vanessa!" I snap back at her, stepping forward with authority. She retreats back into the living room, not running, but putting space between her and I.

"I pay fucking rent here. I don't complain about the fact I'm taking cold showers daily, or that the smell of your over roasted coffee beans is so overwhelming it gives me a fucking migraine, *daily*. I mind my own business, Vanessa. I didn't ask you, the person responsible for this apartment, to replace the furniture, even though Breaker told me it was your brother who left this place in such disarray." I charge forward until her legs hit the couch. She has nowhere left to retreat. For once, she almost looks afraid.

"Listen, I didn't-" she snaps, but I cut her off.

"Shut up. Don't waste your fucking breath with whatever bullshit you've got to say. I didn't ask you to bring your sassy, judgmental ass to my fucking door in the middle of the night, Vanessa, but here we are. You are more than welcome to keep this furniture whenever I leave. Hell, maybe you could even charge a little more to the next tenant and actually get the fucking plumbing fixed. So, I think the words you're looking for are *thank you, Sebastian,* and *I appreciate your kindness, Sebastian.* I'm not really interested in hearing anything else from you tonight." Taking one step closer to her, she shuffles, tripping and falling backwards onto the couch with a huff.

"Estúpido imbécil." she mumbles under her breath, barely loud enough to be heard. Crossing her arms over her chest, she looks away from me, her chin stuck up in the air. So fucking defiant it hurts. I wish that didn't turn me on.

"Excuse me?" I ask, cocking a brow. She replies with another eye roll. "Very well. There are blankets in the hall closet, Ms. Diaz. We can discuss your reason for barging into my apartment in the morning. Don't worry, the new couch is very comfortable."

I don't give her the satisfaction of having the last word. Instead, I pick my pistol up from the kitchen counter and stalk back to my bedroom. Doug follows me halfway down the hallway before I give him a stern look.

"Stay." I tell him, pointing back towards Vanessa. He looks back, glancing at me once more before curling up at the end of the hallway. She gives me a final shocked look, like the interaction between her dog and I is truly out of this world.

"Goodnight, Ms. Diaz." I kick the door closed, stride

across my bedroom, and sit on the edge of my bed. Setting my pistol on the nightstand, I drag my hands across my face.

Why the fuck would I invite this demon into my home so willingly? Opening the drawer of the nightstand, I set my pistol next to the one thing I made sure to bring from home. My fingers trace the edge of the resin, my heart rate calming instantly. I want to go home. I'm tired of running, tired of hiding. But will I ever really be done? Part of me feels like I've been hiding behind falsehoods my entire life. People in my family are like actors who never leave the stage. Always performing, even if no one is watching. Some people wear masks for so long, when they finally peel them back, there's nothing left underneath but the echoes of who they were once meant to be.

nine

Sebastian

IT'S BARELY five when I wake again to the sound of the front door slamming shut. I should've known she'd be up before the crack of dawn, given her profession. I try for the next half hour to fall back asleep, but the whining coming from the living room finally drags me from my bed.

Doug stands right outside my bedroom door, leash hanging from his mouth. Smart pup.

"Alright already, give me a fucking second." I push past him, walking into the bathroom and closing the door behind me. He paws at the bottom annoyingly. That's a fucking habit that will stop. I finish brushing my teeth quickly and open the door to Doug's impatient glare waiting for me.

"You need to learn some manners, Douglas." Stepping past him, I grab a pair of black athletic shorts from the dresser and a matching black t-shirt. Slipping my running shoes on, I don't miss the irony that this is the most laid back I've been since the day I came to this town. Tattoos run the length of my arms and legs, barely an inch of untouched skin visible. It's rare I dress in anything less than Armani. But I don't think I need to be so formal to take Vanessa's dog for a walk around the square. Clipping his leash to his collar, I stop short when I see the cup and plate on the edge of the kitchen island.

Sorry for interrupting your beauty sleep.
God knows you need it.
V

I laugh out loud at the note she left next to the cinnamon scone and travel coffee cup. Even though I talked shit about her coffee last night, I didn't mean it. Her espresso isn't half bad. Popping the lid off, I breathe in the strong aroma of the Americano made exactly the way I like it. I hate it when she does nice shit for me. It makes me feel like I have to be nice in return, which is the last thing I want to do.

Finishing the scone in two bites, I grab the coffee in one hand and Doug's leash in the other. Walking downstairs, I decide to take the route through the coffee shop. I don't know if Vanessa allows pets inside the place, but hopefully she'll make an exception for her own mutt.

Leading Doug through the back door, his eyes bouncing from person to person, I realize this town is more alive in the early hours of the morning than I've ever seen it. The line at the counter is nearly out the front door as Vanessa scurries around behind the espresso machines making drinks and warming pastries. Her smile is bright and cheerful as she converses with all her customers as if she knows their life stories by heart. And maybe she does. She seems like the type to want to get to know perfect strangers just for the hell of it.

Her eyes catch mine, and she stops dead in her tracks, jaw hung open, coffee cup dangling from her hand. I tip my cup to her, tugging Doug's leash as he and I walk towards the front door. Her eyes follow us all the way out of the building, like she can't believe I would do something so mundane as take her dog for a walk. A group of young women waiting in line whisper about me but they're not exactly discreet.

"Jesus, who the hell is that?" One woman asks another.

"I don't know, but I want one. Can you say *daddy*?" Another woman replies.

Vanessa must be able to hear them as well, because she clears her throat. Interrupting their perusal of me, she demands their order in a much more abrupt tone than she's had with any other customer. All I can do is smirk and keep walking. Giving her a quick wink, Doug and I continue towards the front of the coffee shop. Her eyes practically roll out of her skull, and I suppress a laugh.

Opening the front door, I step out into the town square and I'm thrust back into a memory. Suddenly I'm six years old again, begging my father for a puppy. As a boy, I always wanted a dog. Something to keep me company since he traveled constantly. My cousins were always around, but it's not the same when you're growing up in a castle so vast and empty, and all you want is a partner in crime by your side.

One day, I found a dog on the way home from school, and I convinced my security detail, Vigo, to let me bring him home. The 60-year-old grandfather of four had a soft spot for me, and I used it to my advantage many times. I hid the pup in my room for nearly two full days, feeding it scraps from my mother's dinners I'd smuggled in my pockets.

I thought I'd be able to slowly introduce him into the house, and by the time my father noticed, he'd already be a fixture there. In my young mind, there was no way he could say no. I had even bought him a collar and given him a name, Amico. I'd planned out my entire speech, everything I needed to say to convince my father I was responsible enough to take care of a dog by myself.

The very night I planned to talk to my father, he came home early. I always knew if he was in his study, he wasn't to be disturbed at all. Amico and I were playing in the hall outside my room, and suddenly he caught the scent of something. He took off running towards the study. I sprinted after him, hoping like hell to prevent the impending disaster. I caught up to him, grabbed onto his fur right before he made it to the office door. Clutching him to my chest, I let curiosity get the better of me for the first time in my life. My first mistake.

Walking closer to the office, I clutched the puppy closer to my chest, my heart pounding against my ribs. Men were arguing, their voices muffled, but I could still sense their anger. My father sat behind his desk, his guards surrounding him, while some other men I didn't recognize stood on the opposite side of the desk. They all looked upset. Even as a boy, I could tell the signs of conflict and aggression from the outside looking in. The noise got louder and louder as I crept closer, something about money and products, about respect and understanding. One man lunged across the table towards my father, and my father pulled a pistol from under his desk, pressing it against the man's forehead. Amico chose that exact moment to bark, distracting my father and allowing the man across the desk to pull a blade from his belt, slicing my father across the cheek. His eyes met mine for only a moment, anger blazing hotter than I'd ever seen before as blood dripped down his cheek. He pulled the trigger, killing the man in front of him. One of his guards charged towards me, grabbing me by the shoulder with one hand and snatching Amico by the scruff of his neck in the other. My dog yelped to be released, and I kicked at the man, wanting to run for my room.

"Do not hurt the boy," was all I heard from my father before his henchman dragged me away. He threw me into my room and took Amico away. I never saw the dog again, but the shiner on Vigo's eye the next morning told me everything I needed to know.

The sound of my phone ringing pulls me from my memories as Doug and I cross the street into the courtyard of the square. Draining the last of my coffee, I drop the cup into the trash bin and answer the call.

"Teo, do you have news for me?" I ask, scanning the storefronts along the street. Doug seems just as alert as I am.

"Luca has propositioned at least six potential buyers. They're all people you've already declared we won't work with for one reason or another. Some human traffickers, some just scum of the Earth, some have already stolen from us in the past, and we've cut ties. He's trying to build his own ranks against you, obviously. He's stupid for going to any member of the family to do so, but it seems he's managed to entice some of the lower-ranking members. Money makes people do dumb shit. Well, money and drugs, and the promise of some better life they know nothing about." Teo blows out a breath on the other side of the line, and my mind races.

"I don't understand what the fuck I did to piss him off so much. Why now?" Doug and I make a lap of the square before he catches the scent of something in the grass and stops to investigate.

"I don't know, Bash. All I can tell you is he's sloppy. Either he's a fucking idiot or he's not worried about covering his tracks at all." Matteo replies, and anger boils in my veins. This is my empire. My fucking legacy. I've grown it into what it is today, and the way he's tarnishing it is pissing me off.

"I need two men that you trust. I mean *really* trust, Matteo. With my fucking life. I want you to fill them in on everything that's happened so far, but don't tell them where I am. They need to infiltrate Luca's operation, find out his next steps, and report back. I'm tired of hiding here, tired of running. I want my fucking life back." I can feel my blood pressure rising as I grit out the words.

"This is your family, Sebastian. *Our* family. He will not succeed." Teo replies with conviction.

Doug tugs on the leash, distracting me from the conversation. A low growl sounds deep in his throat, and I follow his gaze. We've managed to circle back to where we started, and his eyes are locked on the alleyway between Mug Life and a clothing shop next door.

"I trust your judgement in selecting the men, Teo. I'll be in touch." Hanging up without another word, I slip my phone into my pocket and focus my eyes on the shadows in the alleyway.

"You see something, boy?" I ask, patting his back. It doesn't distract him even for a moment.

I move to cross the street, and someone darts down the alley, disappearing from view. Whoever they were, they were definitely doing all they could to avoid being seen. Doug lets out several loud barks, yanking against the end of the leash, but I pull him back.

"Easy, boy. We can't chase every shadow we see, or we'd never stop running." I tell him, guiding us back towards the coffee shop.

The crowd has cleared out since we left for our walk, and Vanessa is wiping down a few tables alone inside the shop. As soon as we come through the front door, I unclip Doug's leash and he runs straight to her.

"There's my sweet boy! Did you have a nice walk? Can you believe that big, scary man actually took you for a walk? I know, I was shocked too!" She talks to him as if I'm not standing right here.

"You're welcome." Shoving my hands into my pockets, I lean against the nearest table. She always finds the easiest ways to be annoying.

"I didn't say thank you." she says, a cocky grin on her plum colored lips.

"I wasn't talking to you, Bambina. Doug and I have become great friends. He appreciates my efforts. Don't you, boy?" I pat my leg softly, and he strides over to me, sitting at my side. Vanessa's jaw goes slack, and I laugh to myself.

"The utter betrayal, Doug! I'm your mother!" she says, propping her hands on her full hips.

"You know what they say." I walk slowly towards her, my presence making her more and more uncomfortable. "Everybody loves an alpha, Vanessa."

I drag her name out, watching her skin flush red with my words. I know she finds me attractive. She just hates my guts at the same time. Conflict wars in her eyes, and I revel in it.

"Let's go, Doug. Mama has to work." He follows me to the back door, but I stop short, turning back to catch her attention. "We will discuss your reason for knocking on my door as soon as you get done today. So hurry home, dear."

I wink back at her, and she rolls her eyes, scoffing at me.

""I'll talk to you later, now get the hell out of my shop, Sebastard."

ten

Vanessa

BY THE TIME I make it upstairs later that night, I'm dead on my feet. The shop was surprisingly busy today. My weekly delivery came in over 3 hours late, right in the middle of the afternoon rush. Steven, the regular delivery man, must've had something up his ass today because his usual flirty disposition was nowhere to be found. Instead, he grunted every other word before shoving the clipboard in my face to sign. He knows I'm meticulous in going over my orders before signing for them, yet he acted like I was a huge inconvenience today.

Walking through the front door of Sebastian's apartment, Doug meets me with a wag of his stubby tail. He pushes his head into my thigh, and I scratch behind his ears the way he likes best.

"Did you have a great day, my baby? Mama did not."

I drop my phone and purse on the kitchen island, looking around the small space for any sign of Sebastian. I didn't really ask his permission to come back again tonight, but he did say we needed to talk, so I just assumed he knew I'd be here.

"Where is he, boy?" I ask Doug, and he looks down the hall towards the open bedroom door.

It occurs to me right at this moment that maybe I should've called before I just let myself in to his apartment. We're not friends. We're barely acquaintances. But I'm at the point of asking for forgiveness instead of permission now, so might as well push forward.

"Sebastian?" I call out, but I don't hear a reply. Stepping further down the hall, I hear the sound of water running.

Any rational person would turn around, respect someone else's privacy and wait on the couch. But I can't stop my feet from carrying me closer and closer towards the sound of the haunting music and running water coming from the bathroom. Doug nudges my leg, but I push him away, too invested in what I might discover to stop now.

Whatever he's listening to is dark, the bass thumping through the air surrounding me as I step into his bedroom carefully. This space screams *Sebastian*. He's replaced the double bed and mismatched side tables with a dark wood king-sized platform bed piled with even darker linens. Everything about this man is shrouded in obscurity. I hate to admit how beautiful I find it all.

I take two steps closer to the bathroom, the music getting louder and louder. Something about acid and alkaline? The contrast between him and I just as obvious as the lyrics. His scent permeates the air in every inch of this apartment. The faint smell of coffee fades into the background, overpowered by his leather, rain, and bourbon, as if he's just come in from outside, even when he hasn't. Old boots. Old habits. Warm. Familiar. *Expensive.* He smells like money that doesn't ask permission for anything. Like danger that's learned the importance of patience. Like a man who doesn't need to raise his voice to be obeyed. Steam billows from the open bathroom door, and my mind hesitates for only a moment before I step closer, the shower stall coming into view.

I don't know what he's listening to, but I definitely like it. Even through the condensation built up on the glass, I can see the outline of his perfectly sculpted body. I never realized just how completely covered in ink he is until this moment. There is barely any bare skin left on his torso or legs, intricate black swirls and skulls intermingled with dragons and daggers. He is truly a work of fucking art and muscle. Figures he would keep all of that covered with his pretentious wardrobe and not let anyone use him as eye candy. That's just selfish.

Heat races through my body, and I feel betrayed by my own DNA. I don't want him. He drives me fucking crazy. Like, punch-him-in-the-face-repeatedly-just-for-the-fun-of-it-crazy. But standing here, looking at this Adonis of a man literally lathered in soap and dripping wet in front of me...

"Fuck..." Did I say that out loud?

His gaze snaps to mine, and I know my eyes must be as wide as saucers right now. I'm fucking caught. There's no denying I'm standing here ogling him. I brace for the impact, my eyes pinched tight, preparing for the slew of profanity and anger he will rightfully throw my way.

"I'm sorry! I'm sorry! I'm sorry! I'm sorry!" I panic, turning to rush out of the room and slamming my head into the frame of the bathroom door.

"Gesù Cristo!" I vaguely hear the sound of water turning off over the shrill ringing in my ears.

My ass hits the floor, arms and legs flailing as I sprawl out onto the tile. Immediately, my head throbs in pain, blood dripping from my nose. Before my head can fall back onto the tile, Sebastian catches me. The clean scent of him surrounds me, his damp skin warm where it meets mine.

"What the fuck are you doing, Vanessa?" He demands, his voice dark but sounding so far away.

The room tilts as I grip onto his forearm, his bare skin searing into my palm like liquid fire. As the world around me slowly comes back into view, so does my reality. Sebastian is inches away from me, cradling my head as gently as I've ever been touched, still dripping wet from the shower I interrupted, *completely naked.*

"Argggaaahhh!!!" I yell, scooting back across the tile floor until my back hits the wall across the small room from him.

I'm literally eye-to-dick with the most extraordinary and imposing man I've ever seen in my entire life. He is over six feet of muscle, tattoos, darkness, and sarcasm, and all he can do is smirk back at me. I have clearly bitten off far more than I can chew when it comes to everything involving this man.

Slapping my hand over my eyes, I try to ignore the sound of his devious chuckle in the background. Peeking through my fingers, I watch him stand, his unfortunately impressive cock lengthening more and more at my discomfort. Squeezing my eyes tightly again, I try to ignore the heat building in my core.

I don't want him, I don't want him, I do not fucking want him.

God, I want him so badly it physically hurts.

The sound of him moving through the small space is unsettling. I want to open my eyes, to know exactly where this predator is stalking, but I'm too afraid. My heart pounds in my chest, seconds dragging by as we're locked in this moment.

"Look at me, Bambina." He commands, and I have no choice but to obey. Against my better judgement, my eyes mapping the length of his body until I meet his gaze. He stands in front of me, so close I could trace every tattoo with my fingertips if I wanted to. He doesn't necessarily look angry, more stern. Like I'm going to be punished for such an intrusion.

"Get up." He doesn't offer assistance, just stands in front of me, uncomfortably close and still so incredibly naked. How is he so at ease in his own skin this way?

Scrambling to my feet, I attempt to back away from him again, but the heat in his eyes halts me in my tracks. He steps closer to me, so close that our bodies are millimeters from touching. His erection barely grazes the waistband of my linen pants, and I shiver. His head dips low, his lips only a breath away from mine. My heart is practically breaking through my ribcage, all the anticipation of the last few weeks boiling to the surface. My skin flushes, sweat beading across my hairline as he grips my neck, leaning my head back to look into my eyes. Fuck, the man is euphoric.

"Get. Out." He grits, pushing me backwards through the open doorframe before kicking the door shut.

Fuck, I *hate* this man.

Collapsing onto the couch, I cover my face with my arm. Why the hell did I even go in there? Doug climbs onto the couch, and I attempt to shove him off, but he lays his solid body on top of mine, squeezing the air from my lungs.

"Geez, Dougy. You're squashing me." I say, scratching behind his ears. He just releases a sigh.

The heavy thud of footsteps sounds down the hallway, and my eyes snap open. I don't look away from the ceiling, counting the boards one by one in an attempt to disappear from his view. He shuffles around in the kitchen, and I listen to the cacophony of glasses clinking, water running, and cabinet doors closing, knowing there's still some distance between us for only a moment. He comes into the living room, sitting in the chair across from me in a pair of sweats hung low on his hips. Apparently, there's no need for him to bother with a shirt since I've seen more than enough of his body now. His gaze sears into me even though I'm not looking his way.

"Sit up, Vanessa. We need to talk." He demands. I huff out a breath, swinging my legs down and sitting up. Hugging a pillow to my chest, I let my head fall back, staring back at the ceiling. For the life of me, I cannot look this man in the face. Not after I've been inches from his magnificent dick and then tossed out of the room like trash.

"Knock it off. Look at me. We're both adults here. You felt adult enough to barge into my private bedroom, I think you can be adult enough to have a conversation while looking me in the eye." he says, and I groan, finally meeting his eyes. My face flushes immediately. Heat floods through my body, but this time I stand my ground.

"I'm sorry, okay? I just...I'm sorry," I throw up my hands, and Doug scoots his head into my lap.

"How's your nose? Your head?" He asks, and I flinch, embarrassment evident on my face, I'm sure.

"I'll be fine." I reply, crossing my arms over my chest.

"Very well. Please explain what brought you to my door last night." He asks, and my stomach drops.

"Someone was in my house again. I know you and my friends all think I'm crazy, but I'm not. I don't lock Doug out of the bedroom. Not ever. But he was locked out again. And things around my house are moved when I wake up. There's just this sense of...I don't know. It's like I can feel him there." The last words come out in almost a whisper, and I'm embarrassed by the way it makes me feel. I hate the confusion I feel every time my masked man creeps into my home.

"And what do you feel?" he asks, an intrigued look on his face.

I squirm under his gaze. I don't even want to admit to myself what I feel when the masked man touches me, much less tell Sebastian. So, I do the only thing I can in this moment. I lie.

"Fear. I'm scared." My tone is clipped, and I look away, not able to lie to his face as easily as I thought.

"And?" he pushes, and I shift in my seat. Doug groans, my movements annoying him.

"And what? What do you want me to say, Sebastian? I don't want this person in my house. I don't want this person to potentially follow me to my friends' houses and put their children in danger. You were the only person I could think of who seemed like a safe place I could turn to." I reply, hopeful he will drop this subject.

"What do you know about this man, Vanessa?" He asks, pulling out his phone.

"Nothing. Honestly, it feels like less than nothing. I know his mask isn't normal, like a burglar's or anything like that. It's more...ornate. Delicate. Like something I made up in a dream. The only thing I can ever see is his mouth. It's not covered. And his eyes. I can see them, even though they're obscured. I can *feel* them on my skin. He feels like he wants to hurt me and worship me all at once." I say, losing myself in the memories of the masked man.

"Maybe he does," Sebastian's deep voice cuts through the fog, pulling me back to reality.

"What? How can you say that?" I snap, and he smirks.

"Love and pain are two sides of the same blade. You can treasure someone as your most prized possession and still enjoy bringing them a little pain, Vanessa. If this man is real, maybe he enjoys bringing you such fear because it excites him." He suggests, and an uncomfortable feeling brews inside my chest.

I don't want to agree with what he's saying, but the idea stirs something within me I never thought I would feel. I've never entertained the desires inside me that always scream to be heard, to be unleashed and allowed to roam free. The realization grips me like a hand closing around my throat without any pressure, just the certainty it won't let me go. As afraid as I am about someone creeping through my space in the middle of the night, I can't deny the way it turns me on.

"I don't-" I open my mouth to give him another bullshit excuse, but fire blazes in his eyes.

"Do not lie to me, Bambina. Do you think I'm some stupid boy, barely capable of recognizing the look of lust in your eyes just now? You crave that darkness, just as I and many others do. There's nothing wrong with that. Nothing is wrong with you. But do not look me in my face and feed me more lies about how much of a *good* girl you are, Vanessa. It doesn't suit you. You want to be bad? Be bad. But you own it. Don't tiptoe around the idea, don't dabble, jump in with both feet and let it drag you into the depths of the darkness you crave. You may be surprised just how much you belong down here." He smirks, and I want to deny the things he says, but I can't.

He's only saying out loud all the things I've been thinking as long as I've been old enough to experience any relationship. I've always been more than curious about the different ways pain and pleasure can mix in perfect harmony. But I've never felt comfortable admitting that even to myself.

"I can see by the emotions fighting for control in your eyes, I've given you so much to think about. You can stay here, although I believe you should have better security in your home. I'll do my best to keep the door closed when I'm indisposed. Wouldn't want to have another mishap, would we?" His devious smile tells me he's getting far too much enjoyment from making me this uncomfortable, and I want to slap that stupid grin off his face. But he's offering me his hospitality, and I don't want to deny it.

"Thank you," I grit through clenched teeth, my arms crossed over my chest like a petulant child.

"You're welcome. I can't imagine how many ways you'll be at my mercy to show your thanks." And just like that, the devil has brought me into his den. And I let him.

eleven

Sebastian

OVER THE PAST WEEK, Vanessa and I have settled into an uncomfortable routine. She's gone before I wake in the morning, Doug and I enjoy our walks through town around sunrise, and we stay out of each other's way during the day for the most part. I've learned she opens the shop late on Wednesday mornings so she can attend early morning yoga with Rory, and she sleeps like the literal dead, so I'm not shocked she slept through a masked intruder invading her home.

Today, she made herself scarce while Breaker and I argued back and forth about delivery routes and bank accounts as discreetly as possible. Several times today I've left the apartment to field phone calls from Matteo as he relayed information on how our plan is unfolding. The men have managed to successfully win Luca's trust, gathering information on his next delivery disruption and planning their own way to botch it without losing my product or blowing their cover. I don't want to endanger their lives any more than necessary. After all, the men Matteo chose are my family, my responsibility, men who rely on me to make decisions they can trust. But this is the nature of the beast in this life. Nothing in Fortuna Nera is truly safe.

It's nearly nine at night before I have a chance to calm my nervous system. For the first time since I opened my eyes this morning, I actually feel the smallest amount of peace. Vanessa sits on the couch across the room, typing away on her laptop with her legs tucked under her butt. Her brow is furrowed in concentration, but every few seconds she steals glances at me when she thinks I'm not looking.

After the sixth time, I meet her eyes, and she gasps, her cheeks flushing as she looks away quickly. I suppress my laughter and focus my attention back on my computer, responding to several more emails. She continues peeking over the edge of her screen at me, and I break the silence.

"What are you doing, Vanessa?"

"Quarterly taxes, you?" She looks over at me curiously.

"Planning an assassination." I don't bother looking up, knowing I'm not joking. She can interpret it in any way she chooses.

She's quiet for several long moments, mulling over

the validity of my statement before deciding to press for more information.

"What is it you do exactly?" She asks with trepidation.

"Mind my own business. Ever heard of it?" I quipped.

Her expression turns sour, and she sticks her tongue out at me. Scoffing at her behavior, I can't help the question that arises, even though I know the answer already from my extensive research about her.

"Really? How old are you?"

"Twenty five. Well...almost," she replies instantly just as I take a sip of my coffee. I choke. Hearing the truth for the first time out loud somehow feels more jarring than I expected. Twenty fucking four years old.

"You alright over there?" She asks, raising a brow. I brush her off, regaining my composure quickly with a nod. "Why? How old are you?

"Forty. Today." I respond without looking away from my laptop screen. I don't know what possibly possessed me to tell her it was my birthday. Maybe some sick part of me actually loves to be tortured.

The room goes silent. My fingers hover over the keys as I chance a look over at her face. She's staring at me, a creepy serial killer smile painted across her face.

"Yes?" I ask.

"Today is your birthday?" She prods, and regret

swirls deep in my gut. I never should've let that piece of information slip.

"Don't." I snap, but she's practically bouncing in her seat.

"Come onnnnnn!" She barely contains her excitement, chewing on the edge of her lip repeatedly like she's going to literally combust if I don't cave to her enthusiasm.

"I haven't celebrated my birthday in decades, Vanessa." Something like sadness fills her eyes, and I feel even worse. I want her pity even less than I want her festivity.

"That's just depressing as hell, Sebastian." Her brows pinch together in that annoying way they do when she looks at something she finds sad. I hate that I've become so observant of her that I can recognize these expressions.

"Such is life, I suppose." I reply, continuing to work without looking at the sympathy on her face. Something throbs in my chest, a heavy weight settling against my ribs. I don't want to think about the idea that I may have missed out on anything by not celebrating my birth. I do not dwell on things like this, it's a waste of my valuable time.

"Would you...I know you don't want to celebrate. Will you stop me from celebrating?" She asks, her voice barely above a whisper as she peers over at me.

My fingers hover over the keys on my laptop. I can't remember the last time someone offered to do something to celebrate me. Matteo tries to take me out to the clubs every year, but I'm not young anymore. I'm far past the age of gallivanting until the sun rises the next day. Shit, I don't think I ever really had a phase like that. I was too busy learning from my father, doing my best to commit the lessons he was teaching me to memory for as long as I could before he died.

"What are you going to do? It's not like there's much of a nightlife here in Grovewood," I eye her suspiciously, wondering what she's playing at here.

"I don't know what you mean. The froyo place is open until 10:30 pm, Seb. What more can you really ask for?" She smirks, and I can't help but laugh.

Seb. Only my friends call me that. It's strange how Vanessa has begun to feel more and more like a friend each day, despite my better judgement. I don't want to enjoy her company. I don't want her presence in my apartment to make me feel somehow...lighter. But I do, and it does. Maybe I'm just feeling lonely for the first time in my life. A midlife crisis of sorts.

"Don't ignore my question. What are you going to do?" Closing the screen of my computer, my work abandoned for the distraction Vanessa brings.

"Will you let me make you a cake?" She asks hopefully, her caramel eyes wide as she looks deep into mine.

"I don't like cake." I reply coldly. I don't really want to be an asshole. But I'm being honest. Sweets aren't my forte.

"I can make tons of different desserts, Sebastian. My sister Aria went to culinary school back in Miami. She let me help her every time she was perfecting a recipe. I promise I won't kill you. Not by accident, at least." She gives me a devious smile, and I feel a chink in my armor.

"I like..." I pause, feeling exposed. I don't give anyone personal details about myself. It feels too vulnerable, like I'm opening myself up to be too known, too seen. I hate it.

"Tell me. I promise I won't use it to plot world domination." Her smile is wide and beautiful, her tan skin practically glows with excitement that she could learn even an insignificant detail about me that no one else truly knows.

"Tiramisu. I like tiramisu." I grumble.

The grin creeping across her face is criminal. I can see almost every one of her pearly white teeth as she bounces in her seat on the couch.

"Stop," I say dryly, looking away from her. I don't want to admit how fucking cute she looks right now.

"You mean to tell me, out of every single dessert on the planet you could possibly love, you love *COFFEE CAKE*?!" she shouts the last part, and I can't help but bark out a laugh.

"Not the same thing!" I reply, jabbing a finger through the air in her direction. "Coffee cake is a cake. Tiramisu is a religious experience."

"Oh, my apologies. I'm so sorry to offend you,

m'lord." She bows, making a huge show of being dramatic. I don't want to find her funny, but I do.

"You should be sorry. You can make it up to me though. With tiramisu." I smirk, and she claps her hands, giddy with excitement.

"With my over-roasted espresso? Done and done." She winks back at me, scurrying away to the kitchen.

"You know, if you start that now, it won't be ready until midnight?" I tell her, and she nods.

"I'm aware. Past your bedtime, gramps?" She quirks a brow, and my face falls, all humor gone from my expression.

"I'm nowhere near old enough to be anyone's grandfather." I tell her, and she shrugs.

"Actually, in theory, if you had a kid when you were twenty, she would be twenty right now. And she could have a kid of her own. So logically, you could be a grandpa very easily." she says as she lines bowls up on the kitchen counter.

My stomach twists, a sick feeling building there. I don't need any more reminders about the vast difference in age between Vanessa and I.

"That's enough of that talk, thanks. I'll be back." I tell her, standing and walking out the front door, leaving her looking dumbfounded as the door closes behind me.

I need to put some fucking space between us. This woman clouds my mind every time she's near me. I can't think about the fact she's sixteen years younger than me or only hanging around me because she needs something from me. I can't think about anything but those full lips, her luminous tan skin, and gorgeous caramel eyes. I can't fucking focus on the reason I'm here in Grovewood to begin with. Because my empire is standing on shaky ground at best. Doing something as stupid as entertaining my feelings for a quick fuck is the stupidest decision I could ever make.

Walking through the town square, I breathe in the cool night air. It's November, the chill moving in earlier and earlier in the evenings and throughout the days. I miss the Mediterranean climate. I want to go home. Italy is calling my name louder than it ever has before. In my line of work, I've traveled constantly, never spending so much time at home that it truly felt like enough. Miami satiates my need for activity, for constant motion. Spain fulfills my desire for family, my mother's roots running deep there and the culture always welcoming me with open arms. But Italy holds my heart. What little of it still exists.

Looking around this city, the small southern American charm saturating every inch of every street, my bones ache for home. I want to drive with the top down through hundred-year-old vineyards for miles until no one can find me. I want to eat pasta made by women who keep recipes like secrets they're willing to die for. I want to listen to old men argue as they pull swordfish into their gozzi and steady myself on the uneven cobblestones of my homeland. My world may be the dark underbelly of Italy, but I still make time for all the things that make the country truly beautiful. Being so far away is stifling.

My phone vibrates for the hundredth time today in my pocket, and I answer without hesitation.

"What is it this time, Teo?" I sigh, feeling heavier than I have all day.

"You need to come home." He replies, his tone clipped and serious.

"Funny, I was just thinking the same thing." I scoff.

"Luca hit two of our distribution warehouses. Of course, there were minimal supplies being kept there because we had knowledge these attacks were coming. But he knows. He knows there's a traitor in his operation, and he's going off the rails, Bash. He's threatening people's lives. The elders are talking. There's too much upset going on, they need to see your face." Matteo sounds worn out. I hate the toll this is taking on him.

"I can't keep hiding like this. It looks too weak. This isn't the way I've ever ruled before, it's not the leader I've ever been." Breathing in the cool night air, I resign myself to what I have to do. There are no other options for me.

"I have to admit, I'm scared for you. But you're right. You have to show your face, or he's going to run rampant over this family. Fortuna Nera isn't his playground, and you have to show him." Matteo covers the speaker, speaking in hurried Italian to someone in the background.

"I'll be home before the end of the week. Tell no one, I will make my own plans." I tell him, leaving no room for discussion.

"I look forward to seeing you. Oh, and happy birthday, Bash. It's a big one, old man. Don't spend it holed up in that apartment alone." He quips, and I end the call without another word.

Old man.

Fuck him. There's nothing old about me. I'm in my fucking prime. A flash of caramel eyes blazes through my mind, taking up space where it doesn't belong, and I force it out. Vanessa makes me feel years younger than I have in a long time, but I could never admit that to her. It would feel too much like admitting a huge defeat.

twelve

Sebastian

WALKING BACK TO THE APARTMENT, I brace myself for disappointment. I appreciate what Vanessa is trying to do, but this isn't Italy. Surprisingly, I don't feel the need to be cruel or overly critical of her, so I'll try my best to shut up and be grateful someone is trying to do something nice for me on my birthday for the first time in many years.

Ascending the stairs, the faint smell of espresso fills the air, and I breathe it in. It's one of my favorite scents in the world. That mixture of coffee, cinnamon, and vanilla has become a fixture in my space lately, and I've come to crave it. It's purely Vanessa, and I don't know what I'll do when she's not here anymore, taking up space in my mind and on my couch. I open the front door just as she bends over to slide the dish into the refrigerator. The flare of her hips, her thick thighs, her perfectly tanned skin, her presence disrupts the order of my world. Her movements are steady, nothing feels rushed or accidental. I keep my distance because if I ever crossed that line, there would be nothing left of her. My darkness would consume every ounce of light she possesses.

"It should be ready in about an hour or so." She gives me a soft smile, and I feel another small piece of my resolve crumble. She's so fucking beautiful, so sweet it hurts. Her kindness pisses me off more than I care to admit.

"Smells good." I reply tersely, wishing I could ignore every ounce of emotion stirring inside me for her.

"Everything okay with your work?" She asks, the small talk killing us both.

"Fine. I'll be taking a trip soon. I'm not sure how long I'll be away. We should probably discuss what you intend on doing while I'm gone." I take a seat at the bar, watching her move around the small kitchen, cleaning the few dishes she used. She hesitates when I say I'm leaving, trepidation flashing through her eyes.

"Oh. Okay. That's no problem, I'll make sure Doug and I are out by the time you have to leave." She wipes her hands on a kitchen towel, shrinking uncomfortably. Any other day, I would love to see her so uneasy. But something feels like its shifted between us. Her willingness to do something nice for me speaks volumes about the way she feels. She hasn't seen her ghost of a masked man since she came to stay here with me. Leaving her alone and defenseless again feels like a knife in my fucking eye.

"You can stay. If you want to, you and Doug can stay here." The words leave my mouth before I even think about what I'm saying. Letting her stay alone in my personal space? What the fuck am I doing? But her eyes light up hopefully, and I know I've made the right decision.

"Are you sure? I don't want to intrude." She chews on her bottom lip, and I can't look at her anymore.

"You've intruded more times than I care to think about, Vanessa. I think we've passed the point of propriety." A blush creeps up her neck, and I smirk.

"Why don't you like to celebrate your birthday?" She asks, rapidly changing the subject.

"Don't really see the point, I guess. It's just a day." I reply, rolling up the sleeves of my dress shirt. Her eyes track my movements, widening slightly as they slide across the ink there.

"Your parents didn't celebrate your birthdays? Or your other family?" She leans across the bar in front of me, pushing her tits together in a way that feels completely intentional.

"My parents weren't the celebratory type. We had far more important responsibilities to uphold. And Fortuna has bigger priorities." I tell her without thinking.

"Fortuna?" She asks, quirking a brow back at me.

"Just my family. They're responsible for much bigger endeavors than something as insignificant as a birthday. Keeping the business protected, keeping the family on top, those are the only things I was ever taught to prioritize. Everything else was frivolous. But I don't dwell on it. I understand it's just the reality of my life. When you're raised in the world I was, you're no stranger to obligations." I give her as little information as I can, not wanting to give her the ability to draw any conclusions that could put her safety at risk.

"I get that. But I gotta say...fuck that. That sounds like total bullshit! My parents were never ones to celebrate birthdays either. Well, not unless it was for their sweet angel baby boy. But their excuse was that they were too strung out to remember what year it was, let alone the date. My sister and I celebrated each other as best we could. Everyone deserves to feel special, even if it's just once a year, Seb. Even you. And yes, it physically hurts me to say those words to you, because heaven knows you don't need anyone telling you how fucking special you are. But I mean it. I think you take life a little too seriously sometimes. Take time to stop and smell the damn daisies every once in a while, Sebastian. Otherwise, you'll get frown lines and wrinkles on that beautiful face, and that would be an absolute tragedy." She smirks, truth and sarcasm weighing in equal parts in her words.

"Oh, you think I'm beautiful, huh?" I taunt, and she rolls her eyes.

"No, I think you're a fucking menace." She flattens her palms on the counter, straightening her back.

"Thank you, that's the nicest thing I think you've ever said to me." I try my best to suppress my grin, but it's difficult. Vanessa's devilish tongue is surprisingly entertaining. "By the way, I think the expression is stop and smell the *roses.* I've never heard anyone say stop and smell the daisies in my life. Daisies are fucking weeds, Vanessa."

"Maybe you're right, but I don't really give a shit. I hate roses." She shrugs, checking the time with a smile. "Look at that. All of your yapping soaked up an entire hour. We can check the cake!"

"It's not cake!" My tone is abrasive. Tiramisu is not a fucking cake.

She pulls the dish out of the fridge, reaching into the drawer for two forks before setting it down on the island between us. Apparently, we're going to eat it straight out of the pan like savages.

"No plates?" I ask, taking the fork she offers me.

"Do I look like Cinderella? I'm not the dish bitch around here. I don't see the point in creating more mess, especially since I already cleaned up." She shrugs me off, gesturing for me to take the first bite. "Birthday boys first."

"I am most definitely not a boy, Vanessa." I tell her,

sinking my fork into the spongy dish. Bringing the fork to my lips, I pause. "Don't read into what I'm about to say, okay?"

"Okay?" she says, confused.

"Thank you. You didn't have to take your time to make this for me, but you did. I appreciate it. I've been missing home a lot lately, and this makes it feel somehow...closer." I look into her eyes, making sure she sees the sincerity in my words.

"You're welcome. Happy Birthday. Now eat your cake, Sebastard." She beams back at me, a bright smile splitting her lips. Fucking brat.

Taking the first bite, the rich espresso taste saturates my tongue. It tastes like a collision of bittersweetness and indulgence, not unlike what I imagine the creator herself to taste like. The espresso is dark roasted and slightly bitter. I can tell it's the same one I enjoy from her shop daily, soaking into the savoiardi until they're tender but not soggy. She made them from scratch. How the hell did she manage this? The mascarpone cream melts in my mouth, rich and velvety, with a gentle sweetness that feels more luxurious than sugary. The cocoa dusting on top adds a dry, dark chocolate edge that lingers on my tongue, balancing everything out. It tastes exactly as I dreamed it would. Like *home*. A slow, knowing grin splits her lips, but I say nothing. Instead, I savor the delicious treat she made just for me.

"It's good, isn't it?" She inspects my every move. I just shrug.

"It's fine. Espresso is a little bland. If you imported your coffee from Italy, it would be better." I jab, and she takes it in stride, her triumphant smile not wavering for even a moment.

"I'll take that into consideration for next time." She takes a bite, moaning around her fork. The sound is like heroin straight to my cock, and I shift uncomfortably.

"Will you be okay here?" I'm not sure what possessed me to ask. Concern for her safety? Common decency, maybe? This is completely unlike me. "I know your ghost hasn't made himself known lately, but I don't want to leave you unprotected."

She nods wordlessly, as if she doesn't truly believe it, but she can convince herself if she doesn't hear the words out loud. I don't feel good about leaving her here alone. But I have much more important responsibilities, and she's a grown woman. She's more than capable of taking care of herself. I take one last bite, much bigger than the first, before rinsing my fork and putting it in the dishwasher.

"I'm heading to bed. I'll be leaving before the end of the week." I search her face for any sign of hesitation, but her expression is neutral as she nods back at me.

"Good night, Sebastian. Sweet dreams." She gives me a half wave, her smile not reaching her eyes.

"Thank you, Vanessa. Really. It was...it was great." I

don't wait for her response, even though I catch her smile out of the corner of my eye as I stalk back to my bedroom.

I hate dancing around her like this. Grovewood was supposed to be simple, uncomplicated. She wasn't supposed to muddy the fucking waters with her luscious curves and flawlessly tanned skin. She wasn't even supposed to exist for me. Now, the idea of leaving her here alone causes a sick feeling deep in the pit of my stomach.

I could be out of here before I can do something really fucking stupid like give in to the pull I can't seem to ignore every time she walks into the room.

But that's the funny thing about being the king. A king doesn't have to compromise what he wants, he just has to take it.

thirteen

Vanessa

IT'S BEEN weeks since I've had any sign of the masked man. Still, the thought of Sebastian leaving town is terrifying. What if the masked man is watching, waiting for the moment I'm alone and he can pull me under his spell all over again?

I don't know what possessed me to make Sebastian a birthday cake. Or birthday tiramisu, since I've been told a dozen times tiramisu is not cake. Hearing the way he described his childhood, I felt a kind of kindred familiarity. Like I'd lived the same life, in a different time, on the other side of the world. My parents never celebrated any of their children except my brother. Eventually, it became so normal that it stopped bothering me. But I always knew it was fucked up. Parents are supposed to be your biggest cheerleaders, the ones you can depend on for anything in this life. I got completely fucked in that department. But I had Aria, I didn't need much else, and that was fine by me.

Curling up in my favorite position on the couch, I tug my blanket over my shoulders. Maybe I'll do something really outrageous and sleep in Sebastian's bed while he's gone. Not that this couch isn't ridiculously comfortable, because it is. But the idea of being surrounded by his things, his scent, is intoxicating on a completely different level. My eyes drift closed, pulling me into the abyss of a dreamless sleep.

"Diavolina, I've missed you." His fingers caress my cheek, and goosebumps spread across my skin.

No, no, no, no, no, this is not happening. I've eluded him for weeks! Why now?! Why tonight, the night I finally felt the ice melting between Sebastian and me? I can't move a single muscle, every fiber of my being feeling like solid concrete.

"What did you do to me?" I croak out, my voice scratchy.

How the fuck did he even find me here? Where is Doug? Where is Sebastian? There's no way he could've gotten into this apartment without Sebastian waking up. Ice runs through my veins. Did he hurt him? Is Seb dead, and I'm to blame? Emotion lodges in my throat, a sob aching to break free.

"Shhhhh, not to worry. Everything is fine." The gentle tone of his voice, the delicate way he touches my face, although I know I shouldn't trust him, I do.

"Why are you doing this to me?" I strain to get the words out, tears leaking from the corners of my eyes.

"To you? No, amore mio. I'm doing this for you. To show you who you really are. What you really want." He pulls the blanket down my body, exposing my bare arms to the cooler air.

I want to pull away, to shiver and tug myself from his grip. But I can't move. Is this what sleep paralysis feels like? Is all of this really just a vivid fever dream I'm constantly falling into? Maybe I'm sleepwalking every time something has been moved before. Maybe I really have been imagining everything, and this man is just all in my mind.

"I don't...I don't know what you're talking about." Heat flushes through my body, sweat breaking out across my skin.

"There is no need to lie. I can feel it in your pulse, I can smell it on your skin. You want me just as I want you." One dark hand slips around my throat as the other slides down my arm, leaving heat in it's wake.

Swallowing hard, his fingers flex tighter, the circulation slowing as I teeter on the edge of lightheadedness. I've never really been into choking before, but I've also never really had to chance to explore this side of myself. So I can't say if this is something I'm actually turned on by, or if the heightened emotions are just getting the best of me.

Who the fuck am I kidding? I'm definitely turned on by this. Should I be? No, this is insane, absolutely diabolical. I should be committed for the things I'm thinking right now, but that doesn't stop me from leaning in to his touch the slightest bit.

"Give in to me, diavolina. Let me show you how good it feels to dance with the devil." He leans closer to me, his grip tightening.

Spots dance across my vision. I want to reach up and pull his hand from my throat, but I can't. I can't move at all. More and more I feel like my visions of the masked man are nothing more than vivid nightmares, manifestations of my subconscious showing me the deepest, darkest desires of my soul.

"Give me every piece of you, and I will show you who you really are." He squeezes hard, his chest rising and falling rapidly. This is turning him on just as desperately as it is me.

My body feels as if it leaves itself, spinning on the ceiling, skin blazing against his touch. I'm going to die if I spend another moment here in this heat, in the flames he stokes inside me. I've felt this way before when I used to party in Miami and spend all night drinking bottle after bottle, popping pills with my friends just to forget our meaningless lives.

I want to scream, to call out for Sebastian to save me from this evil. But is he evil? He feels so familiar. Like he's touched me this way a thousand times before. Like we've memorized each other's souls in every lifetime, and this is our reckoning.

I'm going to pass out. I feel the light slipping from my eyes. It doesn't quite feel like he wants to kill me, but I'm not so sure he doesn't want to hurt me. The thought should scare me, but it does the complete opposite. I'm so fucking confused, I just want to get out of here.

"Let...me..." I choke on the words, my head beginning to float, my body almost hollow, as if I'm drifting half a step behind reality.

"Mine," he growls, one hand gripping my hip so tightly I know it'll leave bruises, the other stealing the very breath from my lungs.

I force a scream from my chest with every ounce of fight I have left inside me, but it's pitiful. It comes out as barely more than the mewling of a child afraid of the monster under their bed.

"Come with me," is all I hear him say before everything around me fades to black.

Doug barks loudly and Sebastian curses from somewhere down the hall, the commotion waking me from a dead sleep as a sob rips from my throat.

"Sebastian!" I scream, and he opens his bedroom door, confused. Rushing into the living room, Doug hot on his heels. I can't take any time to appreciate how beautiful he is, black ink covering his olive skin, salt and pepper hair mussed from heavy sleep, his boxer briefs doing nothing to conceal the thick cock I know he's packing. Instead, he finds me a sobbing mess on the floor, surrounded by blankets and pillows. Nothing else is out of place. It's as if I've been ripped from a nightmare, and maybe I have. Maybe I am really just losing my fucking mind.

"Are you okay? What happened? Did you put the dog in my room?" He rapid-fires questions at me I just don't have the answers to. Instead of answering him, I dissolve into a puddle of tears, burying my face in my hands as I'm crushed under the weight of my confusion.

"He was here, Sebastian. The masked man. I swear, he was here. He taunts me, telling me things that aren't true. That I'm..." sobs choke me, wracking through my body like waves crashing against the rocks. Doug nudges me with his head, and I thoughtlessly begin stroking his soft ears.

"No one came into this apartment, Vanessa. I have security measures on every exterior door and window. No one could enter this building without alerting me to their presence." He sounds so sure, so confident his systems could never fail. I have to believe him.

That leaves only one logical answer. I'm going fucking insane. This masked man is truly all in my mind. Everything I've been seeing, feeling, it's all just made up, a story I've somehow convinced myself is real. Maybe I really am sleepwalking. I never have before, at least not that I know of. But there's a first time for everything.

"I'm sorry. I didn't mean to wake you. I don't...I don't know what happened. I don't know what's happening to me." I'm sure I look like the most pathetic mess he's ever seen sitting on the fucking floor, my curls looking something akin to Medusa, blankets piled around me, tears streaming down my face as I scream about a masked man tormenting me. But he looks back at me stony faced, his features completely unreadable. Whatever he's thinking, he's not going to let me in on it.

"I need to make a call," he says, turning on his heel and stalking from the room.

What the fuck is wrong with me? How could I walk into this man's life and turn it into such a disaster like this? Maybe my parents were right. All I do is ruin things everywhere I go. Maybe I need to see an actual doctor about these problems, not just assume I know what's going on like I always do.

Climbing to my feet on shaky legs, I try to clean up the mess I've made of the living room, sifting through the blankets to find my phone. The sun hasn't come up yet, so I don't think I'm late, but wouldn't that just be the cherry on top of a stellar fucking day.

After ten minutes, Sebastian comes back into the room, half dressed in black slacks and a white button-down with the front completely unbuttoned. This man will be my undoing, I swear. I'm not sure it gets any sexier than Sebastian at four in the morning.

"It's done. Rory will be here in half an hour to open the shop. She will take Doug home with her when she leaves for the day. We will stop by your home on the way out of town so you can pack a bag. Anything you don't own, we can buy. You should pack enough for at least two weeks." He's speaking basic English, but it might as well be Chinese because I do not comprehend the demands he's making.

"I'm sorry, what?" I stare back at him, barely piecing together what he's saying.

"We leave in 10 minutes. Get dressed." He turns to leave the room again, but my brain finally catches up. Chasing him back to his bedroom, I feel my anger rising. He doesn't get to make decisions about my life like this. I'm not a doll he can pick up and pose however he sees fit.

"Wait just a fucking minute. I can't just pick up and leave. I have a business, Sebastian. I have responsibilities here. I can't just push them off onto Rory like that. She's..." I catch myself, not knowing if she's confided in him about her condition and not wanting to betray her trust in me.

"It's already been taken care of, Vanessa. Rory assures me she can handle it, even in her current state. She said she welcomes the distraction, actually. Apparently, Breaker has been treating her with kid gloves since she found out she is expecting again, and she's growing tired of it. She said she's happy to help." I pull back, a little shocked that she would speak so freely with him. They must be much more comfortable with each other than I thought.

"But I don't-" my argument dies on my tongue when

his eyes meet mine, the look he's giving me that of a hunter, dark and deadly.

He's daring me to fight back, to keep defying him. I get the idea no one ever questions or denies him back home. But my life doesn't belong to him. I don't belong to anyone, and he doesn't get to tell me what to do like a child with no discussion or consideration of my feelings in the situation.

"Do you want to stay here alone? Whether your ghost man is real or in your mind, do you want to face him alone? Or would you rather give your mind a break five thousand miles from here in the most beautiful place you've ever seen? Let me take you to my world, Bambina. Let me show you my home. Where I can keep you safe." he says every word with conviction, and how the hell can I argue with that.

This is the first time he's shown genuine concern for my safety in a way that would lead me to believe he actually *cares* for me. A quiet, destabilizing click like a lock turning, its pins falling into place, something I didn't know was there suddenly shifts. I replay moments I'd filed away as nothing. The way his gaze always lingers when he looks at me, the way his voice softens lately when he says my name instead of the grating way it sounded before. Then it lands, slow and unmistakable, and my chest tightens not with panic, but with a sudden awareness. Like someone just threw open the curtains after a long, dark winter, and light finally floods every corner of this space. The air feels invigorated in this room. Charged. Heavy with what's not being said between us. It's enticing and terrifying all at once. Because now that I've seen it, I can't unsee it. And whatever happens next, something has already shifted.

"Okay," I agree, not knowing what I'm truly agreeing to. But knowing that whatever it is, I don't think I'm ready for it.

fourteen

Sebastian

WHAT THE FUCK am I doing? This is quite possibly the worst idea I've ever had. Yet here we are, climbing the steps of a private jet, Vanessa looking around like a baby deer in the headlights.

"What the hell do you do, Seb?" She whispers as we enter the luxurious cabin.

I hand our bags to the crew member responsible for storing everything before the flight departs. A flight attendant appears from the back of the cabin. She's young and beautiful, the type who usually frequents these kinds of charters because they're ripe with rich playboys who tip well and provide endless entertainment for women like her. She grins salaciously at me, but I ignore her, grasping Vanessa's wrist and directing her to the seat near the window.

"I've told you. It's a family business." I tell her, taking the seat across from her.

Her eyes are wide and mesmerized, taking in the elegance of everything around her. I imagine she's never been anywhere this extravagant before in her life. If she thinks this is fancy, I should probably warn her about my home.

"Yeah, okay. That's very mafia boss of you, Sebastian. How about a real answer? Is it like generational wealth or something? I feel like it's only rich douche bros that fly around in fancy jets like this, and they're all investment bankers or living off daddy's money or both. I don't think you fall into any of those categories. You've gotta give me something here!" She gestures around the cabin. "How in the fuck is this your life?"

"It's safer for us all if you don't ask questions, Vanessa." I tell her as honestly as I possibly can.

"I've heard that before. From Breaker, actually. And it turns out he kills people for a living, soooo..." she shrugs, looking expectantly at me, but I just stare back at her. Letting her draw her own conclusions is probably for the best.

"Breaker is a good man, Vanessa. That is all that matters in the balance of right and wrong." I reply, leaning back in my seat and scrolling through my phone. I send a message to Matteo letting him know I'm on the way home, but no other details.

"I know he is. Don't misunderstand me. I have no

problem with the work he does. If you were to tell me you did the same thing, I wouldn't judge you, Sebastian. The world isn't black and white, and I've never been scared of all the color you can find when you look hard enough. I grew up in a world full of bad people. I've seen people who did bad things for terrible reasons and people who did bad things because they were just trying to survive, just trying to keep their families alive. I see nothing wrong with being bad for the right reasons. Just depends on the way you look at things, I guess." She stares straight into my soul, her beautiful golden-brown eyes captivating me more and more by the second.

"Not everyone believes the way you do, unfortunately." I say, severing our connection before I can fall any deeper into her trance.

"I know that. I just don't care." She leans back in her seat, her cropped band t-shirt riding up several inches to reveal a sliver of skin.

Vanessa may be unsure when it comes to some things, but her confidence shines through in so many ways it's infectious. She's wearing a pair of black high-waisted linen pants and a vintage t-shirt that's cropped just below her lacy bralette. The edge of it peeks out every time she shifts in her seat or reaches her arm up to adjust her messy curls piled on top of her head. Her casual sophistication is nothing like that of the women I'm used to in my world. She doesn't hide her curves under oversized layers of clothing the way many full-figured women do. She doesn't give a damn who looks, she just is who she is.

The women who hang around the men of Fortuna Nera are chic, Italian elegance, but stuck up and only looking for whichever man can get them as high as possible in the family. I have no interest in being anyone's meal ticket, but it's not lost on me that I have no heir to continue my family line once I die.

Should the time come sooner than I expect, Fortuna Nera should pass to whoever I have named my successor. In theory, that is. But there would be a bloody war. Things move much more smoothly when there is a bloodline to follow. Is it an antiquated tradition that holds little weight in modern society? Absolutely. But as they say, Rome wasn't built in a day, and Fortuna will not be rebuilt in a matter of years either.

A vision of Vanessa as a mother flashes through my mind, her perfectly full-bodied curves growing even softer as she grows a child. It's the last fucking thing I should be thinking about while we're both stuck on this plane for a ten-hour flight to Italy, but I can't stop where my mind is taking me. Vanessa dissolving under my touch as she lets me explore every inch of her body the way I wanted to the moment I saw her. Her caramel eyes shuddering closed as she collapses under the weight of her overwhelming desire for me. Vanessa, *mine.*

My cock stiffens behind my zipper, and I adjust in my seat. I need to think about something else, anything else. Scrolling on my phone, I absentmindedly read through several emails as the crew goes through their last-minute checks before takeoff. Vanessa stares out the window silently, her mind a thousand miles away.

"Everything okay?" I ask, and she jumps in surprise, completely zoned out.

"Oh, yeah. Sorry. Everything's great. I mean, I'm not a huge fan of planes or flying, but yeah, I'm good. And I've never really left Doug behind, but I know he loves Rory. And hopefully the shop won't be too much of a burden for her. I hate putting so much on her shoulders. Do you think Breaker will help? Of course not, he has work, I'm sure. I don't know. Do you think one of your henchmen can make sure I locked my doors? I think I did. Do you have henchmen? I feel like this level of luxury means you have henchmen." She word-vomits every thought passing through her mind, which is better than actually being ill, so I'll take it.

Before I can think about what I'm doing, and why the fuck I'm doing it, I pull her out of her seat and into my lap. She lands with a soft thud, her legs draping over mine and extending over the arm of the chair. Pulling her head against my chest, she stiffens for only a fraction of a second before melting into me, tucking one arm into her chest and wrapping the other around my neck. She sighs heavily, letting my scent permeate her lungs and bring her some semblance of peace. And shockingly, it works. Her rapid heart rate slows, her breathing evening out within just a few moments of me stroking her delicate curls.

"It's going to be okay, Bambina. I won't let anything happen to you, to Doug, or to your business. I know these things are important to you." I try to reassure her, but I've never been very good at offering comfort. Honestly, I can't remember a time I've ever wanted to.

"I'm sorry. I'm not a mess, I promise. I don't know why you keep finding me at my worst, but I'm not this person." She sniffles, and I wonder if she's crying as she buries her head further into my chest.

"I know you are a strong woman, Vanessa. I've known since the first time your eyes met mine. Since the first time you called me a bastard. Most people cower in my presence, but never you. Something about your intensity, your soul. There's a hardness in you that the world has continuously tried to carve into. It failed. I feel that same hardness lives in me. You don't bend. You endure. And somehow that makes you even more intoxicating to me." I shouldn't be confessing these truths to her, but seeing her so scared broke something in me. I want to be the one to hold all of her damaged pieces together. Her shoulders shake so slightly, and I have my confirmation that she is indeed crying.

"You're unyielding in the way fire is once it's been set, Vanessa. Beautiful, merciless, and impossible to look away from. There's nothing fragile about you, and that's what makes you so exquisite. You think you're weak because you're tired. You're not. You're stubborn, and the fact you're still standing is proof. I didn't start wanting you despite that. I wanted you *because* of it. Because of how incredibly persistent and strong you are. It's something I need in my world." I stroke her hair, my fingers weaving into her curls as I tilt her head back and force her to meet my eyes.

The red rim around her beautiful caramel irises causes an unfamiliar ache in my chest. Some time between hating and befriending this woman, I've grown to feel something else for her. Something so much deeper than I thought I was capable of feeling. A tear slips from the corner of her eye, and I catch it with my thumb. Her eyes flutter closed, a small sigh slipping from her lips.

"Seb," she whispers, her soft breath fanning across my skin. My name sounds like a plea, an invitation, like desperation slipping from her lips. She wants me to kiss her, to capture her the way she has me. The list of reasons why I shouldn't is longer than I could even begin to imagine, but right now I can't think of a single one.

My resolve shatters. My hand grips tighter into her curls, angling her head exactly where I want it before pulling her body even tighter against mine. She doesn't even have time to gasp before my lips are crushed against hers. I knew they would feel like absolute heaven. But this kiss is anything but sweet, this kiss is not soft, it's a collision. Weeks of restraint breaking all at once, breath stolen, mouths clashing as if our bodies are still under the impression we're fighting. She moans softly and my cock stiffens beneath her. Her nails slide up my chest, drawing a groan from deep in my throat that only serves to spur her on. My tongue demands entrance into her mouth, never asking permission again. This woman is mine, no matter what she believes. No other man will ever know her this way again. If anyone even dared to try, I would gut them from root to tip. They would suffer at my hands before meeting an untimely death. If I thought she was fascinating before, now that I've tasted her very soul, I will never get enough of her.

Her kiss is consuming, soft and warm, a tender ache that has settled deep instead of fading. Nothing has ever compared to this. I'm man enough to admit I've read novels where poets talk about the world shifting on its axis when the right woman comes along. I always thought those people were full of shit, to be honest. Until right now.

Her slender fingers grip the nape of my neck tighter, digging into the muscle and bone there. I hope she leaves her marks behind as proof to the world that I will never belong to any other after this day. My free hand trails down her soft thigh, sliding around the curve of her perfect ass and squeezing. She doesn't break the kiss, both her hands splayed on either side of the columns of my neck, touching me in the most possessive way I've ever been touched. I've had plenty of women try to lay their claim over me before, but none I've ever given a second thought to until this moment. Vanessa is territorial in a way I've never felt before. She shifts, straddling my hips, and deepens this kiss more and more. I'm going to fuck her if she keeps this up, and I won't have our first time be in this reclining seat on a plane. Mile high club sounds nice in theory, but not in reality.

"Bambina, wait." I pull away, instantly missing the feeling of her lips against mine. A whimper escapes her lips, and I swallow it down. Gently, I lift her off my lap and set her down in her own seat, not bothering to hide the way my cock strains against my pants. Leaning down, I trap her in her seat between my arms. She has a dazed look on her face, as if she's barely coming down from a high she doesn't want to lose.

"Look at me, Vanessa. We'll be taking off soon, and you need to buckle up. When I slide deep inside your sweet pussy, it won't be with an audience a few feet away listening in on us. It will be in my home, where no one can hear you screaming for your life."

fifteen

Vanessa

WE SPEND the next nine hours completely avoiding eye contact. I'm so on edge, so utterly alive with tension from kissing Sebastian I could explode at any moment. I hadn't expected him to treat me so kindly when I was feeling so overwhelmed. I have moments of overload where my mind completely goes off the rails and there's no slowing the rapid deterioration of thoughts as they take over. Somehow, Sebastian was able to do what no one else has ever done before. Not my sister, not my friends, not a single therapist I've paid hundreds to help me find coping mechanisms for this problem. He pulled me against his solid chest, and every thought went silent. I couldn't help but curl into him, enjoying the sound of silence.

At some point during the flight, he started working on his computer. The steady drone of his fingers typing away against the keys lulls me into a dreamless sleep for the first time in weeks. I don't see my masked ghost, I don't see visions of anything at all. I simply enjoy the blissful nothingness until I'm enveloped again by powerful arms and that familiar clean leather and rain scent. I didn't think it was quite possible for someone to smell this *expensive*, yet earthy at the same time. Like luxury grounded by the rawness of the elements. Warm, smooth, and clean.

"Did we land?" I ask, my voice weak with sleep.

"I've got you, Bambina. Sleep. I'll wake you when we get to Villa di Arsenio." He kisses my hair softly, shifting my body in his arms as he carries me to a waiting car. He settles me in a soft leather seat, shutting the door without getting inside.

After a few quiet moments alone with my thoughts in the car, my mind finally wakes up to its surroundings. I'm in Italy. In the backseat of a very lavish car. Is this a fucking Rolls Royce? What kind of alternate reality have I fallen into? A man sits in the driver's seat looking straight ahead, totally motionless. If not for the faint lift in his shoulders, I could swear he was a robot. Despite that, I somehow feel so safe here.

It's a strange feeling, being cared for like I'm something precious. I've never been treated as such before. I've never been at the top of anyone's priority list but my own. But something in Sebastian's touch, in the way he looks at me, tells me that might not be true anymore.

There are still so many unknowns between us. But of two things I am certain.

First, Sebastian is carrying a secret too heavy to be harmless. He's told me it's safer not to ask questions, but I've heard that a hundred times before in my life. Usually from drug dealers and suppliers, the people who kept my parents in business for most of my life. The truth he's hiding could destroy whatever this is before we've even had a chance to define it.

Second, and most unfortunately, I don't fucking care. That kiss, the feeling of pure, unadulterated relief I felt as soon as he held me in his arms, it was worth whatever hell could possibly rain down on me because of who he is.

When we were younger, Aria and I used to talk about the kind of people we wanted to end up with. She would always describe someone sassy and fun who loved adventure as much as she did. My list of wants always consisted of someone who satiated my starving soul. Someone who could quiet the constant cacophony of worries all speaking at once. I've lived as long as I can remember with a thousand half-formed thoughts rattling like loose change inside my skull. Even my calmest moments radiate uneasiness, as if something is always about to go wrong. The only thing I ever longed for in a partner was someone who could make all the noise disappear. What I never imagined was finding it in a man like Sebastian.

He's nearly old enough to be my father, but I don't even consider that minor detail. That's at the very bottom of the list of reasons why I shouldn't want him. He's arrogant, overbearing as hell, and I can't imagine what it would be like if he thought he had some type of control over me.

Am I really that delusional? He already does.

The passenger door swings open, Sebastian's large frame crowding me as he slides into the seat next to me. I move back, giving him his space, but I don't make it far before his hand clamps down on my thigh and he drags me back across the smooth leather seat until my body is flush against his.

"Puoi andare, Enzo. Vai direttamente a casa, senza fermarti." He speaks rapid Italian to the man in the front seat, who replies with only a sharp nod.

"The creepy robot has a name?" I whisper to Seb, his face so close to mine I can see every muscle in his jaw flex when he laughs.

"Robot? Who? Enzo?" His brows pinch together as if I've just told the funniest joke he's ever heard.

"Yes, he was so still and quiet. Freaked me out," I shrug, and he leans forward, slapping the younger man on the shoulder as we pull off of the tarmac.

"Lei pensa che tu sia un robot. Il tipo sbagliato di rigido, amico." He jokes, his smooth Italian accent even more intoxicating than I was prepared for.

"I know you're making some kind of joke at my

expense, but I don't care. You can keep speaking Italian all night long, though. Shit, you can read the fucking dictionary for all I care as long as you do it low and slow in that beautiful voice." I lean back, scooting slightly away from him and sliding my phone out of my bag.

My sister texted me six times. With the time difference, she's about six hours behind us. It's only nine in the evening in Miami, and she's probably getting ready to finish the dinner service at her restaurant. I don't want to interrupt her. I send her a quick message letting her know I'm safe, I'm taking a little time away, and I'll call her soon.

Scrolling through several other notifications, I open the thread between Rory and I, wondering how much I should really disclose to her about what I'm feeling for Sebastian. Glancing over at him as the car eases through the quiet cobblestone streets, he seems to be doing the same thing I am. Only he looks far more concerned with whatever he sees on his screen than I do. His expression is suddenly cut from stone, his jaw locked, mouth drawn into a hard, unforgiving line. His eyes are sharp and unblinking, stripped of the warmth they possessed only a moment ago. His brows are drawn low and tense, carving shadows that make his face feel colder and heavier. Instantly, I want to fold myself into his side, to smooth the hard lines etched across his face and bring his joyful expression back, but I don't interrupt his thoughts. Instead, I focus on what

Rory said over the past several hours while we were traveling.

> "Don't worry about your furry child. He's blissfully happy lying out by the pool right now!"

> "Are you in the air? On an actual plane? Don't throw up..."

> "Seb told Break you guys were going to be gone for two weeks!? Bitch TAKE ME WITH YOU!"

> "When you become the next queen of Italy (does Italy have queens? Idk. But if anyone can make it happen, it's Seb) don't forget who kept your doors open, okay? Bring me excellent wine for future use!"

> "Things are running just fine here, and we'll be totally okay. So don't worry. You need to take care of your mental health. And maybe also clear the cobwebs from your lady bits."

She sends a last message with three shrug emojis, and I snort out a laugh. She's fucking outrageous, but I couldn't love her more. The family I've created in Grovewood has brought me more joy and comfort than most of my blood relatives ever have.

"Something funny?" Sebastian asks, not looking up from his screen.

"Just Rory checking in. Nothing more scandalous than usual." I reply, sending her a quick thank you and promising to send her endless pictures and updates.

Sliding my phone back into my bag, I cross my arms over my chest, leaning my head against the soft leather seat. I take a moment to appreciate Sebastian's features. They're anything but cute or soft, but he is still the most attractive man I've ever laid eyes on. Over the past several weeks, I've kept myself from studying him as much as I could, but that hasn't been as effective as I'd hoped.

I haven't missed the way his dark brown eyes pierce straight through me every time they meet my gaze, like a hunter honing in on his prey. Or the way he keeps a small dagger tucked into the waistband of his pants along his back, in case of emergencies, I'm sure. I haven't missed the tension he carries in his shoulders, as if he's constantly holding the entirety of the world on his back, never resting for even a moment because who knows what might befall him if he does.

He drops his phone in his lap. His long fingers flex, the 'VITA NERA' tattoo inked across his knuckles flashing in the moonlight. I want to trace every inch of ink on his skin, map it all with my fingertips. I want to know this man inside and out. But something tells me it will never be that easy.

"Will you tell me where we're going?" I ask, feeling like I'm begging for morsels.

"To my home. Villa di Arsenio." He replies very matter-of-factly, as if it's normal to address property so formally.

"Your home has a title?" I press, but he just smirks.

"My home has a great many things, Bambina. I will show you when we arrive. Be prepared though. It may be a little more...vast...than you're accustomed to." His expression gives little away, but I'm even more confused now than I was when we got on the jet.

"How vast are we talking here, Seb?" I ask, and a sharp gasp sounds from the front seat.

Sebastian meets Enzo's eyes in the rear-view mirror, and the men share some unspoken conversation I'm not sure about. Did I say something wrong? Am I asking too many questions? I don't really know the protocol for traveling with your not-boyfriend to foreign countries with no knowledge about who he really is, where you're going, or what you're gonna do there.

Enzo's harsh gaze finds mine for only a second before Sebastian is holding a gun to his temple, even though he's still driving the car. He swerves slightly, correcting himself quickly, and I gasp, not knowing how to process what's happening in front of my eyes and how an innocent conversation turned into this so quickly.

"This I will say in English so it is crystal clear. Be careful with your eyes, Enzo. Before you lose them. You will show her the respect she deserves, or you will answer to me, captio?"

"Sì, capo. Mi scuso." Enzo says, his expression morphing from hardness to one of respect instantly. *Capo*?

"Do not apologize to me. Apologize to her." He points back at me, not removing the barrel of the gun from Enzo's temple for even a moment. The man is fucking unhinged.

"I'm very sorry, I did not mean to offend you." Enzo's accent is thick, and he looks truly remorseful. I give him a nod in return, unable to speak a single word.

Maybe my initial assumptions about Sebastian weren't far from the truth. What the fuck have I gotten myself into, and why did that make me want to fall to my knees for this man? He exudes power in a way I have never before seen in my life, and it is euphoric. He's impossible to deny, impossible to ignore. I've been trying for weeks now with no success.

"Good. Now that we have that cleared up. Enzo will be in charge of your security while we are here in Italy. Should you need anything and I'm not around, Enzo will be there." he says so plainly, like bodyguards are a regular occurrence in everyday life.

"La proteggerai come se fossi me. Se le succede qualcosa, la pagherai con la vita." He speaks to Enzo, and whatever he says makes Enzo's eyes widen before he nods his understanding sharply. I don't speak Italian, but I can use my context clues well enough to understand he said something about *paying with your life.*

"I'm going to have to learn some Italian if I want to keep up around here." I joke. Sebastian smiles, but it doesn't reach his eyes.

"But it's so much easier for me to talk about you when you have no idea what I'm saying, Bambina" The bastard actually has the audacity to wink at me, and I wonder if all of this is one big dumpster fire and I'm holding the matches.

"Welcome to my world," he whispers against the shell of my ear, and I swear I feel a tear slip down my inner thigh.

sixteen

Vanessa

WE DRIVE miles outside of Rome, slowing every once in a while for Sebastian to show me landmarks as the sun rises across the beautiful countryside. We pass a beautiful nature reserve that he promises we can come back to sometime before my time here is through. Before I can ask him what else we can see, we turn onto a long driveway. We drive for nearly half a mile before coming to an entrance that feels more formal than any home I've ever seen, as though it requires reverence just to enter the grounds.

Tall stone pillars rise on either side of black iron gates, the stone softened by age and wrapped in thick ivy. Ornate ironwork tops the gate, intricate and old-world, more decorative than defensive, yet unmistakably authoritative. Even though they're small, I don't miss the cameras tracking our movements as we pull closer to the gate. It swings open, and anxiety clenches in my gut. I'm not equipped for this kind of lifestyle. What the hell was Seb doing renting my shitty apartment when he lives like a fucking *king* at home?

"Don't go there, Vanessa," Sebastian interrupts my internal downward spiral, and I blink over at him.

"What do you mean?" I play dumb, masking my emotions.

"I can hear your mind spinning into overdrive from here. I'm surprised smoke isn't pouring out of your ears by now." The corner of his lips tip into a smile, and my shoulders relax slightly.

"How could I not be nervous? Do you see this place?" Pulling the edge of my bottom lip between my teeth, the thoughts in my mind shouting my inadequacies.

I don't belong here.

He doesn't want me.

He's just biding his time.

His hand clamps down on my thigh just above my knee, and my mind goes silent. I don't know how, out of every other human on this planet, I found the one that makes the chaos become order. We pull up to the front of a circular gravel drive, pale stone columns rising in perfect symmetry around the prodigious double front door. Everything is embellished, slightly weathered by time rather than neglect. A wide portico stretches the length of the villa. The architecture feels reverent, almost ancient, as if the house was built to be approached slowly, like a museum. It's beautiful, so beautiful I want to explore for hours and hours, losing myself in the history of this place. At the center, tall iron doors stand open beneath an arched transom of stained glass, framing a glimpse of green space beyond, maybe a garden? Sculpted stone drapery and figures guard the front doors. It's expansive, almost haunted.

"This place is incredible." My voice is hushed, barely above a whisper, as I take in everything around us.

"My father would've loved to hear your praises." He replies, his thumb grazing back and forth across my skin.

"You grew up here?" I ask, looking back at him as he watches me intently.

"I did. Many of my fondest memories are held on these grounds. Many of my worst as well. But this is my home. Please consider it yours. There are very few places you cannot go, but my men will make sure to guide you away from those areas for your own safety. The entirety of Italy is at your disposal, Bambina." He smiles back at me, and I feel a little more of my reservations slip away.

"I think we still have a lot to discuss, but I want you to know how much I appreciate this. You could've left me to fend for myself, and I'm not sure how I would've managed. But this...I never could've imagined this, Sebastian." Leaning over, I kiss his cheek softly, lingering far longer than necessary.

Before I can pull away, his hand grips my throat,

tilting my head back and capturing my mouth in a kiss so feral, I can't catch my breath. His tongue delves into my mouth, taking what he wants without permission. His touch is brutal, every fingertip putting the most delicious amount of pressure against my skin. The darkest part of me hopes it will bruise, branding me with his marks, at least for the moment. A car door closes, startling me, and I pull away. We're alone, Enzo standing outside the driver's door silently.

"I wasn't done with you yet," he says, his voice deeper than usual.

Heat creeps up my chest, and I laugh nervously. I can't imagine what the people here must think of me already. Seb is obviously their boss in some way. And here I am, some American bimbo he flew in to maul in the Rolls while the bodyguard waits to hold the door. What the fuck is wrong with me?

"I think I need a nap. And definitely a shower. Is there anybody who can show me where my room is?" I pull away, avoiding his predatory gaze.

He looks surprised and almost hurt. I'm too confused to delve into the emotional gang bang going on inside my mind right now. I just want to put some space between us for a little while. He nods silently, opening the door for me and stepping out. Extending his hand, he helps me out of the car, squeezing mine a little harder than necessary.

"Rosetta will show you to your room. She takes care

of the daily operations to keep this villa running. If you find you have a problem with something in your room, or need anything we don't have here, all you have to do is tell her and she will take care of it. Please show her the utmost respect. She is a vital part of this household. I have a few things I need to take care of, but I will be back before dinner. Feel free to explore the grounds, or rest if you need to." He places a soft kiss on the back of my hand, not meeting my eyes before walking down a long corridor, leaving me standing in the entry of this palace.

I'm speechless, and a little cold. Did my pulling away really upset him that much? Enzo hovers in my periphery, and I guess this will be my new normal for the next few weeks. An older woman emerges from the same hallway Sebastian just disappeared down. She looks to be in her sixties, but she obviously takes excellent care of herself. Her dark hair is swept back in a loose bun at the nape of her neck, and she seems to glide across the stone floor in an elegant cream pantsuit. I could only dream of being that chic when I'm her age.

"Buongiorno, signora. I am Rosetta. Welcome to Villa di Arsenio. I wish Mr. Arsenio had given me a little more notice, I could have been better prepared for your arrival. But it's no matter. I'm happy to welcome you and to get you anything you need for your stay." She smiles warmly, patting my hand. "Please follow me this way. I'll show you to your room."

"Let me just grab my things from-" I turn to retrieve

my suitcases from the car, but Enzo stands silently behind me with them already tucked under his arms. Fucking creeper.

"Enzo will follow with your belongings, Ms. Diaz. Right this way." She leads the way through several short hallways while giving me a miniature history lesson about the property, the area surrounding us, and the culture of this region.

I take in as much as I can. There are beautiful sculptures, paintings, and tapestries in nearly every room we pass. I feel like we're in an endless labyrinth of hallways and staircases. God forbid I need to go anywhere in this house by myself. There's no way I'd make it out alive. Rosetta continues talking, saying something about the original home being built in the 1400s and then renovated nearly two hundred years later. It's obviously been modernized much more recently. We've passed at least half a dozen doors with biometric scanners, and there are cameras in every corner, making sure there's not a single inch of this property unmonitored. Even with all the high-tech upgrades, they've still kept most of the natural beauty of the villa intact.

"Here we are, your room." She opens two French doors, letting me into a bedroom just as lavish as the rest of the property.

"Thank you so much, Rosetta. I appreciate your kindness, and I would love to hear more about the villa whenever you have time." I reply, not having much energy left for socializing.

"I'm happy to tell you anything you'd like to know, Ms. Diaz. Please take your time freshening up and getting some rest. Enzo will be posted outside your door, and he can call on me any time should you need anything. There are clean linens in the en suite. I recommend taking advantage of the sauna feature in your shower. It's worth it." She gives me a smile. I don't waste time wondering how she knows my name. She seems like the type to know all and be everywhere at any given time.

"That sounds like a dream. Thank you so much. And please, call me Vanessa." I reply, and she nods, backing out of the room.

Once I'm alone, I collapse on the bed, wondering how I ended up five thousand miles from home in a place so beautiful it takes my breath away, and I still can't shut my mind off. My business is taken care of for the time being, and Doug is living his best doggy life. For maybe the first time in my adult life, I don't have a single responsibility to manage. Yet, I'm more scared than ever before.

Deciding the only thing I can do to clear my mind right now is to shower, I strip off my travel clothes. Laying them on the end of the bed, I grab my essential toiletries from my bag before padding into the bathroom.

Smooth marble walls wrap the room in pale warmth, subtle veining like soft movement beneath still water. The color palette is restrained, creamy whites and gentle beige, with sharp black accents. The space creates a balance between luxury and class. Nothing here is excessive, and it reminds me so much of Sebastian himself.

Turning the water on, a wide rainfall shower head pours from the center as water sprays from six different jets on the opposite side of the stall. This is opulence, pure, and beautiful. Stepping into the hot water, I let it scorch my skin. It's probably much hotter than it should be, but I don't care. What is it about women and our love for scalding hot showers? I know it's not good for my naturally curly hair or my skin, but right now I don't care. I want to wash the haze away from my mind, and this is the only way I know I can do it without relying on Sebastian's touch.

Letting the water rain down on my face, I close my eyes, breathing slowly as the adrenaline of the day and all the events leading me to this very place catch up to me. Tears burn my eyes, but I can't see them, can't feel them fall as they blend with the water falling down my cheeks. I don't really feel sad, or scared, not even angry. Just overwhelmed to such an incredible degree. I don't feel capable of holding my emotions inside anymore. Pressing my palms into the cool tile in front of me, I let them fall.

There's nothing like the feeling of a good emotional cleanse. At least in here, no one can see or hear the sobs wrecking me. I cry until I feel completely devoid of all the emotion I've kept bottled up the past few weeks. The tension I've been ignoring between Sebastian and I, whatever the fuck I've been dreaming up with the masked man, the weight of feeling like I have no family, nowhere I truly come from or belong, everything I've let strangle my soul before now. I let it all wash down the drain.

"This does not make you a weak bitch, Nessa. Some days are just heavy." I tell myself out loud because I need to hear the words.

The tears slow as I finally feel like I can take a deep breath. After what feels like an eternity, I go through the motions of a quick shower. There seems to be an endless supply of hot water in this room, and I wonder if that's just the beginning of the never ending comforts I'll find here. There's a panel on the wall just outside the shower stall, and I assume that controls the sauna Rosetta was referring to before. I make a mental note to definitely take advantage of that as soon as possible. Perhaps at a time when I don't feel like I might collapse from exhaustion.

Over an hour has passed when I finally shut off the water, ending my emotional breakdown. I rush through the process of raking product through my curls, wrapping them in my favorite silk scarf so my hard work isn't ruined by the coma-worthy nap I'm about to fall into. When I was young, there was no end to the number of times I heard things like "Oh I would pay so much money to have beautiful curls like yours!" Yeah but do you have any idea what it takes to care for hair like this, Karen? Doubtful. I hated my hair then. It was way more work than I wanted to put into my appearance. But over the years I've learned how to take care of it so efficiently it's almost second nature.

Pulling another plush towel from the warming rack, I wrap it tightly around myself and walk back into the bedroom. I'm grateful the heavy drapes are barely open, only casting a small amount of light across the space. The four-poster bed piled high with cream linens looks like the most inviting dream I've ever seen. I almost feel like running towards it, but you couldn't pay me enough to run anywhere. I make it to the edge of the bed before a deep voice shatters the silence around me.

seventeen

Vanessa

"ARE you not pleased to be here?" he says, and I swear I jump three feet in the air.

"Gaaahhhh!! Jesus fucking Christ, Sebastard!!! What the fuck are you doing creeping around in the dark?! I fucking HATE being scared like that!" My hand flies to my racing heart as he sits, unmoving, in a chair in the corner.

His face is obscured in shadows, but the tension is palpable in his tone. The idea of him sitting here waiting for me to get out of the shower should be creepy as hell, and it is. But I can't help the way my skin heats knowing he was lingering here for me.

"Your fear is your problem. Why are you crying? I brought you here, to this beautiful place, and yet you're still not happy." He seems almost...angry.

"I'm not crying. Not anymore. And I'm not unhappy,

Seb. I was just feeling a little overwhelmed. A girl is allowed to have feelings, ya know." I clutch the towel tighter around myself, feeling exposed.

Even though I can't see his eyes, I can feel them burning into me. The intensity crawls across my skin, racing through my veins like pure adrenaline. My core clenches, sweat beading down my spine. We're in a standoff, neither of us willing to break this tension. I know he can see me, so this hardly seems fair.

"What? What do you want? I told you the truth. I'm allowed to fucking cry, Sebastian. I understand that you have no fucking emotions, but the rest of us normal people actually feel things. Crazy, right?!" I'm practically screaming at him, letting my anger get the better of me.

Before I know what's happening, he's stalking across the room, gripping my throat as he backs me into the bedpost. The bite of wood against my spine cranks my anger up another notch. My towel falls open in the front, barely covering my body. His fingers flex around the column of my throat, but they don't squeeze. This isn't an assault, it's a threat. I'm dancing on the edge of his patience, as always. But part of me loves to watch it unravel. Loves to see the control he holds so tightly slip away, thread by thread, until I've completely unwound him.

"You think I have no emotion, Bambina? You caused me pain when you pulled away from me in the car. You knew that. I don't care what your reasoning was. You can tell me your pretty lies until your face is blue, but I know you've wanted me just as badly as I've wanted you. You may be confused about what that means, but I am not. Between that pain and the way you look, I'm so fucking obsessed, I can't think about anything else. Can't focus on any of the work I need to be doing. Because my mind is so full of you, Vanessa." His voice is low and even, millimeters away from my ear, his accent growing increasingly thick with each passing moment in his homeland.

The words are like a single match on kindling in a drought-stressed forest. My entire body ignites, flames consuming me from the inside out. I grip the hair at the nape of his neck, dragging his lips to mine in a kiss just as dominating as the one on the plane. For a moment, he doesn't release my throat, gripping tighter for only a heartbeat before both hands slide down my body, stripping me bare and hoisting me up into his arms effortlessly. He never makes me feel like my body is a burden the way others have in the past. I'm not a small woman, I never have been. I have fat on my body, the way we all do, but I don't feel ashamed of it. Sebastian worships my body with such dominance that I've never questioned his attraction to me. I don't break our kiss, I'm not sure I could if I wanted to. I want to crawl inside his body and never leave. Clawing at his dress shirt, my fingers slide easily across the silky material.

"You're too dressed," I breathe, panting against his mouth.

"Because I didn't come here for this," he replies, and I give him a seductive grin.

"Didn't you? Why else would you be waiting here for me at the one time I would most likely be completely naked? Just trying to even the score, huh?" I laugh softly, my laughter dissolving into a moan when his mouth descends down the column of my neck.

His touch is possessive, territorial in a way I've never felt before. I've been touched by lesser men, but nothing has ever felt as dominating as Sebastian's touch. He pulls my body even tighter against his, the solid ridge of his cock grinding against my pelvic bone. A whimper escapes through my lips, and he swallows it down.

"So fucking ruinous," he murmurs against my lips, and my entire body aches for him. He stalks forward, tossing me onto the bed so he is towering over me. Any other time I might feel self-conscious, like I need to cover myself up under this intense scrutiny, but not now. Not here. I want him to take in every single inch of me, because this is all I have to give. If he doesn't like it, he can leave the same way he came in. But the look in his eyes tells me I couldn't pry him away if I tried.

His fingers work the buttons on his shirt so quickly, I'm not sure I've seen him so manic. Discarding it behind him, he makes even quicker work of unbuckling his belt and slipping it out of the loops. The sound is almost inappropriate in the relative quiet of the room, the only other noise coming from our panting breaths. I've never had the chance to study the ink on his chest so closely before, so I take my time as he pushes his black slacks and boxer briefs to the floor.

"Touch yourself. Show me what makes you feel good." His cock springs free, heavy and solid in his hand. Giving himself a few quick tugs, he raises an eyebrow, waiting for me to follow his instructions.

It wasn't an ask, it was a command. He's demanding my submission, and for once in my life, I give it willingly. Reaching down with a shaky hand, I swirl two fingers lightly across my swollen clit, a moan clawing its way up my throat. My eyes roam over his body, mouth watering at the sight of the bead of precum already dripping from the tip of his cock.

"Are you just gonna stand there watching?" I pant, the pleasure building in my core.

"I could," he places one knee on the outside of my thigh, his eyes locked on my pussy.

"Touch me," I tell him, reaching for him. The fucker has the audacity to push my hand away.

"No," he guides my hand back to my clit, working my fingers in time with my racing heart. "Not until you're begging me to."

"I'm already fucking begging you, Seb." I tell him, beyond frustrated.

He teases me, dragging the head of his cock against

my clit until I'm a writhing mess beneath him. My mind is hazy, intoxicated with lust and irritation. I want him to just give in, to lose himself in me the way I'm so fucking lost in him. But he wants me to beg. I beg for no man.

"You know what to say, Vanessa. How to make your suffering end. Give me what I want, and I will give you what you want." He smirks, and I want to slap his perfect face.

"Get off of me!" I shove at his shoulder, hoping like hell he doesn't listen to me.

"I'm trying to get inside you." He kisses me, a kiss so devastating my body tells me my pride isn't worth it anymore.

"Fuck you, asshole. Just fuck me! Please!" That's all it takes for him to close the last of the distance between us.

He slides inside me in one stroke, burying himself completely and without warning. My mouth falls open in a silent scream as the sharp intrusion slowly melts into an exquisite ache. I'm gonna feel him for days, but every moment with Sebastian is already far better than any other sexual experience I've ever had. I bury my face in his neck, my teeth digging into the tendons there until he growls.

"Be careful, I bite back." He laughs darkly, and I whimper.

He pulls back, almost pulling out completely before

slamming back into me. I scream, pleasure and pain swirling through every inch of my body. His control is obliterated once I rake my nails across his back and hook one leg around his hip, using my heel to urge him deeper inside me.

He thrusts into me, a punishing pace I should've expected from a man like Sebastian. He dominates every room he enters, every conversation he's a part of, why would this situation be any different? We fight for control, both of our strong personalities warring for power.

"So fucking sweet, Vanessa, how you think you have even an ounce of control in this room. Always so sweet, even when you're spitting venom at me." He trails his tongue down the column of my neck, and I gasp.

One firm hand grips both of mine, dragging them over my head, trapping them in his grasp. He pistons into me, his hips slamming into mine so hard I'm sure I will bruise tomorrow. Fuck, I hope so. I know my soul will never recover from this encounter. I love the thought of having something physical to remind me of his claiming, fleeting as it may be.

I feel my climax building faster than I ever thought possible. I've never been easy by any interpretation of the word. I wouldn't say I'm a tease, but I definitely make men work for it for sure. Sebastian barely has to lift a finger before I'm a fucking puddle on the floor for him. I feel unhinged as he fucks me into the mattress without mercy, spurred on by my cries and nails digging into the back of his hand. His free hand comes around my neck, squeezing harder than really necessary. Just how I like it, how I've *always* known I wanted it.

I detonate, my inner walls clamping down around him so hard it almost causes me pain. I've never come so hard in my life, a scream ripping from my lips, but barely squeaking its way up my throat. His eyes bore into mine, and for a moment, I'm worried he might not release me. Spots dance across my vision, but my orgasm doesn't dissipate. In fact, it builds again as his thrusts continue pummeling into me.

"I know you've got at least one more for me. Give it to me, Vanessa." He commands, and I thrash, trying to pull my hands from his grip.

My head feels lighter as a panicked, urgent need to breathe overrides rational thought. My lungs scream for air, yet my body still seems to follow his commands. This strange version of fight or flight is something I've never experienced before, and I don't know how to handle it.

His head dips down, capturing my nipple in his warm mouth, and my body feels completely at his mercy. I can feel him growing thicker inside me. I know he's just as close as I am, but I can't hold off any longer. My orgasm crashes through me, devouring me whole as the world collapses beneath me. White blurs across my vision as he releases my hands, his fingers suddenly digging into my hips. He thrusts once more, groaning loudly as he unleashes everything he's been holding back into me. I feel warmth flooding me as he comes so deeply inside me, I'm not sure where I end and he begins. Before I can enjoy the afterglow of what we both just endured, my lizard brain takes a backseat and logic starts functioning again.

He just came inside me. I don't remember him putting on a condom. I don't use birth control. The hormones drive me quite literally insane. How the fuck could I be that stupid? I don't want to have little Sebastian's running around me night and day! Do I?

Do I?

He collapses onto the bed beside me, panting heavily with a satisfied smile on his face. Already, my mind is racing a thousand miles an hour, but he looks blissfully fuck-drunk.

"I'm fighting every impulse in my body that's telling me to punch you square in the fucking jaw. I just want you to be proud of my control right now." I say, my breath coming in heavy pants. My silk scarf is barely hanging on to my head, my wild curls sticking to my forehead.

He laughs. Actually, full-bodied, ab-clenching laughs. Fucking. Bastard.

"I would tell you I'm sorry, but I am not," he sits up abruptly, sauntering into the bathroom like the cocky god he is. And I wish I could say he wasn't deserving of the title, but after the way he annihilated my body just now, that would be a complete lie.

He comes back, a washcloth in hand, and I give him a confused look. He definitely doesn't seem like the aftercare and cuddling type by any means. But he leaves me dumbfounded, sliding the warm cloth across my slick skin, cleaning up the evidence of what we just did. He stops when he reaches the apex of my thighs, his dark gaze observing his handiwork with pride.

"I'm not on-" he cuts me off, not bothering to listen to what I have to say, or not truly caring, one of the two.

"I'm aware of what you're thinking right now. And I have to admit. I can't find it within me to care. Keeping you here, tied to me forever, sounds like heaven to me." He cleans the most intimate parts of me more gently than anyone has ever touched me before, gentler than I would ever expect. All the while admitting something that should make my fucking blood boil. So why am I not fuming? Why am I not so mad that I could literally kill him right now?

"That's insane, Sebastard! I hate you!" Even as the words leave my mouth, they taste like poison on my tongue. That dark smile graces his perfect face again, and I hold back a groan.

"Keep telling yourself those pretty lies, Vanessa. Maybe you'll believe them one day. But you know I can give you a life bigger than you've ever dreamed." Without another word, he gets dressed, walking to the door. He pauses, looking back at me with a longing on his face that tells me he'd rather die than pull himself away from me right now. "Dinner is at six, please be there."

The door closes with a thud, and I'm lost again, a mess of emotion and irritation. I have a life, a damn good one, back in Grovewood. I can't stay in Italy as some Italian Adonis's sex slave permanently, and just accept this as my life. I love my independence, I love my business, and the family I've created back home. The only thing I know for sure is that it was the best sex of my life. I've let him into my body, into my heart, and into my mind, and I'll never get him out now.

eighteen

Sebastian

MY SHOES MAKE a rhythmic scuff as I pace the dining room floor, scrolling through what feels like a thousand messages from various people demanding my attention now that I'm home.

"If you wear a hole in the floor, Rosetta will kill you." Matteo's voice echoes through the dining room, and I smile.

"She would never do the dirty work herself, brother. That's what she has you for." I smile, pulling him in for a hug. "It's good to see you."

"I'm glad you made it home safely. And the men tell me you've brought back a souvenir." He smirks, and I shoot him a dark glare.

"Do not call her that." I snap, my features stony and unyielding.

His expression is one of surprise at first, but quickly

turns amused. I immediately feel like I've given too much away. While Matteo has never been one to poke fun at anyone I was interested in previously, I've never really been interested in anyone long enough for him to learn their names.

"Ah, struck a nerve?" He chuckles, and I drop my shoulders.

I know Matteo would never disrespect me, or anyone I hold dear. It's not his way. But he would endlessly tell me 'I told you so,' if I were to admit I had feelings for someone. He's been dying for me to find someone for years. He knows better than anyone that I'm lonely, even though I would never admit such a weakness.

"Fuck off. Are you staying for dinner?" I want him to meet Vanessa, but part of me wishes I could keep her hidden away, all to myself.

"Of course. I have to meet this person who has captured your attention so completely. She must be quite a woman." He smirks, and I already know I'm in for a hell of an evening.

"Quite a woman? Talking about me, are you?" As if I've manifested her from thin air, Vanessa comes sauntering into the room wearing a pair of high-waisted black linen pants and a white cropped shirt.

She is so different from any other woman I've known, so simple yet still sophisticated in her own way. Her dark curls are piled in a messy twist with tendrils framing her face, and I don't think I've ever been so tempted to kiss her before. But I'm interested to see how this plays out. She brushed me off when we got here, making me feel like she didn't want anyone to know anything about us. I'm not a fucking teenager. The allure of sneaking around for midnight trysts is completely lost on me. If that's what she's looking for, she'll have to find it somewhere else. Even if the idea of her finding anything from any other man makes me feel a murderous rage I've never experienced before.

"Of course. Please join us. Vanessa, this is Matteo Gallo. My oldest and closest friend. Matteo, this is Vanessa Diaz." She takes his hand, and my fists clench at my sides.

"Ms. Diaz. The pleasure is most definitely all mine, I assure you." He kisses her hand softly, exaggerating his accent. He's only doing this to get a rise out of me, and unfortunately, it's working. "Had I known they were keeping such ravishing women in America, I might have spent more time there."

"Oh, you're one of *those* men, Mr. Gallo?" Vanessa replies, and I almost laugh out loud. She got his number right from the start.

Matteo's brows raise in shock. She never fell for my charm. I don't know why she would ever fall for his. Matteo is a good man, truly one of the best I've ever known. He would lay down his life for those he loves. But he is the very definition of Casanova himself.

"I should apologize, Teo. I should've told you she's

completely immune to the seductions of Italian men. Unless your name is Sebastian, of course." I circle behind her, watching her shiver at my words.

Pulling out the chair next to mine, I gesture for Vanessa to sit, and she obeys. The simple act shouldn't turn me on, but my cock stiffening behind my zipper has different ideas. Pushing the thought from my mind, I take my seat at the head of the table. Matteo watches Vanessa skeptically, as if she's a puzzle he's trying like hell to solve.

The chef, Marco, a younger man I poached from a Michelin-star restaurant in Rome, comes into the dining room to greet us. His eyes immediately find Vanessa, lingering on her perfect, shapely body a second longer than I find acceptable. I clear my throat, glaring at him in a way that conveys my disdain. He quickly straightens, hurrying around the table to pour the wine.

"Good evening, Mr. Arsenio. I've prepared a fantastic menu for you tonight to celebrate your return home. Coda alla vaccinara, your favorite. Antonio will return in a few moments with your first course." He nods, turning to leave the room.

But he must be the dumbest fucker that ever lived, because his gaze rakes over Vanessa yet again and my blood pressure spikes. Matteo laughs under his breath, watching my patience quickly unravel.

"Marco, please wait one moment." I do my best to regain my composure. I don't want to terrify the man. I really do enjoy his cooking. But he needs to understand there will be consequences if he doesn't control his actions.

"Is there something I can do for you, sir?" Marco asks, a slight tremor in his voice.

"Yes. You can keep your eyes and your thoughts off Ms. Diaz, unless you would like me to remove both from your skull." Slipping the dagger I keep tucked into the back of my waistband into my hand, I spin it once, looking him dead in the eyes before stabbing it forcefully into the wood of the table in front of me. The glassware clinks together, and Vanessa jumps slightly, but says nothing. Matteo wants to laugh so badly, but he's doing his best to hold it together. He knows I'm deadly serious. I've given less warning to better men before removing fingers, ears, or chunks of flesh as repayment for their disrespect.

Marco stares around the table, stunned and possibly unsure if I mean what I'm threatening. But deep down, he knows this is not a threat. This is a promise of what's to come if he doesn't change his behavior. Realizing no one here is on his side, he quickly straightens, nodding his understanding.

"My apologies. To you and Ms. Diaz. Antonio will be in with hors d'oeuvres as soon as possible." He bows slightly, rushing from the room.

As soon as he rounds the corner, Matteo dissolves into a fit of laughter. Fucker. Pulling my blade from the wood, I smooth over the divot it created. Rosetta is going to kill me. This table is over a hundred years old, handcrafted in some monastery in Spain. It is a truly beautiful piece, but after a hundred years, it's bound to have a few nicks and gashes.

"Was that really necessary?" Vanessa asks, seeming a little irritated by my outburst.

"They will learn what is appropriate in your presence and what is not. This is how." I say simply, leaving no room for argument.

"Yes, I understand. But did you have to take it out on this beautiful table?" She glides her hands across the smooth wood, and I find myself wondering if this woman is just as unhinged as I am. Have I met my match in her?

"Jesus fucking Christ," Matteo mumbles, rubbing his head. "È perfetta per te, fratello."

"If you're going to say things about me, say them in English. At least until I can learn the language," Vanessa replies, rolling the stem of her wineglass between her fingers as she peers over at Matteo. Her expression is mischievous, and I'm glad someone will finally give him a run for his money.

"He said you are perfect for me, Bambina." I tell her, and her slight smile tells me she agrees.

"Oh, I already knew that. I'm beautiful, I'm hilarious, I'm successful, how could I not be perfect for anyone?" She sips her wine, and Matteo snorts out a laugh.

"And so humble, don't forget that attribute of yours," he says, and she nods her fervent agreement.

"Yes, that too. That's actually my best quality." She throws back at him. These two will be the death of me, I can already see it.

Dinner goes off without any other fireworks. Matteo shares stories of our youth, giving Vanessa all the blackmail she could ever possibly need. But for once, I don't feel uncomfortable with someone learning such personal things about me. I've never invited another woman into my home to meet my family in such an intimate setting as this. I always feared they would assume it meant far more than I was willing to commit to. But with Vanessa, it feels like this is where she belongs. By my side, in my life, learning the chapters of my history the way no one else has ever heard them before. The idea terrifies me but feels oddly comforting at the same time. I want to show her my world. But will she be able to handle everything she finds here? Something tells me she can. I have to believe she will.

My mother preferred to remain ignorant to the darkest parts of Fortuna Nera. As long as it kept her up to her ass in designer handbags and gave her all the luxuries she felt she deserved, she didn't ask questions. I don't think Vanessa would expect the same lifestyle. She wants to know things, to be involved in decisions being made about her life. I can't fault her for that at all.

"Oh, bella donna, it has been a genuine pleasure to meet you. I am so glad I have been able to bask in your company this evening." Matteo drowns her in compliments, but she just rolls her eyes.

"You are quite the charmer, Teo. I don't know how the women survive around you without losing their hearts...and clothes." Vanessa replies, and I choke on my wine.

"You flatter him far too much. He's not nearly as smooth as he seems. He's only trying to steal you away." I tell her, a part of me hoping she'll give me some kind of validation.

"That would imply I'm capable of being stolen. I'm not so easily swayed by Mr. Gallo or any other man." She sips her wine, a simple gesture, She sips her wine, a simple gesture, not understanding the impact her words have just had on me.

"Well, thank you both for a fantastic meal. I look forward to seeing much more of you in the future, Ms. Diaz. Please keep my brother here in line once you're back in America. He has a tendency to find trouble, even when he doesn't look for it. If you'll both excuse me, I have some business I need to attend to." Matteo excuses himself, leaving Vanessa and I alone in the dining room.

She's looking everywhere but my face, but I can't stop tracing every perfect line of hers. I never expected to feel so strongly about her, to feel such a need to protect and care for her, but I do.

"Can I ask you a question?" She breaks the silence, and I nod. "What do you do? And don't brush me off or give me some bullshit non-answer. Tell me the fucking truth. You want me to let you into my life and into my body, I want you to be honest."

"I can respect your need for answers, truly I can. But I need you to trust me when I tell you there are so many things that are safer for you not to know." I don't want to lie to her.

But in Fortuna Nera, the more information you know, the bigger the target on your back. If she wants to be with me, she'll have to understand that being at the top of an organization like this means someone is always trying to remove you from power. Like the situation with Luca, there will always be someone who wants what I have, and there is never a shortage of struggles. But in a way, I do feel like I owe her some kind of explanation of what kind of life she would be in for if she chooses this.

"Then I need you to give me something I can know. Because I will not live in the dark, Sebastian. I won't blindly follow you into the darkness. But I will walk by your side, with my eyes wide open, as long as I get to make my own choices in the matter." She speaks with such assuredness. I want to put my faith in her, to trust her completely, even though everything I've ever known has always told me that's not possible.

"Fortuna Nera is hundreds of years of tradition, Bambina. Hundreds of years of maintaining the family name and business to uphold that tradition built through generations. No matter how legal the means of maintaining such things may or may not be. We hold more power than the law, more control than the Prime Minister or your American President, for example. We are global, and I've worked hard to spread our business ventures as far as I possibly can. I'm still growing this empire, still building this family. And I'm proud to be a part of this legacy, no matter what it's taken to get to this point. There is blood on my hands, Vanessa. Many would say I am not a good man, and they would be right." I've given her as much information as I'm willing to for now. Hopefully, it's enough to satisfy her curiosity.

"If I ask you yes or no questions, will you answer them?" She pries, and I lean back in my seat, crossing my arms over my chest.

"Possibly. But if there's something you don't need to know, I will not tell you." I reply honestly, and she nods, chewing the inside of her cheek.

I can see her mind working a thousand miles a minute, trying like hell to decide what information she wants to know and what she can live without.

"Does the work you do prey on those less fortunate than you?" She asks, and I feel a knife twist in my heart.

"Not a fair question. Do you see this home? Everyone is less fortunate than me, Vanessa." I'm not trying to brag, it's just the truth.

"Fair point. Does it harm children?" She cocks a brow.

"No. We don't deal in people, Bambina. It's a nasty business and one I've actively protested against in my... industry. I do not allow any of our products to be sold to children, either. What happens once it's out of my hands is something I cannot control, but I do what I can. I don't intentionally harm the innocent or prey on the weak. That's not my style." Much to the disdain of men like Luca, I don't believe in human trafficking. I don't care how much money can be made from it, it's not worth the price it would cost my soul.

"Drugs or guns?" She asks calmly, seemingly unaffected. I really should've paid more attention to the background check I asked to be done on her when we first met. I know her family is involved in low level dealing, but I don't know much past that.

"Both. I don't discriminate. I have several different avenues for generating revenue, both legal and illegal. Real estate, investments, Fortuna owns a lucrative law practice, and a popular bank in New York City." I reply, and she nods her head silently, absorbing everything.

I wait in silence for what feels like an eternity, knowing she could run. She could decide this isn't any kind of life she ever wanted for herself. Hell, she already did when she left her family behind and moved hundreds of miles away to Grovewood. Now I'm dragging her back into the same mess she never wanted in the first place. But if she stays, if she accepts me for the man I am and the things I have done, I can give her a life unlike anything she has ever imagined.

"Okay. I can live with that." She pushes back from the table, holding her head high with so much fucking grace it takes my breath away. She is incredible. Unlike any woman I've ever met, and so much more than I could ever deserve.

Walking towards me, she drapes an arm over my shoulder, bending down to kiss my cheek. Turning my head, I capture her lips, pulling her into a deeper kiss. Tasting her, all dark vanilla and cinnamon, is a heady experience. I've never been so completely addicted to anything in my life before her. She deepens our kiss, her fingers curling into my hair, and I can't suppress the groan that rumbles in my chest. Fuck, this woman tastes so good. I could go on this way forever and never get enough.

Standing, I lift her into my arms, wrapping her legs around my waist as I make my way to my bedroom. My fingertips dig into the soft flesh of her ass. Every part of her is so incredibly soft, such a contrast to every one of my jagged edges. Her fingers tighten in my hair, holding me so close we're sharing the same breath. Her tongue explores my mouth, sliding across mine as her sweet taste explodes on my tongue. Carrying her towards my room, I kick the door open, never breaking our kiss. I'm so completely intoxicated by this woman. She's rooted herself in my life and under my skin, I can't escape her. Setting her on the edge of the bed, the cream linens surround her, making her look as ethereal as she is. I let her go just long enough to unbutton my shirt, and her hands find my skin instantly, nails raking down my chest. Grabbing her hands in one of mine, I stop her advancements.

"I want you. Fuck, I want you so badly it pains me, Vanessa. I used your body so thoroughly this morning, and I have no apologies. But I don't want to exhaust you. And I've come to learn quite a few things about you over the last several weeks. I don't want you thinking the only reason I'm interested in your company is because of what you can offer me physically." Kissing her hands, I step away for a moment to take off my slacks, draping them over the chair in the corner before returning to her.

She stares up at me, her eyes wide and mouth slightly open. She looks mesmerized, almost speechless, and I don't quite understand why. Her eyes look a little glassy, emotion building there. Did I do something wrong? Make her feel rejected in some way?

"What's wrong?" I press, lying down on the bed next to her, propping myself up with my elbow.

"You constantly surprise me. Every time I think I've got you figured out, you do something I don't expect. I don't really know how to handle it all." Her lip quivers slightly, and I pull her into me. Wrapping my arms around her, I nestle her against my chest, covering us with the duvet.

"I know. I'm quite incredible. I don't know what you did to get so lucky." I kiss her head softly with a smile, holding her tighter. I think I've smiled more with her in the last few weeks than ever before in my life.

"And then you speak and I remember why I prefer you to be silent and nice to look at." She settles further into my hold, and for the first time in what feels like ages, I fall asleep without war waging in my mind.

nineteen

Vanessa

I WAKE UP ALONE, the space next to me cold and empty. Yesterday, Sebastian took me shopping in Rome. Even though I'm not much of a shopper, it was nice to walk the streets of a beautiful city on the arm of a gorgeous man, while shopping for anything and everything I wanted. People parted like the Red Sea when Sebastian walked through the streets. At first, I thought it was the way he simply commands attention everywhere he goes. But it didn't take long for me to realize it's actually because everyone, every man, woman, and child, knows exactly who he is here. We walked down the streets and they treated him like royalty. We ducked into shops and they fawned over him as if it were a visit from the King. And I suppose, to them, in a weird sort of way, it was. Sebastian bought me the most beautiful black silk dress I'd ever seen in my life. It came from a local shop where the owner was most definitely flirting with him, but I didn't care. The dress was worth the jealousy.

Rubbing the sleep from my eyes, I see a note sitting on my nightstand.

I didn't want to wake you, but I had to leave. Enzo will take you anywhere you want to go. Please be safe. I left you a gift on the balcony.

Seb

I could get used to this boyfriend thing. Is that what Seb is? My boyfriend? It seems like such an odd word for a man as intense as him. Boyfriends are silly creatures who toy with your emotions and leave you on read when you piss them off with foolish things like affection and feelings. Sebastian doesn't play those kinds of games.

Kicking the blankets off my legs, I stretch my arms over my head. Padding across the room, I push open the double doors to the balcony and find the most beautiful view I've ever been fortunate enough to see. The hillside seems to stretch on forever, the sun rising over the landscape, bathing every inch in a golden glow. This feels like a place where time softens, not just passes. The countryside rolls out in gentle, velvety waves of green, the hills layered one behind the other like brushstrokes, fading into the hazy blue of the morning sky.

The sun is low, spilling gold across the land, turning the fields into something almost luminous, like they're glowing from within rather than simply being lit. Narrow paths wind lazily through the hills, and workers walk by each other calmly, not truly in a hurry to get anywhere. It's incredible. I understand now why Sebastian felt so homesick. I'm going to miss this beauty so much when we go back home.

I don't have to search long to find the surprise he's left for me here. A new yoga mat, foam blocks, and grippy socks sit on the table to the left of the door, and I can't help but smile. The man is learning what makes me tick. I rush out the door of Seb's room, hoping my suite isn't hard to find from here. Instead of finding a wide open corridor, I run straight into a wall of solid muscle. Enzo grunts as we collide, gripping my arms so I don't fall back on my ass as I bounce off his chest.

"Mi scusi, Miss Vanessa," Enzo says, helping to steady me.

"That's okay, I should've been looking where I was going. Can you help me find my way back to my room?" I ask, and he looks a little hesitant. "I just need to grab a change of clothes. I'm not making a run for it."

I don't know why I feel the need to explain myself to Enzo, but something in his expression tells me Sebastian didn't want me going back to my own space. Honestly,

I'm completely fine with that. I'd rather spend the rest of this trip wrapped up in his arms every night. But I can't exactly wander the halls naked or in the same clothes every single day, so I have to restock.

"Of course, ma'am. Right this way." Enzo turns, walking down the hall.

I expect to follow him through turn after turn in this labyrinth of an estate, so I'm shocked when we turn one corner and stop at a familiar doorway. My room was less than twenty steps from Sebastian's this entire time.

"You've got to be fucking kidding me," I mumble under my breath, and Enzo scoffs.

"He's ridiculous, you know that, right?" Enzo just shrugs, knowing his boss is more than just controlling, while also understanding he can't be changed.

Whirling through my room like a tornado, I grab a few changes of clothes, change into my spandex workout shorts and sports bra, and slip an oversized t-shirt over my head. Grabbing my hair care products and scarf from the bathroom, I toss them into my bag and head back to Sebastian's room. Enzo doesn't meet my eyes when I walk down the hall, and does everything he can to avoid looking at me as I walk in front of him.

"Something wrong, Enzo?" I ask, confused by his sudden change in attitude.

"No, ma'am. I just value my eyes. If the boss knew anyone else saw you dressed this way, I can't say what he'd do, but it wouldn't be pretty." He nearly runs straight into the wall, but stops short, turning and looking away as I lean on the frame of Seb's doorway.

"I see. Well, I would never want to get you into trouble. But I answer to no man, and most definitely not when it comes to what I wear." Pushing off the door frame, I leave the door open, walking straight outside to the balcony and pulling my t-shirt over my head. I may be a curvy woman, but I'm not ashamed of my body.

I've never worked out in any other clothes besides these, I see no reason to change now. If Sebastian wants to be with me, he'll have to adjust to my lifestyle, just like I will to his. Rolling out the new mat, I sit in easy pose in the center. The landscape surrounding the villa is incredible. I'm beyond lucky to be experiencing such a beautiful place with almost nothing to worry about. Closing my eyes, I spend a few moments meditating. The one thing I've always loved about yoga was the ability to clear my mind of all the noise and heaviness of the world around me, even if only for a few moments. I fold into child's pose, my hips sinking back toward my heels. My torso drapes over my thighs like it's finally allowed to rest. My arms stretch forward as far as I can reach, my shoulder muscles relaxing slowly. I feel the tension unfolding in my lower back as emotion builds in my chest.

Moving into a runner's lunge, I take a deep breath, holding it for a few seconds before releasing it. My spine lengthens as my chest lifts, oxygen carving space through the front of my body. I feel the energy flowing through me, the weight of the world sloughing off my shoulders as I release shaky, deep breaths. Despite my best efforts, tears sting the back of my eyes. Pushing through the emotion, I stretch into upward facing dog. My palms press firmly into the mat beneath my shoulders, arms straight and firm as my chest arches forward. The tops of my feet root down, my thighs hovering just off the mat. My back curves into a deep bend, my shoulders spreading wide as my heart lifts toward the rising sun. Tears stream down my face in earnest now, but I ignore them. I'm getting so tired of the emotional dams continuously breaking in this fucking place.

I fall into hero pose, kneeling with my knees together and sit back between my heels. The tops of my feet press into the mat as my thighs settle, heavy and grounded in place. I rest my hands on top of my thighs, palms down to steady myself. I wanted this to be relaxing and cleansing, but I can't understand why my emotions keep getting the best of me. Breathing deeply, I empty my body of every sensation that feels unnecessary. Hopefully, I can get back into my regular yoga routine, and this won't feel like such an intense experience.

"Miss Diaz?" Enzo's voice breaks the silence, and I wipe my eyes.

"Yeah? You can come in, Enzo. And please open your eyes. I don't need you breaking your nose and convincing Sebastian I'm abusing his staff." I laugh, and I think I actually see Enzo crack a smile.

"Would you like to see my favorite part of the villa?" He asks, still avoiding eye contact.

"Depends. Is it in any way a torture chamber?" I joke, and he glares at me. "Lead the way."

"Please put a shirt on or something. I can control myself, but some of the younger men...they will run their mouths, and then it will cost them their lives. Terrible business really, could all be solved with a t-shirt." Enzo's lips quirk into what could almost be considered a smile as I grab my shirt and slip it over my head.

"Hold it! Hold everything! Did you just make a joke?" My smile is sly as he tries hard to hold back laughter.

"In a way, yes. But also no. The boss will kill them for their disrespect without question." He shrugs, and I roll my eyes.

While I find Sebastian's tactics archaic, I understand the need to rule with an iron fist. If you allow leeway, you allow anarchy. Invite it even. And that's how empires fall.

Slipping my feet into my green platform Vans, I gesture for Enzo to lead the way to wherever it is he's taking me today. This villa is massive, and I haven't experienced even a third of it. I want to leave the grounds, but I don't think I'd feel comfortable leaving without Sebastian by my side. So for now, I'll see everything I can from inside the safety of these stone walls. We walk mostly in silence, Enzo stopping a few times to describe some of his favorite pieces of artwork. He really is a man of few words.

"Enzo, can I ask you a personal question?" I prod, not knowing what he's allowed to reveal or not.

"I suppose it depends on the nature of your question, Ms. Diaz. I'm not sure the boss would feel comfortable with me giving you personal details of my life." Enzo grimaces, echoing my thoughts.

"Well, I'm gonna ask anyway because he's not my boss. How old are you?" I question, and he looks a little surprised.

"Oh, that's not very personal. I'm 29." He looks straight ahead, navigating the halls with ease.

"How long have you been with Fortuna Nera?" I ask, my voice quieter this time. Is this supposed to be a secret? Surely everyone here knows who funds this lifestyle, right?

Enzo's brows raise in surprise, as if he's shocked I know anything at all about the Fortuna name. He gets a faraway look, maybe deciding if he's able to give me an honest answer or if he should tell me nothing at all.

"I've been a part of this family since I was 17," he finally admits, dipping his head slightly. I walk alongside him, nodding slowly.

"So much life to have lived in just 12 years." I tell him, offering an understanding smile.

"Yes, but I've been given opportunities in Fortuna I would never have known had I stayed where I was before. I didn't have the easiest upbringing. Mr. Arsenio offered me a way out, a second chance to build a life of my own that was actually worth a damn. I will be forever grateful to him for such a thing." He speaks with such admiration, it's hard not to believe in Sebastian's character.

We're almost outside. I can smell jasmine in the air as the breeze blows through several open doors. The air somehow feels fresher here. I've never felt suffocated by my life in Grovewood, but something about being here in this incredible place feels so much more...free.

"One more question. Then I promise I'll give you some peace and quiet." I try to suppress my smirk, knowing what's to come.

"Doubtful, but please. Proceed." He takes a deep breath, like he has to brace for impact before answering my questions.

"Do you carry a gun?" I ask, watching his eyes widen slightly before he schools his features again.

"Yes." he replies.

"Can I shoot it?" I ask, my grin so wide I can't contain it.

"No." he shuts me down instantly. I knew he would, but I had to try.

"Buzzkill." Rolling my eyes, I catch the hint of a smirk on his face out of the corner of my eye. If I'm gonna be stuck with a babysitter all week, Enzo isn't the worst of the worst.

"Here we are. Il giardino dell'Eden" he gestures, allowing me to walk ahead of him through the large open double doors.

I'm led into the most beautiful garden I've ever seen, a true oasis on Earth. It feels unmistakably Italian, shaped by patience, sunlight, and years of reverence for beauty. Symmetry guides my eye around the space, but the overwhelming abundance of greenery softens it. Roses spill from beside clipped boxwoods, their champagne color complemented by the Mediterranean light.

Tall cypress trees stand like twin guards, narrowing the sky and directing attention toward beautiful fountains and statues. Stone paths, worn smooth from years of generations making this place a home, invite me further into the expansive space.

"Oh, Enzo. This is incredible." It's almost as if you have to whisper here. Anything else feels too intrusive.

"Beauty, right?" Enzo says, smiling as he looks around the garden.

Terracotta pots brim with citrus and herbs, all orange blossoms, rosemary, and sun-warmed leaves. Beyond the garden's edge, the yard opens to a shimmering pond. This is a place meant for afternoon strolls and late conversations, where time can truly stand still.

"Thank you so much for showing me this place. I've been constantly impressed by the beautiful things Italy has to offer." I offer him a genuine smile, bending to the side to hug him. But before I can wrap an arm around his side, I'm pulled the opposite way against a wall of solid muscle.

"I do not know what's going on here, and I do not care. But if you touch him again, he will not live to see the sunset. Is that what you wish for him, Bambina?" Sebastian's silky but firm voice skates across my skin, and as pissed as I am about him ruining a perfectly innocent moment, I can't help the way my body reacts to him.

"Boss, I was only showing Ms. Diaz the gardens. I apologize if-" Enzo steps back, putting plenty of space between us.

"Absolutely not. Do not apologize, Enzo. And let me go right now." I wrench my body from his grasp, letting my anger overpower my desire for him. "Nothing about our conversation was in any way inappropriate, and you have no right to dictate who I speak to, who I hug, or who I do anything with, at all. You don't *own* me. If you think you have any shot at a future with me, you need to think very carefully about the way you speak to me. Maybe you were able to treat the women before me like cattle, but I am not the one, Sebastian." I shove his chest, pushing him away from me and turning on my heel.

"Thank you, Enzo. I appreciate you showing me the gardens. They are beautiful." Enzo looks at me wide-eyed, unsure what he should say or do.

Sebastian doesn't say a word, glaring down at me with fire in his gaze. He's pissed, and I don't give a flying fuck. Stomping through the open doors, my mind reels. Who the hell does he think he is? He says all the right things when we're alone, but his overwhelming possessiveness at the least opportune moments is wholly unwelcome.

Turn after turn, I lose my way in the labyrinth of the villa. All I want is to find my room and lose my fucking mind on my own, but I can't even do that. Tears sting my eyes the way they always do when I'm pissed off, and I swipe them away. Curse my Latina fire for making me so quick to anger, but also just as sensitive when my feelings are hurt. My vision blurs again as I round another corner, bumping straight into Rosetta.

"Oh, God! I'm so sorry! I wasn't paying attention! I'm so sorry, Rosetta!" I frantically wipe my eyes, schooling my features.

"I'm quite alright, Miss Vanessa. But you don't look so well. Can I help you?" She offers, and I give her a watery smile. "Maybe I can lead you back to your room? A little rest can go a long way. I could bring you some tea, perhaps?"

All I can do is nod as she takes my hand and leads me back to my room. Suddenly, the shine of this life and palace feel more like walls closing in, faster and faster. But who knows, maybe my mind will feel clearer after some rest.

twenty

Sebastian

I PACE back and forth in my study. Never in my life has anyone ever spoken to me the way she does. I can't stand her defiance. But at the same time, it turns me on more than anything ever has. She doesn't understand the nuances of this world, doesn't understand where the boundaries are. It's my job to show her. But I can't do so if she's constantly behaving like such a fucking brat. She's driving me insane. The self-control I've perfected over a lifetime seems to evaporate in her presence.

Deciding I can't give her a moment more to behave this way, I make my way directly to her room. This back and forth, unknown boundaries, and wondering where the other one stands ends now.

Coming to the door, I turn the handle and find it locked. You've got to be fucking kidding me. She locked me out of a room in my fucking house?! I have no more patience for this. Rearing back, I kick the door open. Wood splinters as the latch gives way. Vanessa shrieks, shrinking back on the bed where she was sitting.

"What the fuck are you doing, you psychopath?!" she screeches.

"Honey, I'm home. It's been such a long day already. And we have much to discuss. Like your fucking mouth." I growl, stalking across the room.

She stares at me, speechless. Her eyes are red-rimmed. She's obviously been crying. She thinks I am to blame for her distress, but I'm not. If she's going to live in this world, she's going to have to learn her place in it.

"Please, just leave me alone, Sebastian. I'm tired and I need some space from you right now." She tells me, and I hate the sound of that.

"Well, I hate to tell you this, but that's just not an option for me." She needs to know what being with me is going to be like if she intends on making this work. And I hope she does. I never expected to care for her as deeply as I do, but I can't stop it. I never saw myself planning a future with anyone before Vanessa.

"Sebastian, please, can we just talk later?" She does look and sound tired. But I can't push this off. I can't let my mind continue to go down a never ending rabbit hole.

"No, Vanessa. I don't understand why you're upset. I won't apologize for my nature. I can't stomach the idea of another man touching you in any way. I don't understand why you won't just let me care for you. Let me... just...*love* you." The word just slips out, my frustration breaking down all my defenses.

I know immediately that I've said the wrong thing. She looks at me with rage in her eyes, as if I've betrayed her in some way by admitting too much. I can't lie to her anymore. I don't want to.

"How dare you say something like that to me, Sebastian! Something so fucking manipulative!" She explodes, lashing out at me in an unexpected way.

"Manipulative? By admitting to you that I fucking love you?! How could that be manipulative?!" I match her energy, anger building inside my chest.

"Because you don't want to love me, Sebastard!" She screams, coming chest to chest with me. "You want to hold me captive here with you, suffering and compliant until we both wither and die together! Because then at least you don't have to be alone!"

Her words feel like acid against my skin. She feels like staying here with me is the same as captivity?

"But that's the difference between you and me, Sebastian. I would rather be alone forever than spend it trapped in this fucking prison of self-loathing and jealousy!" Every word feels like a slap to the face. I feel like I've done all I can to make sure she's spent all her days here in comfort.

"Stop! You're done! If you want to spit your fucking poison at someone, you can do it to someone else. I'm done being your punching bag, Vanessa. You are a fucking brat, and I'm tired of it. I've given you all the possible comfort I can give, and you've made no concessions to even try to accept me or my lifestyle. You demanded my truths, and I gave them to you. You have no idea how difficult all of this emotion is for me, but still you act like every time something doesn't go your way, you're ready to walk out the fucking door." I tamp down my rage, knowing it can be impossible to come back from if I don't control it. But she started this.

"You think I want to feel the weight of this empire looming over me every fucking day, all day, balancing on a knifes edge, and then come back to this bullshit? You have no idea what kind of responsibilities I have to manage. I don't need you adding to the fucking list, Vanessa!" Resting my hand against the bedpost, I pant, my shoulders heaving. Adrenaline courses through my veins, my heart pounding against my ribcage.

"Sebastian-" her voice is softer now, but I can't hear it. I can't be nice to her right now.

"No. You want to go, then fucking go. I'll have Enzo inform the pilot. All you have to do is tell him you're ready. The choice is yours." Turning, I leave her behind.

Walking back into my suite, I slam the door behind me, the sound echoing through the cavernous room. Fuck, she drives me absolutely mad. I've never felt rage like this before, and I've killed men for less. This morning, Matteo and I spent the day devising a plan to catch

Luca in his lies. But no matter what I did, I couldn't shake the thought of her from my mind. I couldn't wait to get back to her.

But as soon as I did, I found her with her arm wrapped around another man. Was it innocent? I'm sure. She's never given me a reason to doubt her, and Enzo is as loyal as they come. But seeing her hands on another man filled me with a ferocity I couldn't contain. I wanted to rip Enzo apart with my bare hands. A man I've known since he was barely more than a child, who I've seen grow into a dependable soldier I know I can place my trust in.

Maybe something in me felt like the two of them looked better suited than Vanessa and I do. He's much closer to her age and can probably relate to her on a level I can't. But the very thought of another man ever getting the chance to be in my position makes me want to wage wars. Stripping off my dress shirt, I drop my clothes to the floor. I'm never one to leave my things in such disarray, but my mind is a fucking mess and I can't stop the spiral.

I turn the water in my shower as hot as it will go, hoping the hot water and steam will make me think more clearly. Everything feels so fucking heavy. The weight of my responsibilities to Fortuna, my feelings for Vanessa, the secrets I still hold back from her, they all feel like chains around my neck. I've never let the people who depend on me down. But now this woman feels more important to me than any obligation, any family blood, and I don't know how to handle the confusion. I've only ever known my responsibility to Fortuna. It's the only thing that's ever mattered to me, what I've built my life around. Is there truly any hope for a different path for me?

Stepping under the scalding stream, I hiss before letting the heat settle into my bones. I shouldn't have yelled at her. A man who raises his voice at the woman he claims to love isn't a man at all. But no one has ever gotten under my skin the way she does. Resting my forearms against the tile, I let the water rain down on me. What if she does choose to leave? I know there isn't a corner of this world I won't search to find her. But I don't have the time to devote to such a feat right now. I have to focus on what's going on with Luca. I can't let myself get sidetracked, no matter how much it would kill me to know she's gone now that I know what needing her tastes like.

I'm so dissolved in my own mind, I don't hear Vanessa come into the shower behind me until she's pressing her body against my back, her arms snaking up my chest as she kisses my shoulder.

"I'm sorry." She whispers, and the walls I've perfected over decades to keep everyone at bay shake.

"No. I should never have raised my voice at you. Even when you anger me, it's not okay." I grip her hand, relishing in the warmth of the water, and her body leaning into mine.

We stand this way for minutes, hours maybe. She brings me solace unlike any I've ever known. I'm not sure I would've been able to survive the night had she decided she wanted to board the plane home.

Her hand slides down my body, delicate fingers wrapping around my shaft lightly at first, then increasing the pressure as I grow harder in her grip. She pumps me slowly, and I love the way she takes command of my body without waiting for permission. As if she'd need it. My knees buckle slightly, my arms falling forward against the cool tiles as she picks up her pace. My breaths are coming out in pants, lust enveloping us both. I'm close to the edge already, my chest rising and falling with the rapid pounding of my heart.

Turning, I surge forward, my hands spearing into her curls as I take control of our kiss. I devour her, body and soul, pouring every ounce of love I can into her. I tug harder, angling her head exactly where I want it to be, taking what I need from her lips. As much as I love the power I exude over her, I don't want to overdo it. Until she opens her mouth, and I'm completely undone.

"Punish me," she moans, and I'm a fucking goner.

"Bambina, do not play with me," I warn her, my lips trailing across her collarbone.

"I know I have to learn how to fit into your world.

Teach me," she breathes, and I'm lost. So fucking lost for this woman.

Tilting her head back, I kiss her deeply, implanting the memory of me permanently into her mind and body. She'll never get me out of her system, as if she would ever try. I place one last soft kiss on her lips before pushing her to her knees on the shower floor. Her nails drag a path down my torso as she drops, and I revel in the feeling. She wants to claim me just as desperately as I do her. I won't stop her. I would be a fool to pretend I don't belong to Vanessa completely.

Before I can command her, she wraps her lips around my swollen head, taking me as deep as she can without gagging. Her tongue traces every vein along my shaft, her curls plastered to her face as her head bobs to the rhythm of my racing heart. I can't suppress the animalistic groan that rips from my chest, and I wrap my fist around her dark hair. Her eyes meet mine and I could come right now from the need blazing there. She is all heat and fire, pure dark energy that fits so perfectly with mine. She gives me a small nod, allowing me to take the control I crave, and I tighten my grip on her hair, thrusting into her throat. She rubs her thighs together, an attempt to relieve the ache building at her core, I'm sure. But this is supposed to be a punishment.

"Don't you dare come." I tell her, my voice hoarse as I use her for my own pleasure. She whimpers, her hands finding my thighs, nails digging into the muscle so deeply I'm sure she'll leave marks.

"This isn't for you, Bambina. This is for me." I tell her, my breathing labored and strained. I wish I could enjoy the feeling of her sinful mouth for an eternity.

She moans around my shaft, and my hips jerk in response, a small growl escaping her lips. I don't need her words to know she's loving every second of this. I never dreamed of finding a woman like this goddess, this temptress on her knees before me.

"Are you gonna take me all the way down that perfect throat of yours and swallow everything I give you?" Her beautiful eyes flick to mine, a devious, knowing look hidden there.

I grip her hair tighter in my fist, fucking her mouth faster until I ignite, coming down her throat in long bursts. She swallows every drop, her fingers flexing against my thighs as she chokes on my release. Sparks dance across my vision, her mouth feeling like the most divine heaven I've ever encountered. When I finally come back down to Earth, I release her hair. Her mouth falls open with a wet pop. The sound feels obscene, but so are the millions of things I want to do to her right now.

She falls back on her ass, looking up at me. Her eyes are a little glassy, but she looks satiated. Even though she wasn't chasing her own pleasure, she still looks as though this was just as satisfying for her as it was her me. A devious smirk breaks across her face, and I'm dying to know what's running through her mind right now.

"What are you thinking, my little devil?" I ask, my thumb skating across her swollen bottom lip. She leans into my touch, her eyes closing for only a moment before a soft smile graces her gorgeous face. When they open again, her honey eyes are perfectly clear.

"I love you too, Sebastian." She replies, and my final defenses are obliterated.

twenty-one

Vanessa

THE PAST FEW days with Seb have been an endless stream of bliss. He disappears for most of the day, but spends his nights having dinner with Matteo and I, and telling stories about their ridiculous escapades. Every night I fall asleep wrapped against his chest, cocooned in warmth and protection.

Today, however, he seemed more tense than usual when he kissed me goodbye. He lingered a bit longer, almost as if he were afraid to let me go. I've spent all day trying not to dwell on the look he gave me. Instead, I buried myself in work. Even though Rory has been running the day to day operations back home, I still have obligations that require my attention.

After going through the online inventory, ordering the regular supplies, and arguing with my paper-goods supplier for over an hour about the lack of medium cups apparently sweeping across the entire United States right now, I'm exhausted. Settling into a comfy leather chair in the sitting room down the hall from the dining room, I pull up Rory's number on my phone. I need to update her on a few things, and honestly, it would be nice to just hear her voice. She picks up on the second ring, her usual sarcastic tone a welcome sound to my ears.

"Well, if it isn't my favorite world traveler. How is Italy? Divine, I assume?" She asks and I snort out a laugh.

"I'm hardly a world traveler, Aurora. I've barely left Seb's villa. But it is divine. I could easily fall in love with this place and never come back." I sigh, and I swear I hear her smile through the phone.

"Uh huhhh, I'm sure you could fall in love...with Italy." She's fishing, but I won't make it that easy for her.

"Beautiful artwork, the most romantic scenery. I mean, what's not to love here, right?" I tease.

"You're going to make me drag it out of you, aren't you?" She gripes, and I snicker.

"I have no idea what you mean." I feign ignorance, knowing this is driving her crazy. I know Rory thinks something is going on between Sebastian and I. She's right, so I can't really deny anything.

"Had any of that delicious Italian sausage on your trip yet, Vanessa?" she blurts out, and I choke.

"Oh, my fucking god! You are deranged!" I screech.

She cackles through the line, her laughter absolutely contagious as I dissolve into a fit of my own.

"Well? That wasn't a no!" she prods for more information, and I hope she can hear my eye roll through the phone.

"Things are...good." I say, my voice at least two octaves higher than usual.

"Good?" she asks, and I groan.

"Great." I reply, knowing I'm selling the situation way too short.

"Just great?" She should interrogate for the CIA.

"Ughhhh FINE! They're amazing! *He's* amazing! Aurora, he's incredible. He's so sexy, and smart, and fuck, the intensity the man exudes is unlike anything I've ever experienced in my life." I feel like a teenage girl with her first crush all over again.

"Ah, I remember this feeling so vividly. Actually, I still have it on the daily every time I look at my husband. Are you just stalking on the DL or are the feelings mutual?" She asks, and I smile.

"Most definitely mutual." I hesitate, wondering if I should reveal the depth of our relationship. But who the hell else am I supposed to talk to about all this if not Aurora? "He told me he loves me, Ror."

Silence drags on though the line. I fold my lips between my teeth, waiting for Rory's response, but all I hear is her steady breathing.

"Did you have an aneurysm?" I ask, and she snorts.

“I don’t even know what to say. In the few years I've known Sebastian, I’ve never even considered him falling in love. He's just so...serious.” she says, and I can’t argue.

“You’re not wrong. The way he speaks to me, the way he makes me feel, it’s never felt more serious, Aurora. And if I’m being honest, it terrifies me. I don’t know how to be loved that way. Or if I'm even capable of loving someone else like that. I know I want to, and I’m willing to try. But what if...” A heavy sigh escapes my lips and I bury my free hand in my hair.

“What if what?” She sounds so motherly, so soft and gentle.

“What if I fail him?” I finally speak the words I've been afraid to since the moment his lips first met mine.

I would be truly heartbroken if I became another responsibility for him, another weight on his shoulders that wasn’t even worth carrying.

“Vanessa, I wish I could hold your hand when I say this. But please, just listen to me. Shut the fuck up. You know you could never fail anyone you love. That is absolutely not something you’re capable of. You put your heart and soul into everything and everyone you commit to, and Sebastian would never be anything less. If anything, he would be so much more. I know you’ve been let down by your family time and time again. And you’ve been toyed with by boys before. That’s a whole ass man you’ve got there, honey. Trust me, it’s a whole different ball game.” I know she’s right. She’s only echoing the exact words my logical mind has been telling me.

"Can I ask you something? Will you give me a completely honest answer?" She asks, and I already know what's coming.

"Of course," I reply, bracing myself. Confessing my feelings to Seb is one thing. Telling the rest of the world how I feel is something completely different. It feels so much more vulnerable, so much more intimate.

"Do you love him?" She questions, and I don't have to think about my answer.

"Yes. I love him." I reply, unable to stop the smile that overtakes my face.

"Fuckin' knew it!" She shouts, and I laugh.

"He drives me absolutely insane, but I do." I reply, dark brown eyes flashing through my mind.

"Oh, you'll come to learn that's the very best part. You think Break is all sunshine and roses? No, that man is certifiable. He makes me question my sanity daily. But I know he is the only person on this entire god-forsaken planet I would ever want by my side. He's walked through hell to protect me, and I know he'd do it again without question. He is every missing part of me. I know all those perfectly healed women talk about how you have to stand on your own and you can't love someone else if you're not complete as you are, and that's fine. For them maybe. But I know I would absolutely die without that man." She speaks about her husband in the way I've always longed to feel for another person. In the way I feel every time Sebastian is near.

It's scary, the feeling of needing someone so much it's as if your heart won't beat without them. It's amazing how quickly your mind and body forget how they ever functioned before that person came into your life. I've always dreamed of finding someone who could truly understand my soul and accept it without judgement. I never thought it was in the cards for me until Sebastian strolled into my life, all Armani and attitude, and ruined all my perfectly laid plans. I was happy to be a bitch forever. Well, maybe not happy. But content. Now, I'll never be the same without him.

"I don't think I could ever have predicted this happening. I mean, don't get me wrong. The man is fucking gorgeous. I definitely knew that going into this situation. But I didn't expect him to also be so thoughtful and kind, so much of a challenge to my mind and my heart in the best way. He was completely unexpected. It would've been so much easier to hate him." I tell her, and she snorts out a laugh.

"Would it, though? Then you wouldn't get all those fantastic orgasms I know you're living for right now," I can hear the sly smirk in her voice, but she's not wrong so I can't argue.

Something crashes in the next room, the sound of rapid Italian shouting filtering through the doorway, jolting me upright in the chair. Enzo comes around the corner, his expression more severe than I've ever seen.

"Aurora, I gotta go. I'll call you back later. Love you." I hang up without another word, setting my phone on the table and standing.

"Enzo, what's wrong?" I demand, and his brows crease.

"I think you should retire to your room, Ms. Diaz. There is some business that needs to be attended to. I will come get you as soon as things are resolved here." He lies. It's all a lie. Something is seriously wrong, and he's refusing to tell me.

"Tell me what's going on right now," I demand, but he looks away.

Someone shouts louder, the urgency in their voice sounding so dire though I can't understand what they're saying. Something about the chaos going on in the background, the way Enzo is trying to dismiss me, my anxiety is rising higher and higher by the moment.

"Ms. Diaz, I really think you should-" he tries again, but I cut him off.

"Do not placate me. Tell me what's going on right now, or I'm going to find out myself!" I command, and he flinches. He hesitates for only a moment more before taking a deep breath.

"Things did not go to plan this evening," is all he can say before I'm pushing past him.

Matteo's voice is clear above everyone else's,

shouting loud commands in hurried Italian. Tears already sting my eyes, and I will them away. I hate that I cry in serious situations. I want to be strong under pressure, and I know if I'm going to be a part of this world, I need to grow thicker skin. As I navigate my way towards the voices, I listen for Sebastian's. I hear nothing. Panic builds in my throat, anxiety burning through my veins.

Just give me one word. Just one. Anything.

Matteo shouts again, this time something about needing *medico.* A doctor? I break into a sprint, running straight for their raised voices with Enzo close behind me. Turning the corner into the dining room, I'm thrust into a room full of men I don't recognize. All of their eyes land on me, their expressions grave and discerning.

"Vanessa, please," Enzo whispers aggressively, but I ignore him.

Matteo is yelling commands at the head of the dining table, while someone lies nearly motionless on the table top. We just had dinner there last night. The most delicious homemade pasta I've ever had in my life. And now all I can see are the faces of these men and the severity in Matteo's eyes.

"Matteo," I shout, and he looks up for only a moment, wincing at the sound of my voice.

"You shouldn't be here, Ness. Enzo, get her out of here." He snaps, but I shake out of Enzo's hold again.

I push past the man, finally coming to the side of the table. Sebastian lies in the middle, his white dress shirt completely soaked through with blood. Two small holes puncture his left side as blood slowly pools beneath him. His usual olive skin looks pale and peaked, and I feel my heart rate begin to spike. Rage boils hot and lethal beneath my skin. My fists clench at my sides, nails digging into the flesh of my palms until the point of pain.

"Who hurt him?" I demand, my voice darker than I've ever heard it before.

"Things got a little out of hand. We were supposed to be meeting an associate. A known ally. And evidently, that wasn't the case. We were ambushed as soon as he let the security team leave the room. I barely got him out the door." Matteo's explanation is rushed as he applies pressure to the gunshots on Seb's abdomen. Sebastian groans in pain, and I grip his hand tightly.

"Where the fuck is the doctor?!" I shout, tears streaming down my face. I don't let my emotions break free, but I don't hold them back either.

"Vanessa, I really think we should-" Enzo grips my arm.

Before I know what I'm doing, I reach into the holster still attached to Sebastian's shoulder and pull out his pistol. Lining the barrel up with Enzo's chest, I look him straight in the eyes. A collective gasp sounds from every man in the room, followed by Matteo cursing. Enzo releases me, holding his hands up and stepping back.

With one finger on the trigger, one hand holding Sebastian's, and all eyes on me in this room, I decide now is as great a time as any to make myself perfectly clear to this boys club about where I stand when it comes to their boss.

"I'm going to say this one time where every single one of you can hear me, so feel free to spread it like the vicious little gossips I know you all are. If any one of you suggests I need to leave this room again, I will put a hole in you to match Sebastian's. Ask me to leave his side again, and you will burn for it. Do we have an understanding?" I raise a brow at Enzo, and he nods once. Matteo laughs softly in the background.

"Something to say, Teo?" I ask, training my gun on him.

"Definitely not, regina mia. This is where you belong." He dips his head to me, and I lower my gun, setting it on the table next to Sebastian's side.

An older man enters the room carrying a black doctor's bag like the one you see in movies. He couldn't be more of a cliché if he tried. He's wearing a pressed wool suit and a dress shirt with a starched collar, it feels far too formal for such a house call. His silver hair is neatly parted, and his face carries the calm gravity of someone who has seen far too much to be easily rattled. He must be a regular here.

"Why was he not brought to the medical wing? I cannot treat injuries like this on a dining table, Matteo."

The man scolds Teo, and for the first time he looks as though he's been put in his place.

"This was as far as we could make it before he lost consciousness. I thought it best to stop the bleeding before going further and call you here." He clenches a fist at his side.

"Very well. Clear these men out of here. I do not need an audience to perform. You, woman, go to the medical wing and get me a sterile surgical tray, saline, and everything needed to start an IV." The doctor snaps, and I look around wondering who the fuck he thinks he's talking to. Surely it's not me.

Grasping Sebastian's hand tighter, my other hand flexes around the grip of the pistol. I meet Matteo's eyes, and even without a word he tells me to grin and bear it. Unfortunately, that's just not my style.

"Enzo, go," Matteo commands, and the doctor gives him a stern look.

Enzo leaves without another word to fetch the supplies, and most of the other men clear out of the room as well. Matteo is uncomfortable around the doctor, which puts me on edge as well. I'm putting the life of the man I love in the hands of someone I don't trust. But what choice do I have? I don't want to watch him die right before my eyes, so I have to let this man do his work.

Sebastian groans, his eyelids flickering open and shut. He mumbles something completely incoherent, and my heart skitters to a stop in my chest. If I wasn't sure about my feelings for this man, they are crystal clear now. Seeing him this way is like fucking torture.

"Ness..." he says, his voice strained as he grips my hand tightly.

His jaw clenches tightly, the pain evident in every inch of his body. He's in agony and there's nothing I can do about it. I squeeze his hand back, just letting him know I'm here. I don't know how conscious he really is.

"I'm right here, Seb. I'm not going anywhere." Tears stream down my face, but I ignore them. There's no time for my emotions right now. I have to remain strong for him.

The doctor rolls up his sleeves, turning Sebastian onto one side. Every muscle in his body contracts in anguish, but he remains silent, refusing to show weakness in front of his men. I want to cause this doctor the kind of pain he's causing Sebastian, but right now he's a necessary evil.

"I don't think he would be conscious if the bullets hit any major arteries. The internal damage, however, I cannot tell you the extent until I am able to get him to the medical wing and retrieve the bullet. Only one of them went all the way through, the other appears to be lodged in his rib, if I had to make an educated guess. He will lose consciousness again soon, and he will need surgery." Panic settles into my bones with every word the doctor speaks.

Enzo comes back into the room with the supplies, and the doctor busies himself with packing Sebastian's wounds and starting an IV. Everything moves so fast, yet slow all at once. All of a sudden, I'm taken back to a memory from when I was a little girl. Aria took me on a carousel at the park close to our house. I begged her to take me for a ride. I'd been mesmerized by the beautiful lights and intricately painted ponies. But once the ride started, I was terrified. We were standing still while the world around us seemed to move so quickly, and I panicked. I cried in her arms the entire time until the ride ended. I feel the exact same way now as I did that day on the carousel.

"Ness, please listen. He's gonna knock me out. And I need...you to do something..." Sebastian's eyes lack their usual fire, his voice thready and thin.

"Anything. What is it?" If he asked me to fling myself off the top of this villa right now, I probably would. I can't imagine a single thing I wouldn't do for him.

"I need you to go home." he says, and the earth shakes beneath me.

I can't imagine a single thing except that.

I stare at his face for a few long moments before I realize he's not kidding. Why he would be kidding at this moment, I don't know. But why would he be asking me to do something so unthinkable? I can't imagine being separated from him. Even the thought of being in the next room makes me feel ill. He wants me to be an entire ocean away? I don't understand.

"I'm sorry, I just hallucinated. What?" I ask when I finally snap out of my stupor and process what he's asking me to do.

"Leave this place, Vanessa." He winces, maybe from the pain, maybe from the demand he's making.

"I can't just leave you, Sebastian! You can't ask me to do that!" My voice is shrill, barely less than a screech, but I don't care. I feel completely panic stricken by his request.

"He's ready, we need to go now." The doctor says, and my brows furrow.

Everyone in the room is looking at me like I'm going to blindly obey his command, but I've never been the kind to mindlessly follow anyone or anything. Why would I start now?

"Teo," Seb says, calling him over, and Matteo comes closer.

He whispers to him so closely that only Matteo can hear what he's saying. I'm stuck looking back and forth between the men, my hand still wrapped tightly around Sebastian's, as they decide the fate of my future. There's no way I can get on a plane and leave here not knowing if Sebastian will live until tomorrow. Sure, he's talking to me right now, but things happen during surgery all the time. And he told me we were supposed to be in this together. That I could trust him. Trust him to send me away at the first sign of trouble?

"I'm not fucking leaving! You can't make me leave you, Sebastian! You don't get to do this to me, you fucking bastard! You don't get to make me fall in love with you and then send me away!" I scream, not caring how absolutely insane I look right now. He looks almost remorseful before he kisses my hand.

"You are not safe here. You have to leave. This will not be the end for us…" he winces, and I know I'm delaying his care, but this feels like an impossible situation.

"We need to go *now*," the doctor urges, and I wish I'd put a bullet in him when he came through the door. Through anyone who dares take him away from me.

"Please, Seb. *Please* don't do this to me," I sob, clinging to him for dear life.

"Tu sei la mia anima," Sebastian says, barely loud enough for me to hear. I should've learned more Italian before coming here, should've known I'd need it around him.

"Let him go, Ness. They have to take him." Matteo pries my hand from Sebastian's, pulling me away from him entirely. Somehow in the shuffle, Enzo manages to take the gun out of my reach as well. That's probably for the best. The rage I feel right now would definitely end Matteo's life.

I watch helplessly as a few men move Sebastian onto

a hospital bed and rush him from the room. I want to scream. I want to break every fucking bone in Matteo's body right now because he's the one holding me back from following Sebastian.

"I hate you," I tell him, but he doesn't loosen his grip.

"I can live with that." He replies.

"I wish it were you on that fucking table," I know my words are venomous, but I can't contain them. I hate the feeling burrowing into my chest right now.

"So do I, regina mia. Trust me, so do I." He holds me up, my body going slack in his grip. The fight in me is draining as Sebastian gets further and further from my reach.

twenty-two

Vanessa

I TRIED to fight Sebastian's ruling, but it was no use. Matteo has been standing guard at my door for nearly an hour as I pack my things as slowly as humanly possible.

"You know this isn't right." I tell Matteo, but he avoids looking at me.

"It doesn't matter what I know." He replies, typing furiously on his phone.

"What did he say to you? Before they took him... what did he say?" I ask, and his eyes snap to mine. I can see the pain there. Sebastian is his best friend. I know this is killing him.

"Nothing for your ears, Vanessa." He bites back, anger barely banked.

"That's bullshit, Teo. Tell me." I demand, folding the

black silk dress Sebastian bought me in Rome into my bag.

I never wanted material things from him. I only wanted him. But a part of me feels like I need something to remind me my time here wasn't all a dream or a fantasy I made up in my mind. That his love for me was real, I felt it, I wrapped it around my heart and my body just like my silk dress. I cross my arms over my chest defensively after I zip my last bag closed, staring back at Matteo for an answer.

"He told me to make sure you got on the plane. And I intend to do that. Now, let's go." He hefts my luggage onto his shoulder, turning on his heels and leaving the room without another word.

The drive to the airstrip is silent, both of us completely lost in our thoughts. Am I going to have to fly all the way back home alone? I suppose this is how I will have to face my life for the foreseeable future, so I might as well get used to it again. My taste of a life with Sebastian was barely more than an appetizer. I don't know why I thought it could have been more than that. Part of me feels like I should still be crying. But the tears won't come. There's only an emptiness inside of me that feels cavernous, endless, like a pit that will never be filled by anything or anyone but Sebastian.

"Go back to the apartment. Sebastian thinks it will be safer." Matteo says, and I scoff.

"I don't really give a fuck what Sebastian thinks right

now, Matteo. If he truly cared for my safety, he wouldn't be putting an entire ocean between us right now." I lean my head against the window, watching the beautiful countryside pass by.

Once we reach the airstrip, he passes my bags to the crew robotically. He doesn't spare me a second glance, and for a moment I think he might even leave without telling me goodbye. But I'm shocked when he climbs onto the jet behind me, taking the seat across from me. He doesn't look happy about it at all.

"What are you doing, Teo?" I ask, and he avoids my gaze.

"Following orders, Vanessa." He replies, and something in my chest squeezes.

"You...he told you to come with me? I don't...I don't understand...you are supposed to protect Fortuna in his absence." I'm confused by what's happening, but I have my suspicions. I don't want to believe they're true on the off chance they're not. The disappointment would hurt worse than Sebastian sending me away.

"It seems he decided something else was more important to defend. Someone was more important to him. Never in all the years I've known him has he ever given priority to anything over Fortuna Nera, Vanessa." Matteo meets my gaze, intensity burning there. I can't quite tell how he feels about Sebastian's decision, but it doesn't look good.

He chose to send his right hand to protect me, to see

me home, rather than leave him here to guard the family in his absence? This is his way of showing me I am more important to him than Fortuna Nera? The weight of his decision settles around us in the plane's cabin.

"Please understand what I'm going to say very clearly, Vanessa. Never has Sebastian ever put anything or anyone over Fortuna. *Never.* It's not in his nature. He was born and bred to live and breathe for this family. But in you, he's found a different kind of family. And I am grateful to you for showing him there is more than the darkness that has lived inside of him for so long. Give him some patience. I know this isn't what you want, but it's what he truly believes is best. He wouldn't choose this if he believed there was any other alternative." Matteo pleads Sebastian's case. But honestly, there isn't a need. My anger with Sebastian has fizzled out.

As much as I hate being separated from him, I understand every move he makes is calculated. Now, I only want to hear word that his surgery is complete, and he's okay. I know he will be. Internally, I'm manifesting it as hard as I possibly can. My sister always told me manifestation was the best possible way to attain your dreams, along with determination and hard work. I've done the work, I've paid all the dues, now I just have to bring it into existence that he will come out of this stronger than before. We will find each other again. I refuse to do anything but manifest the hell out of this shit.

"Have you heard anything from the doctor?" I ask, and Teo flinches.

"He's still working on him. I imagine it will be several hours, he's a very meticulous man." Matteo grips his phone in his hand so tightly I fear it might snap.

"What's with you and the doc? You have some kind of beef with him?" I might be overstepping, but I might as well pry as much as I can now if we're gonna be stuck on this plane for the next ten hours.

"Nothing. It's nothing." Matteo dismisses me, his eyes shuddering. He looks out the window as the door of the jet is sealed.

"Bullshit. May as well lay it on me. What happens on the plane, stays on the plane, Teo." I shrug, buckling my lap belt.

"There's really not much story to tell. Old men hold their ideals tighter than a virgin's knees, Vanessa. I grew up in this organization, but that doesn't mean it was always the path I envisioned for myself. Once Sebastian was sure he wanted to take over for his father, I had no doubt I would take over for mine as his right hand. But my uncle, he didn't let go of my dreams as easily as I did." Matteo leans back, holding up a hand for the flight attendant to bring him a drink.

"So the doctor is your uncle? God, your family is so intertwined in this organization, it's ridiculous. Fortuna wasn't always your dream? I can imagine the money and power must have felt like an overwhelming temptation, especially at such a young age." I tuck my feet under me, wrapping my arms around my waist.

"Money and power were never the problem. I had more money than I knew what to do with. It was the sense of responsibility that is hammered into you from the time you're old enough to speak in Fortuna. I grew up with the understanding that no matter what I did, no matter what path I chose, it was to be in service to The Family. That kind of pressure is so heavy for anyone, let alone a child. I wanted to be a doctor, wanted to help people. And I probably could've gone to medical school if I really wanted to. But no matter what, I would've been in service to Fortuna Nera. So I chose to accept my fate sooner rather than taste freedom and spend my life fighting against what I knew. I love my brothers and I love this family. I have more opportunities here than most can ever imagine. But it can be suffocating. My uncle, the doctor from today, prefers to live with his head in the sand. He ignores the uglier side of what Fortuna Nera does until he wants the paycheck. Then he's happy to take their money. I don't tolerate hypocrites, so he and I don't see eye to eye. But the respect for elders runs deep in my bones. It's hard to align the two feelings in my mind." Matteo takes a long drink of the dark liquid in his glass, and I nod at him in reassurance. I am truly thankful he shared something so vulnerable.

"I understand what you mean completely. My family

assumed I would go into the family business as well. When I turned them down, you would think I spat in the face of my ancestors. My parents built their living, if you can call it that, from selling drugs to an already broken community. I refused to help them continue to prey on the weakest of society, and that really pissed them off. I loved the beautiful community where I grew up. The culture and the people were so vibrant. Everyone helped one another when they were in need. Until my parents ruined everything. They brought poison onto those streets and devastated families, all for their own financial gain. I wouldn't contribute to that. I wanted to follow my own path, my own dream. And ultimately, I'm glad I did, because it led me to Grovewood, and to Sebastian. But in their eyes, I am their greatest disappointment." I watch the clouds shrink beneath the plane as we climb higher and higher in the sky.

The fear I felt flying to Italy less than two weeks ago seems so insignificant now. My mind is too consumed with thoughts of Sebastian. Is he okay? Is he stable? Should I have told him to fuck off and stayed anyway? I could worry myself to death, but it's no use at this point. I'm already miles away from him, heading in the opposite direction. All I can do is pray to whatever gods might be listening to me that they will bring us back together.

"Do you have a moral problem with drugs, Vanessa? Because if you do-" Matteo asks, but I shake my head.

"No, it's not that. What people do with their bodies

and their money is their own choice. I don't feel one way or another about drug dealers who sell to adults who are capable of making their own choices. But my parents, they target the junkies, the ones who are fresh out of rehab or a step away from an overdose. And kids. They never have a problem selling to children. That I have a problem with. If some rich playboy wants to snort coke off a stripper's ass, or some suburban mom is more interested in ecstasy than diet pills, that's their business. But children? It doesn't seem like a fair customer base to me, ya know. At least give them a fighting chance." Silence drags on between Matteo and I, and I wonder if I've said something wrong.

"I won't pretend the work we do is righteous. It is far from it. But Sebastian has very strict rules for our distributors. That is part of the reason there are so many we refuse to work with. A mafia boss with a conscience? It's a conundrum, for sure. I often wonder if it will be his downfall. But he has this ability to...turn it off. When it's necessary." Matteo finishes the last of his drink, leaning his head back against the seat.

A loud ringing breaks the silence in the cabin, and my heart stops. He answers without hesitation, speaking rapid Italian to whoever is on the other side of the line. I really need to join one of those language apps or something because this shit is getting old, fast. His eyes find mine as he continues his conversation. I can't discern a single thing from the look he's giving me, but he doesn't look away. The tension in his shoulders doesn't release either. Panic grips both of my lungs, squeezing until all the air has been expelled from my body. His conversation is quick, and his face looks severe when he hangs up.

"Give me something here, Teo." I beg, my voice shaking.

"He's okay. He's going to be okay." The words come out of Matteo's mouth, but they feel a thousand miles away.

A sob rips from my lips before I can stop it. I feel like I've been holding my breath since they carried Sebastian into the dining room, and now I can finally exhale. My head drops into my hands as I let the tears flood down my cheeks. I thought I would feel devastated by the knowledge he's okay and I can't be by his side. But right now, the only thing I feel is complete and utter relief. I don't think I've ever felt such a selfless love for another person in my life as I do right now, knowing that even if I can't be with him, he's still safe and sound somewhere in this world.

"Enzo said he's resting now. He'll keep me updated on his condition." Matteo exhales, the tension finally relaxing in his shoulders.

"Go back. Once we land, after I'm home safely, you have to go back. I don't know what he told you to do, Teo, but I don't want you to stay with me. He needs you more than I do. I'm more than safe in Grovewood. But I need to know he's just as protected. And the only way I will know that is if you're by his side." I wipe my face, breathing deeply for the first time all day.

"Get some rest, Ness. It's a long flight. We'll talk about it when we land." He brushes me off.

"I'm serious, Matteo. Please let me love him the same way he's loving me. Take me home and then go back to him. I could never live with myself if something happened to him again and you were thousands of miles away." I plead, and he seems to be seriously considering my words.

"It's not that simple, Vanessa. Sebastian gave me an order. I cannot just defy him." He sighs, and for the first time, I find myself feeling truly exasperated by this world.

"Can I ask you...what did you call me earlier? In the dining room with Enzo? Regina Mia? What does it mean?" I ask curiously, wondering if it means the same thing in Italian as it does in Spanish.

"Caught that, did you?" He smirks, running a hand over his face. "You are a strong woman, Vanessa. I've known Sebastian a lifetime. I've long wished for him to find someone like you to walk by his side. Someone who could help shoulder the weight of his responsibilities, without complaint or judgement. Someone who would defend him just as fiercely as he defends all of those he loves, an equal. A partner to challenge him in the best way possible. Only a Queen is strong enough to stand beside a King, Vanessa. You have the makings of a true Queen. But that kind of position, it takes from you as well. It takes away from the life and dreams you always envisioned for yourself. This family, this lifestyle, while it may seem enticing, it is not for the faint of heart or the weak minded. Once you're part of Fortuna Nera, you can never leave." His words are solemn, not meant to sway me one way or another, but more to make me understand the weight of the decision.

Being with Sebastian isn't as easy as just falling in love like every other woman. I can't live some soft fairytale dream where everything is sunshine and rainbows, and my boyfriend works a boring nine-to-five job at a cushy bank and comes home every night for us to watch Netflix in matching PJs. If I choose a life with Sebastian, it will be unlike anything I've ever dreamed, in every beautiful and dark way I could imagine. But now, knowing him in the way I do, and having felt his soul intertwined with mine, I could never envision a life where I didn't belong to him. There are still so many secrets left to uncover about each other, so many nuances left to unfold. But I know there is no one I want to spend the rest of my life learning about more than Sebastian. No one has ever challenged me, or annoyed me, worshipped, or infuriated me more than that man. He was either born in hell or heaven sent, either way and without doubt, he's mine.

twenty-three

Sebastian

I WAKE WITH A GASP, pain radiating from my left side. A machine beeps steadily in the background, my vision slowly becoming clear. Dr. Gallo shuffles around the room, drawing up something clear from a vial before injecting it into my IV. It burns like fire flooding through my veins, and I fight the urge to jerk my arm away from him.

"Calm yourself, Mr. Arsenio. Just antibiotics. It would be a travesty for such a great man to be taken down by something as trivial as infection now, wouldn't it?" He raises a brow, and Enzo shifts uncomfortably in the doorway.

He doesn't have to say a word. I know most of the men hate Dr. Gallo. He's a vain, self-righteous man. He believes himself to be so far above this family that he could look down and still barely see us. Only ever coming down long enough to get paid. Unfortunately, we do require his expertise from time to time. Like tonight, apparently.

"Enzo," my voice is strained as I try to sit up in bed. My abdomen flexes and every muscle screams in pain. I'm getting so fucking tired of being target practice.

"Sir." He stands at my bedside, shouldering the doctor out of the way.

"Where are they?" I ask, and something like pity flashes across his face.

"They should be landing in South Carolina any moment now. She was...less than pleased to be going." He rubs the back of his neck, looking away uncomfortably.

"She will get over it." I tense, scooting back in the bed. I feel like he has more to say, but won't speak in front of mixed company.

"Thank you for your work tonight, Dr. Gallo. Your payment will be sent shortly. You're dismissed." I excuse the older man from the room and he looks shocked.

"B-but Mr. Arsenio, there are things to be tended to. Your wounds, they are quite serious, and I should-" I hold up a hand cutting him off.

"I assure you. This is not the first time I've been shot, nor will it be the last. I have highly trained staff who are more than capable of taking care of these things, just as I am capable of caring for myself. You may leave the antibiotics and go." I dismiss him again, and a small smirk twists the corner of Enzo's mouth.

"Very well. I will be looking for my payment." He huffs, shoulder-checking Enzo as he flounces out the door dramatically.

"Speak. I know you have more to say." I tell Enzo.

"We've got to find a better fucking doctor than that asshole. His face is the kind you just want to punch. Repeatedly." Enzo shrugs, and I choke out some semblance of a laugh.

"That's not what I meant, but I agree with you. We'll find someone eventually. I know you have something to say about Vanessa, so say it." I lean my head back, staring at the ceiling.

"It's not my place, sir. Your decisions are not made to be questioned." Enzo states, straightening his spine. He is a loyal soldier, a quality that is becoming harder and harder to find without incentive. Most don't know he and I share a bond much closer than any other soldier in my army, that we share blood, and he prefers it that way.

"I'm not asking for your response as your Don, Enzo. I'm asking for your opinion as my brother, as her friend." He seems caught off guard by my referring to him as her friend, but I know that's what she would consider him. She sees most people as friends, even though she puts on this tough exterior.

"Sir, I believe Ms. Diaz is truly special. And I don't

want you to think that means I see her in any way but as the kind of woman who could actually best you. Someone who could match this world we live in, and not let it devour her. I understand your need to send her away, to get her as far from danger as you felt necessary. But if I can offer you my advice, don't keep her there for too long. She's smarter and more capable than I think any of us give her credit for. She might surprise you. After all, I've never had anyone threaten to shoot me if I dared to separate them from you before." He scoffs, and my brows raise in surprise.

I had begun to convince myself that it had all been a dream. Something hazy in my mind plays out the scene of Vanessa holding my gun inches away from Enzo's chest, his hands held up in surrender, the rest of the men backing out of the room. It felt like something out of a movie, something wild and feral where a beast defends its kill. Only she was defending me, begging in the most savage way not to be taken from me. And I sent her as far away as I could.

I don't dwell in regrets, it's not in my nature. I make decisions and deal with the consequences. My only solace comes in knowing there is no one on Earth I trust more to keep her safe than Matteo. The thought crossed my mind when I told him to follow her that I was sending my second in command out of this country while I was completely unable to lead my men, to protect them if something else should go wrong. The entire purpose of Matteo's role in Fortuna is to lead when I cannot, and I told him to go. But her safety is more important to me than anything else has ever been. When I think of someone hurting her, of anything even coming close, it's a devastation I cannot stomach.

"I know the great fortune I found in her, Enzo. I am only trying to protect her the best way I know how. By keeping her as far away from me as possible. This world is dark and dangerous. It seems too hard for someone as phenomenal as she is." I feel my strength slowly fading. I need rest, my body begging for relief. Enzo laughs lightly, and I raise a brow at him.

"Sir, forgive me. But have you met the woman? Dark and dangerous seem to define her in almost every way." He replies, and I can't help but smile.

I know he's right. First, I will heal my body, then I will dismantle and rebuild this organization. I will make it the family I've always intended it to be. The kind I can trust to protect Vanessa for the rest of our lives. Because the further she gets from my reach, the more my heart constricts, squeezing like a vice. I feel more and more like I might die if I can't touch her soon, if I can't feel her next to me.

"You may be on to something there, Enzo. Luckily for us all, I don't plan to let her get away. I just need...time."

twenty-four

IT'S BEEN two weeks since I got home from Italy. Two of the longest weeks of my life without a single word from Sebastian. Matteo didn't listen to me, of course. As much as I begged him to return home, he's been squatting in the apartment on the same couch I called home a few months ago. Rory has lingered in the coffee shop, helping with the day-to-day tasks even though I don't really need her to. I think she's just trying to keep tabs on me more than anything else. It's as if she's worried I'm going to shatter at any moment if I have to spend another day without Sebastian returning to sweep me off my feet.

Even though I miss him desperately, I'm not the type to sit around waiting for my prince to come to my rescue. I have my own life, my own responsibilities to fulfill here. I can't just abandon them to wait around for a savior, no matter how much I love him. So for now, I'll keep moving through each day, keep running my business and living this life, hoping I'm just one more day closer to seeing him again.

"Do you think your Italian shadow will live here forever?" Rory asks, and I snort out a laugh, steaming my hundredth cup of milk for the day.

"Very doubtful," I tell her, shooting a glance at Matteo reading a book in the corner of the cafe.

Every day has been the same. I wake up before the sun, attempt to rouse Matteo like the sleeping teenager he is, take Doug for a morning walk, and open the shop. I wouldn't call it robotic, but it does feel like going through the motions. Doug was beyond excited to see me, and I felt the same. He's spent every night since I've been home sprawled across my body in bed. As much as I missed him, being covered in a hundred and forty pounds of dog isn't exactly my idea of a good time.

"Shame. He's not terrible for business. I think the female population of Grovewood has been coming in for coffee at least three times a day since he's been in town." Rory laughs, and I can't help but agree. Matteo smirks, and I know he's eavesdropping on our conversation.

"Mind your business, Gallo," I shout over the sound of the espresso grinder as I make one last drink for myself.

"I'm gonna wipe down the last few tables and then

head out, unless you need anything else from me," Rory says, and I nod.

"That sounds perfect. Thank you so much for your help. I'd say you don't need to keep coming in, but I don't think you'd listen to me in the first place, so I'll see you tomorrow." I smile at her, and she winks back.

"You know it, babe." She finishes cleaning, tossing the dirty rag into the sink behind the bar and grabbing her purse. "Love you!"

"Get home safe!" I wave, rinsing the drip trays and setting them aside to dry.

"You don't need to hover here, either, Matteo. It's a little stalkerish of you, honestly." I raise a brow at him, trying to suppress a smile.

"Stalking you relentlessly is my job, Ness. Sebastian would kill me if anything happened to you in my absence." He replied, not looking up from his book.

"Nothing is going to happen to me here in Grovewood. Nothing ever happens here." I busy myself wiping down counters then finish the last of the dishes.

He looks conflicted, like Sebastian really told him to never let me out of his sight for even a moment, or he'd lose his position. Or maybe something worse, like his life. I don't say a word, letting him process on his own. After a few moments, he closes his book, standing to shake out the sleeves of his suit jacket. The man has been wearing suits every single day since he's been here, no matter what I've said to convince him this is a casual town.

"Very well. I will take the mutt for a short walk around town before bed, then. I could use some space to clear my mind as well." He exits through the back door, and within moments I hear the apartment door open and close.

I lock the front door, flicking off the overhead lights and pulling the front blinds closed. Turning on one of my favorite deep, moody songs perfect for end of the day cleaning, I tie my hair half up out of my face. The baseline thrums as I sweep, getting lost in the lead singer's words as he talks about being close to the end and becoming who you are. I let my mind wander, mindlessly cleaning the floors and tabletops until I'm nearly done for the night before the power goes out, the room suddenly plunging into total darkness. The sound of the back door closing startles me, and I squint against the inky blackness. A figure stands just inside the doorway, silent and unmoving. My heart rate kicks up a notch, but I take a deep breath. It's Matteo. It must be.

"Wh-who's there? Teo?" I ask, my voice barely above a whisper. But he can hear me, I know he can.

No response comes from the shadows, and my heart pounds harder against my ribs. I can't get behind the counter to where my gun is hiding without being forced to go through him first. It would be my fucking luck that as soon as I told Matteo to leave, that everything in

Grovewood is safe and sound, someone attacks me in my own shop. The man is shrouded in shadows, so still as if etched in stone, which puts me on edge even more.

"What do you want?" I demand, anger building deep inside me. I'm so fucking tired of being afraid.

"Oh, diavolina. What do I want? I have only ever wanted you," the man says, and instantly I recognize his voice. My masked man has returned.

He steps from the shadows, the slivers of moonlight glinting across his beautiful mask as he steps closer towards me. The skin on his hands and jaw are as black as the night surrounding us, and my heart drops to the floor. Surely I'm hallucinating?

"You're not real. I already...you're just a dream. Just something I made up in my mind." I say, my voice shaking as I back away from his advances.

"Do I look like a figment of your dreams, diavolina? You honor me. To think you've been dreaming of me while you've been so far away, while you've been under a different man." He steps closer and I take another step back.

"I don't...he's not...leave him out of this!" I lash out, stepping towards him for the first time, anger boiling in my veins.

I don't care what he does or says about me, but he won't threaten Sebastian. Surely Matteo will return before he can do any real damage. I'll finally know the true identity of this phantom.

"Worried about your boy toy, my dear? I won't hurt him. Not much, at least." He grins that devilish grin and I snap.

Lunging towards him, we collide, my fist making connection with his jaw. He seems shocked for only a moment before he wraps himself around me, his arms locked around my torso from behind, forearms crossing low and tight across my stomach, pinning my elbows to my sides before I can react. His grip is solid, unyielding, meant to stop my movement, not hurt me. There's no squeeze, just a controlled pressure, enough to restrain without injuring me. His breath is still, while mine becomes frantic. He is very, *very* real. And my body is reacting to him the way it has since the first moment he touched me.

"Let. Me. Go." I grind out through gritted teeth.

"Calm yourself, and I will." He replies, something about his demeanor so incredibly familiar, as if we've danced this dance before.

"Calm myself? How about you kiss my ass," I snap back, and he laughs, a full-bodied laugh that sends chills through every nerve ending in my body.

That laugh. This touch. I am intimately familiar with both. Desperation and betrayal war for equal footing in my mind as I come to terms with my understanding of the masked man's identity. As if my body has known all along, as if it's been screaming at me to understand, to recognize, to open my fucking eyes and see the predator in front of me. I go still, the struggle in me dying. His grip around me loosens slightly, and I use the opportunity to jab an elbow directly into his left rib. He hisses in pain, his arms falling away from me, and I know I've proven my suspicion.

Turning to face him, finding the void where his eyes hide sunken behind the mask, I stare him down. Even though I can't see those eyes, I know what I will find there. He drags in a ragged breath, and before I can think, my hand wraps around his throat, squeezing as hard as I can. His jet black hand grips my wrist but doesn't pull me away.

"All this time, and I couldn't see what was right in front of me? That you were making a fucking fool out of me?!" My voice raises an octave at least, the anger coursing through my veins.

"You are no one's fool, *Bambina*" He uses that term of endearment I've come to cherish, and I squeeze harder as he squeaks out the last bit.

"Enough! No more! No more lies!" I walk him backwards, and he stumbles as I back him against the nearest wall, caging him in the way he's made me feel since he first began haunting me. "You used me, targeted me from the very beginning."

"I did." he says it so plainly, the words slice through my heart.

"Why? Why would you do this to me?" I ask, begging for some kind of understanding. "I thought I was losing my fucking mind! Seeing things that weren't there! But all along it was YOU!"

My grip tightens to the point of white knuckles, my fingers burning against the sensation. Tears burn like pinpricks in the backs of my eyes, and I will them away. I won't cry for this man, won't let this betrayal take anything more from me.

"You want the truth, or do you want more pretty lies?" he says, and I choke down a sob.

Pretty lies...

"Do you know how to tell the fucking truth?!" I scream, all hope for control lost. His neck will bruise where my fingers hold him, but I don't give a fuck. He deserves every mark. I've never wished I had a gun in my hand more in my life.

"I've given you all of my truths, Vanessa. Every last one of them now. For all of my life, I've hidden the darkest parts of myself away from everyone, to keep them safe, to protect them from the depravity that runs soul deep inside me. This mask has become like a second skin to me for so long, I'm not sure where it ends and I begin. Hiding behind the mask became my way of choosing distance over exposure. A deliberate act of showing this vessel. Something calm, charming, confident, yet still savage, all while keeping my true self hidden away underneath. The mask became a buffer, a shield that let me move through the world without being fully seen, or ever completely known." He speaks with such fervor, such rawness, my fingers lose their grip. He takes a deep breath, his familiar sad smile the only piece of him peeking out from the edge of the mask.

"Behind it, I have all the control. I can decide what I allow people to see. I can smile without feeling much of anything at all, revel in the fear I cause. It dulls my vulnerability, but sharpens my power. Over time, it began feeling lighter than the truth, safer than honesty, even necessary. Like I couldn't have any intimate connection without anonymity. Until the line between the mask and what's real began to blur. It's been my protection, of course. But it also feels...lonely. Because the mask not only keeps danger out, but it keeps intimacy out with it. Until I met you, and you shattered every single notion I ever held of what I thought I knew or wanted." He swallows, the remnants of truth lingering in the air around us.

I want to be angry. I want to feel this betrayal for the rest of my life and never let this grudge die. And maybe before Sebastian, I would feel that way. I've always had this anger inside me, this ability to carry a chip on my shoulder that I just couldn't brush off. But now, knowing the way he was raised and the kind of man he's become in spite of it all, I can't bring myself to feel even an ounce of contempt towards him. He's softened all my serrated edges by pairing them down with his own. From the outside looking in, he's not a good man. He's manipulative, he lied to me, but he's also opened my eyes to a life unlike anything I ever thought imaginable for myself. He's shown me I don't have to be ashamed of the darkness I carry inside myself because it's mirrored in his own.

My hands glide up the columns of his neck, and he bristles momentarily before relaxing into my touch. I slide my hands up his jaw, pushing the mask up with them. The inky black color obscuring his face fades to the familiar olive tone I recognize around his dark eyes. His gaze bores into me, filling me with every ounce of uncertainty and fear, all of his reservations. But I also find something else there, something deeper.

"Hear me. Clearly, please. I understand that mask kept you alive. It made you untouchable when the world wasn't kind, when you felt like you had to hide these parts of yourself away," I step closer, our bodies flush against each other. "I'm not asking you to be anyone else. I'm only telling you I don't want you to hide behind the mask with me, Sebastian. I see you, the real you, and I love every part of you."

I thread my fingers through his hair, slipping the mask off his head and placing it gently on the table next to me. It really is beautiful. No wonder it haunted me for months the way it did, the way he did. There was always this invisible thread pulling me towards him, my masked man, something that told me he was meant to be in my life. Finding Sebastian behind the mask only proves to me this man is my destiny. Pushing up onto my tiptoes, I hold my lips only a breath away from his. His eyes dare me to kiss him, to give in to this depravity for the rest of our eternity, and I have no reason to hesitate.

"If you need to, take the mask off slowly. Let me learn you the way you are now. You don't have to be so strong with me. You don't have to be feared. You're safe in my love, the way I am in yours." I take a small breath in, looking into his deep brown eyes, showing him I mean every word.

"I have never known anything that measures against my love for you, Vanessa. Beyond time. Beyond any apprehension. Beyond everything that will inevitably try to end us. I will never give you up." He grips my neck, crushing my lips to his in an all-consuming kiss.

twenty-five

Vanessa

TIME STOPS the second Sebastian's hands touch my skin. The world may be spinning still, but I can't feel anything but his lips against my skin. His kiss is commanding, as always, and heat floods my body. How he can make me want him so desperately with just one touch, I'll never know, but I don't care either.

"I've missed you," I breathe between kisses, smiling against his lips.

Feeling shameless, I grab the fabric of his dark jacket and drag him back to me. He guides my leg up and around his hip before lifting me off my feet and placing me on the table next to us without breaking our kiss. The edge of my skirt rides up my thighs, but I don't care. Hell, Matteo could walk back in right now and I wouldn't give a damn. Let the world watch. Right now, I'd let this man strip me bare and fuck me on the steps of the Vatican. I'm not Catholic, what does it matter to me? His demanding hands rake across my curves, and I groan, soaking in every sensation.

"The way you make me feel, the way you touch me, I've never felt anything so addictive." I whisper, my voice husky and strained. My nails scrape across his scalp as he bites my lower lip. Pinpricks dance across my skin, and I struggle to maintain any sliver of control.

"When I touch you how? Like this?" He asks, trailing his fingertips down my neck and across my collarbone. Goosebumps cover my skin, causing me to shiver. He drags his fingers across the collar of my shirt, gripping the fabric in both hands before ripping it down the center. "I can smell what I do to do, Vanessa. I can see your skin react to my touch."

I gasp, staring daggers back at him. I love this fucking shirt. I raise a hand, rearing back to slap the silly little smirk off his face, but he catches my wrist before I get that far.

"I loved this shirt, Sebastard. I would've just taken it off if you'd asked." Rolling my eyes, I try to wrench my wrist from his grasp, but he squeezes tighter.

"But my way is much more fun. Admit it, you like me savage. I can see it all over your face, I can smell it all over your perfect skin," his tongue darts out, tracing a path between my breasts. I can't suppress the groan that falls from my lips every time he touches me like he owns me.

"If you think I smell good, you should see how good I taste," I say, tempting him even more. I'm going to get what I want from him sooner or later, but I prefer sooner.

Sebastian flashes the sexiest smirk I've ever seen, his face still partially covered in the black body paint, and drops to his knees without another word. His palms flatten against the outside of my thighs and drag up towards my hips, pushing my skirt up with them. His fingertips meet black lace, and he hisses out a breath.

"Gesù Cristo, Vanessa. I want you so badly. How have I gone two weeks without this perfect body? Just waiting for me to unwrap this delicious pussy and devour it?" He squeezes my hips so tightly, I know he'll leave his marks behind and I groan.

"You enjoy making us both suffer. Fucking masochist." I say, bracing my hands on the tabletop behind me as he places one hand in the center of my chest and pushes me back.

"Don't move," he commands, and I look down at him.

So quickly, he pulls out the knife he usually carries at his back, tracing the tip up my inner thigh. I shiver, loving the feeling of the cold steel against my skin. One wrong move and it will bite into my flesh. The darkest parts of my soul want to know how it feels to bleed for him. My thigh muscles quiver, and he grins.

"Don't move, Bambina," he sings, and that silky

smooth voice slinks through my veins like sweet poison. I'd die a satisfied woman if these were my last moments.

The sound of fabric slicing rings in my ears, and the cool air hits my core moments before his lips descend on me. He closes his mouth around my clit and sucks hard. Crying out, I'm unable to stop myself or remember that we're currently in a public place, *my* public place, right now. My hand threads through his hair, drawing his face even closer to me, and he comes willingly, licking and biting in even strokes. My nails rake across his scalp and he growls, the vibration shaking me to my core.

"Jesus fucking holy, Sebahhhhh!" He sucks harder, adding two thick fingers deep inside of me, and my back arches, nearly throwing me off the table. The point of the knife grazes against my inner thigh again, and I shudder into it.

"So fucking delectable. Be my good girl and come on my face, Vanessa. Show me who I belong to," he commands, his voice raspy as the heat of his breath brushes my skin, and he laps at my core furiously.

My orgasm hits me like a bolt of lightning, like pain and pleasure colliding at once, and I don't bother suppressing my scream. Let the neighbors call the fucking cops. The only business open at this hour is Grovewood Ink, and god only knows the sounds I've heard through the walls at all hours of the night from that place. I'm just giving them a run for their money for once.

He stands, wiping his mouth in the most sinful way before crashing his lips against mine once more. Tasting myself from his tongue is the most devious indulgence I've ever consumed. I never thought the serenity I find in Sebastian's touch would ever be a reality for me. His darkness tangles with my own, and completes me in the best way.

He's only inches from being inside me, only his layers of clothing between the two of us, and I can't stand it any longer. I need to feel him, and it's taking everything in me not to take control of this situation and climb him like a fucking tree.

"You want my cock, diavolina?" He grins that wicked grin, the one the masked man has haunted me with for months, and my core clenches. Trailing the edge of his blade across my collarbone, I shudder, my nipples pebbling as the tip of the blade traces the curve of my right breast.

"I think you have too many names for me. You're gonna have to pick one and run with it, Seb." I pant, slowly untucking his shirt and releasing the clasp on his belt. The tip of his knife hovers over my heart, and I'm shocked he has yet to slice into my skin. I know it's sharp, devastatingly so.

"How about wife?" he says, and I swear the Earth shifts off its axis.

I gasp, my eyes shooting up to his. His eyes are fixated on the spot where his knife presses against my skin, transfixed by the sight of it. He can't be serious, can he? There's no fucking way he's serious. But...he speaks about our relationship in terms of eons. Like we have no true end. It only makes sense that one day I would be his wife, right? Do I want to be anyone's wife? I don't think I've ever thought seriously enough about anyone to consider the title before now.

"Tell me to stop," he says, his eyes still locked onto the knife's point. The pressure is nearing pain, but I still won't stop him. If it pierces my skin, so be it. He will never cause me pain in the ways others have, of that I am sure. I trust him completely.

"Never." I tell him, and his smile spreads deviously.

The blade bites into me, breaking the skin, and I hiss as he drags it across my heart, the curves drawing his familiar letter. I will gladly wear his brand for the rest of my life. How could I be anything less than his wife, than the queen of his kingdom?

"Tell me you'll be mine. Forever." It's not a question, more of a demand. Of course, coming from this brute of a man, everything is a demand.

All I can think to do is laugh, and his eyes flick to mine, confusion brewing there. We make quite a pair right now. If anyone were to walk in on us right now, we'd both be thrown into some kind of institution. But that only serves to further prove to me how much I belong in his arms and by his side until the very end.

"I love you, Sebastian. And I will love you until the

sun burns out, until the stars crash into the sea. Give me all you can, all your darkest impulses. And I will always stay by your side." Blood trickles between my breasts, and my core clenches, my body begging to be filled by him.

"Mine," he growls, gripping the back of my neck and pulling me towards him.

Our lips collide in a furious kiss, the sound of his buckle clinking against the table, his zipper sliding down, his desperate inhales for breath filling the air around us. There is no hesitation before he slides deep inside me, and my head falls back on a silent scream. I'm so incredibly full of him, my body having waited far too long to feel him moving inside me. This is exactly what I needed to feel complete. Him, always him.

"Look, Vanessa. Watch my cock sliding into you. See how perfectly we fit together? We were fucking made for each other." he says, guiding my head down and forcing me to watch where we're joined. I whimper and feel him grow thicker inside me.

"Fuck, Seb. Harder. God, you feel too good." I groan. I don't think he's supposed to be engaging in sexual activity this vigorous so soon after a major abdominal injury, but I can't find it in me to give a fuck at the moment. We're not too far from the hospital if his orgasm causes some kind of massive internal bleeding, and at least he'll go down satisfied.

His tongue traces the bead of sweat trailing down

the side of my neck, and I roll my hips, causing a groan to rip from his chest. He pounds into me like a man completely possessed, like a fucking beast. I know his fingertips will leave bruises where he's gripping my hips and neck, but I don't care. My nails rake down his back, and that's all it takes to send him over the edge. He spills into me, claiming me in every way, and I cling to him.

After our breaths finally even out, he slowly pulls out of me, tucking himself back into his pants, his cocky smirk firmly in place. My pussy throbs, a combination of our wetness dripping out of me. Sebastian cocks his head to the side, catching it with his fingers and pushing his cum back inside me. The act is completely obscene, a deep blush creeping up my chest and heating my face.

"Don't go getting all embarrassed on me now, Ness. I just fucked you in the middle of your coffee shop, and you didn't even pull the front blinds down all the way. There's really no need for embarrassment." He laughs, and my cheeks burn hotter as I look toward the front of the building.

The blinds on the front door sit halfway down the front window, and I die a little inside. God help me if anyone felt like taking a late night walk tonight. They must've gotten a hell of a show. My chest heaves, the adrenaline finally settling in. Sebastian steps away, pulling the front blinds completely down and grabbing a clean towel from the counter and wetting it before coming back to me. He shrugs out of his black dress shirt, draping it across my shoulders to replace the one he ripped from my body. The man had a thing for ruining clothes tonight. He presses the towel against my chest, and I hiss, the cut stinging.

"You shouldn't have let me do that." he says as we both study his handiwork. A skillfully sliced letter *S* lies right above my heart, the skin already red but not really bleeding much anymore.

"You're right. I should've let you finish the whole name," I smirk back at him, and he stares at me, completely dumbfounded. He mumbles something unintelligible in Italian before gripping my jaw between his thumb and forefinger and kissing me hard enough to bruise my lips.

"Ti amo, anima mia," he whispers, and I don't need to be fluent to understand that one at all. *I love you, my soul.*

"I love you. And I meant what I said," I tell him, threading my fingers through his dark hair. "I'm not afraid of your darkness, Sebastian. The only thing I fear are the secrets you keep from me. So show them all to me, and I will love every part of you."

Wrapping his shirt around my body, he scoops me up from the table and carries me towards the back of the shop. There's a whole new mess I need to clean before opening in the morning, but right now I can't begin to give a shit. I've missed him more than I thought possible, and all I can think about are his hands on my body until the sun rises.

"Wait. Matteo. I'm not about to spend all night with him creeping on us from the other room. That's a fetish I'm not interested in exploring." I joke, but really...I'm not joking.

"I've already sent him to stay at your house with Douglas. Even though he was quite excited to see his father, I had to postpone our reunion until tomorrow. Right now, all I can think about is getting you under me." He sets me on my feet, pushing me towards the back door to lock up, and I find myself wondering how he moves so effortlessly in the shadows and if I'll ever be that good.

"Douglas," I scoff.

He gave my dog a proper name, completely fucking unhinged. He follows me silently up the back stairs to the apartment where we began, his hand burning a path up my spine. Burying his face in my neck, I fumble with the keys to the apartment. I don't understand how he can still make me so fucking nervous, yet here we are.

"Open the door, Vanessa." He growls against my skin, and I laugh uncomfortably.

"Get the hell off me and I will, Sebastard." I reply, shrugging him away.

"I'm starving," he groans, desperation lacing his tone.

"Oh, really?" I ask, already knowing what he's going to say.

"Feed me, so I can devour you." He replies, biting into the muscles between my neck and shoulder, and I melt into a puddle at his feet.

Okay, so I lied. Not at all what I expected. It seems this man will continue surprising me for the next hundred years, and I think I can live with that.

I WAKE to the sound of my alarm blaring on the bedside table. Sebastian groans in bed next to me, the feeling of his strong arm wrapped around my waist, a comfort I didn't realize I needed this much.

"Make the evil stop," he grumbles, and I smack the screen until the alarm quiets.

Drama king.

"Go back to sleep. I'm going to open the shop," I attempt to lift his arm off my waist, but he holds me tighter. I can't help the smile that spreads across my face. "Not sure if you remember but I have a little mess to clean up this morning," I tell him with a wide grin.

"Don't leave me," he says, burying his face in my curls. Being wrapped in his powerful arms is intoxicating. I never want to leave this dream, but reality pays the bills.

"Go back to sleep. I'm just gonna open the shop, I'll be back later." I slide out of bed, dropping his arm back to the mattress.

"Wait for Teo. He'll be here in ten minutes." He mumbles into the pillow, his voice heavy from sleep.

I'm obsessed with this version of him. Knowing no one has ever had the pleasure of seeing this side of him fills me with a kind of privilege I didn't know I would want. Many have loved and lost before us, and many will love after we are gone from this Earth. But this love, here in these moments, however fleeting they often feel, is mine.

"I'll tell him to meet me downstairs. I love you." Kissing his temple, I brush his messy hair out of his face, tracing the lines of tattoos down his shoulders and torso.

"Keep doing that and I won't let you leave this room," he says, and I laugh softly.

"I'll see you in a little bit. Take your time, I do have actual work to do." Stretching until our fingertips no longer touch, I finally leave the apartment and make my way down to Mug Life.

The dining room sits just as we left it last night, and I smile at the memories. As angry as I felt when he finally removed his mask, the night he spent worshipping me, body and soul, definitely made up for it. Righting the table and chairs, I busy myself wiping everything clean, erasing the evidence of what we did here last night.

Starting my morning duties, I pop my earbuds in, my favorite upbeat music making everything feel like my life is finally falling into place. I know Sebastian still has uncertainties in his business. I know there are still problems on the horizon. But after last night, after the things he said to me and the promises we've made, I can't seem to care about anything or anyone else right now. Faintly over the sound of my music, I hear the click of the back door. Matteo must be arriving finally.

"Wow, that was way less than ten minutes. For once you're early, Teo. I'm impressed." I laugh, pulling my earbud out and turning to greet him.

Suddenly I'm face to face with a man I don't recognize. He appears young, olive-skinned, with striking green eyes and a large scar trailing down one cheek. His features look familiar, but I've never seen this man before. His face is completely devoid of emotion, cold and empty, yet his smile looks almost sinister. The expensive suit he's wearing tells me he's not here for coffee and a pastry, but likely for something far worse.

"W-who are you? What the hell are you doing here?" I attempt to take a step back, but he steps closer.

"My associates were correct. You are exquisite, Ms. Diaz. I can understand what my cousin sees in you." He twirls a lock of my hair around one finger, and I shiver. Cousin? This man is an enemy if I've ever seen one, I feel it in my fucking bones.

Yet again, I find myself only feet away from the gun I

keep behind the counter. How do I keep getting into these situations? I can throw a decent punch, but that would only serve to piss this guy off. He's got at least a foot of height and a hundred pounds on me. There's no telling if he's alone. Surely, Teo will be here in just moments. I could scream, that would likely wake Sebastian. But in the meantime, this man could slit my throat in a matter of seconds. I slip the earbud in my hand into the pocket of my linen pants.

"What do you want?" I ask, shuffling backward, bracing a hand on a table. He advances, a predatory look in his eyes.

"What I've always wanted. To hurt Sebastian. And this is how I finally accomplish that goal." His wicked grin widens, and I turn to make a run for the front door.

I only make it a few steps before he grabs me by my hair, ripping my head back towards him. A scream rips from my throat, but he slaps a hand over my mouth. I bite into the fleshy part of his palm hard enough to break the skin. The taste of iron floods into my mouth, and I feel a sense of triumph knowing I made the fucker bleed.

"Fucking bitch!" He rips his hand away, backhanding me with the other.

The slap surprises me, stinging like a brand across my cheek. Tears spring to my eyes involuntarily, but I will them away. Only one man can bring me to my fucking knees, and it's definitely not a man as weak as this one. He grips my throat tightly, and I wince.

"You try that shit again and I will kill you. You do not matter to me, cunt. I will tell your worthless father you were collateral damage and call it a fucking day, do you understand me?" He growls and I'm so fucking confused.

My father? What does my family have to do with any of this? And how does this shit keep happening? Moments when I'm most vulnerable, the few minutes I'm left unguarded, the wolves descend every time.

"We're going to take a little drive, and you're going to come quietly. Or I'm going to shoot you in your pretty little face, understand? I will burn this building to the ground with your man sleeping upstairs. That would be so much easier for me, honestly. But I need him to willingly give me the keys to his kingdom first if I want the elders to obey. So you're going to follow the rules, and we're all going to have a good day, got it, sweetie?" His lips press against my cheek and bile rises in my throat.

I nod as his fingers tighten in my hair. A whimper escapes my throat, and I wonder what's keeping Matteo. Why is no one here to interrupt this encounter? Tears spring to my eyes again, spilling over my lashes.

"I think Sebastian will be a little distracted when he wakes, my dear. You see, Matteo is his closest friend. And imagine the devastation he will feel when he discovers I burned that shitty little house of yours to the ground with him locked inside." There is joy in his voice at his admission, and I can't stop the sob that rips from my chest.

Oh Matteo. My Dougy. My home.

All the memories of the life I've built with my own hands from the moment I came to Grovewood, everything stolen by this monster. I can't begin to understand what he wants from me. But I know, with the nature of Sebastian's family, it can only be power. It will always be power they come for. I vow to myself in this very moment, they will never strip it from him because of me.

"Let's go, Vanessa." He hisses, pushing me towards the back door.

He shoves me into the passenger seat of a black sedan, slamming the door and speeding down the alleyway. He navigates the streets of Grovewood with ease, as if he's done it a thousand times. The thought makes me sick to my stomach, because he likely has. There's no telling how long he's been here, watching us, waiting for this very moment. We drive in silence towards the coast for an eternity, the feeling of peril building in my chest. I should've screamed. I should've fought harder. My life has been an endless stream of knowing what I should've done only after it's too late to change a situation.

Now I'm stuck here, not knowing whether I'll live or die today, not knowing whether Matteo has already given his life for such a stupid cause. Tears fall from my eyes, staining my green satin shirt. This day started so well. Cute outfit, great hair day, wrapped in the arms of a gorgeous man. What a turn it's taken in such a short amount of time.

"Where are you taking me?" I ask quietly, and the man smirks.

"We're going to have a little family reunion, Vanessa." He grips the steering wheel hard, the leather creaking under his hands.

"I don't understand how my family is involved in any of this. I haven't even seen them in years. They know nothing about my involvement with Sebastian. How are they-" I ask, but he cuts me off.

"See, that's where you're wrong. They know all about your boyfriend, sweetheart. You can't imagine how proud they were when I told them you bagged one of Italy's most eligible criminals. They were shocked, you can guess, when I told them it was the head of the Arsenio empire. The same man who refused to work with them many years ago when your father approached one of Sebastian's suppliers in Miami looking to expand his enterprise. It seems my cousin was unimpressed by your father's more... immoral business practices. Can you imagine being the head of an empire such as this one and possessing something as restrictive and useless as a conscience? Disgusting. Your parents were more than willing to help me find you once I promised them a seat at the table when I rule this family." He speeds down the back roads, the salty ocean air seeping in through the car vents.

The sound of ship horns, trucks, and seagulls resonate outside as he slows down, driving through city streets again. We must be close to a shipyard. He pulls the car through a dark, gated entry, driving through rows and rows of shipping containers before stopping next to what looks like an empty warehouse next to a long dock.

"Listen to me right now, Vanessa. You do anything to try to escape once we go inside, and I will shoot you. I will not hesitate. I'm not your little boy toy. I don't give a fuck if you live or die today. You're nothing but bait to me. Don't fuck up my plan and make me shoot you in front of mommy and daddy, okay?" he says, and I want to stab him right through his beady little eyes.

After hand cuffing me, he pulls a gun from the small of his back, presses it against my temple, and drags me from the car. I'm done crying. I've moved past fear and on to anger. I'm so fucking tired of being a pawn in this war. I will not be taken down by this shrimp-dick motherfucker.

"What makes you think I won't just make you kill me now? Try to run again and lose every chance of leverage you think you have for getting Sebastian here?" I snap, yanking against his grip. The sting of his hold on my hair is painful, but nothing compares to the rage I feel inside.

“You think I’m an idiot, Vanessa?” He laughs.

“You don’t want me to answer that.” I reply, pulling against my restraints.

“I brought a special kind of incentive. Just for you, baby.” He whispers in my ear, kissing my cheek again. His hot breath against my skin makes my stomach roll as he kicks open the warehouse door.

In the center of the room, my parents are huddled together, looking just as ragged and guilty as they always have. But my heart shatters at the sight next to them. Sitting tied to a chair, her face bloody and bruised, is one of the very few people I would stay in hell for. She doesn’t have to open her eyes for me to know they are the mirror image of mine.

Aria. *My sister.*

twenty-seven

Sebastian

I WAKE IN A COLD SWEAT, a nightmare clinging to the edges of my mind. My phone blares with alarms. Did I set an alarm? No, the sound is wrong. That's not the alarm I wake up to. That's the security system for Vanessa's house. Jumping out of bed, I grab my phone and pull up the cameras.

Everything is offline.

I open the feed of the shop downstairs.

Offline.

Someone pounds on the door to the apartment, and I tug a pair of slacks up my legs, grabbing my gun from the island as I make my way to the front door.

"Seb!? Ness?! Anybody, please!!" Rory's voice filters through the door, and I unlock it quickly.

"Aurora? What are you doing here?" I ask, confused.

"Is she here? Tell me she's here, Seb! Please! Vanessa?!" she shouts, pushing past me into the apartment.

"She's downstairs opening the shop, Rory. What's going on?" I ask, following closely behind her.

"No, she isn't! She's not down there, Seb! And her house..." she sobs, tears streaming down her face. "Her-her house is..."

She's crying so hard I can barely understand anything she's saying. I've never seen Aurora so shattered. She's always the most collected woman, always the most calm in a crisis. Grabbing her shoulders, I stop her frantic search and force her to look at me.

"What about her house, Rory? Where is she?" I demand, and she dissolves again.

"That's what I'm saying! I don't know!" She screams, her head falling against my shoulder.

It's only a moment later, and her husband is barreling through the apartment door. Breaker's eyes meet mine, and I see something there that never bodes well. Pity.

"Did you find her?!" Aurora asks, and he shakes his head.

"She's not in the shop?" I ask, grabbing a shirt and slipping my shoes and holster on before making sure both of my guns have a round in the chamber.

"No. But that's not all, Sebastian. Her house..." Breaker says with a grimace.

"Matteo is there. He was supposed to be coming to

open the shop with her. We'll go there first." I slide my knife into the sheath at my back, pushing past him.

"It's gone, Sebastian." he says, stopping me in my tracks.

"What do you mean gone?" I ask, my tone glacial.

"Burning to the ground. I got an alert that someone cut the power to her security system. By the time I got there, the fire was out of control. There are at least half a dozen trucks still trying to put it out now. But there won't be anything left of it. We came straight here to find her, but she wasn't in the shop. There was...it looks like there was a struggle, Seb." He replies, fury building in my chest.

"FUCK!" I roar, knowing I should never have allowed myself the comforts of rest when things were so unsettled.

"Matteo?!" I ask, desperation in my voice. I didn't see any missed calls or messages from him. If the house was engulfed, I can only imagine...

"We didn't see any sign of him either, Sebastian. I'm sorry." Breaker replies, and without hesitation, I put my fist through the drywall next to the front door.

Pulling his number up on my phone, I call and listen to the phone ring and ring. He's not dead. I know he isn't. I would know. I've known him almost all my life. He's closer to me than nearly anyone else on this planet. I would know if he were dead.

"Pick up your fucking phone, Teo. Pick it up, pick it

up, pick it up..." I mumble to myself. Break and Rory exchange worried glances with one another, like they're sure I'm losing my mind. Maybe I am.

My best friend is missing, possibly burned alive in his bed. My woman, *my world*, has been taken from me. My empire is under attack. And my army, the bulk of my men, is in Italy. I could maybe scramble a few dozen from Florida within a few hours, but I have no idea what Luca's end game is here. I don't know where he is or what he's doing to Vanessa as we speak.

I try calling Enzo after I get no answer from Matteo, knowing no matter what happens next, I need some kind of reinforcement here. His phone goes straight to voicemail. Am I too late? Has he already targeted my home in Italy?

"Do you have any way of tracking her?" Breaker asks, my mind barely able to focus for more than a second.

"I don't know if she has her phone." I reply, and Rory's face falls.

"I found it on the floor downstairs." she says, dropping it onto the counter.

"Nothing else? You've got to get her some jewelry. When this is over, I'll send you the info for my dealer. All of Aurora's jewelry has tracking devices built into it," Breaker says, opening an app on his phone.

"I just love how obsessively controlling you are," Rory says, smiling up at her husband.

"Scold me later, it keeps you safe." he says, scrolling

through several screens. "Does she have any other devices? A watch? Anything like that?"

"She's worse than me about tech. Her watch isn't even digital." I reply, threading my fingers through my hair. The inaction is killing me. I have to do something.

"What about her earbuds? I only found the case downstairs. Maybe...maybe she has them?" Rory says, and Breaker smiles widely, kissing her square on the lips.

"You brilliant, beautiful woman! I have to get to a computer. I think I have a backup next door at the tattoo shop. I'll be right back." he says, turning to leave.

He only makes it a few steps before someone collides into the doorframe. A body, bloody and bruised, props himself up against the wood. His face is covered in black soot, half his chest and right arm burned and ravaged. Matteo pants, looking half dead, barely holding himself on his feet.

"Holy Jesus fucking walking dead!" Rory says, rushing to his side.

She eases herself under his good side, taking his weight and helping him onto the couch. He needs a fucking hospital, but there would be too many questions. The skin on his chest and arm is charred, the burn severe. It should've been me.

"We need clean linens, not towels. Grab a sheet and run it under some cool water. Rory, go downstairs and grab some honey from the shop. As many bottles as you can." Breaker jumps into action, already calling someone on his phone.

I rush to the bedroom, grabbing the sheet and running it under the kitchen tap. I've made many advantageous friendships in my life, but Breaker is definitely one I don't think I could live without. My mind can't stop to process all the things he's asking for as he answers a dozen questions to whoever is on the other end of the phone. Iris maybe? Or one of the other guys from the tattoo shop? I know they frequently work together. At one point, they were all in the Marine Corps together. Some kind of specialized unit where they learned things like how to triage major burns in the field without access to a hospital, apparently.

"Yes, he's coherent. He's looking at me right now, Sanaa," he says into the phone. "Okay, we'll keep him conscious. Aurora will be here with him. Yes. Yes. I'm not a complete dumbfuck. Good point. Okay. Thank you."

Rory comes back with the honey and several bottles of water, setting them on the table in front of the couch. I bring the soaked sheets to her side, and she rips them into strips. It's so odd these kind of things seem so common in their lives, but I'm not asking questions.

"Spread the honey across the burns and layer the wet cloths on top, it will help to prevent the spread of infection until Sanaa can get here. I have to go and get my laptop. I'll be right back," Breaker says, kissing his wife's head and rushing out the front door.

"Bash," Matteo groans, and I drop to his side.

"I'm here. You're gonna be fine. I will kill Luca for this, I promise you that. He will die by my hand." I vow, and he smirks.

"Yeah, that sounds good. But Bash, the dog..." Teo says, coughing harshly. Rory winces as she drapes the cloth strips over his chest.

"Don't worry about him, Matteo. I know you did everything you could. Vanessa will understand that it was-" I say, but he shakes his head.

"Bash, the dog ran. He's the one who alerted me to the fire. I was able to get out because he was pulling me out of bed. I tried to get to the front door, but the ceiling collapsed. That's how I got this," he says, gesturing towards his burns. "We were trapped. He pulled me through the house to the back door. When I kicked it open, he ran. He's out there somewhere, Sebastian."

"Jesus fucking Christ. Who would've thought Douglas was such a hero?" I reply, dragging a hand down my face. "We will find him. Just rest. Let us take care of you, too."

"You have to drink this, Matteo. Burns cause dehydration very quickly, you have to drink way more than you think is necessary." Rory tells him, holding a water bottle to his lips and helping him drink.

"Okay, I think I might've found her," Breaker says, coming back into the apartment with his computer in one hand and a backpack in the other.

“Well, that was quick.” I reply.

“There are very few times that statement has applied to me, but when it comes to my job, it’s accurate.” he says, and Rory snorts.

“Gross. You found her?” I ask, gesturing to his computer.

“Yeah, she must have her earbud on her. It’s pinging her location near the shipping docks outside of Charleston. Only about half an hour from here.” He replies as I retreat to the bedroom.

Grabbing my duffel bag from the closet, I unpack the small arsenal I have stored here. I never imagined a war breaking out from the apartment, but I’m always prepared for anything. Walking back into the kitchen, I set the bag on the island before shrugging into my suit jacket. This ends now. I won’t tiptoe around Luca any longer, he will die today.

“I’m coming with you,” Matteo says, attempting to sit up from his position on the couch.

“Easy there, killer. You’re not going anywhere,” Rory says, pushing his good shoulder back down. “He cannot go. These burns are way too severe. He won’t survive a gunshot or worse. Honestly, I’m not sure he would survive the car ride, Sebastian.”

“She’s right, Teo. You have to stay here. You have a doctor on the way?” I ask, and Breaker nods.

“The best doc I know. Sanaa was Navy, attached to

our unit for years. Matteo is in expert hands. I can go with you, Seb," he replies, and his wife tenses.

"I won't ask this of you. You've done enough to help me, and I'm incredibly grateful. But this is my mess, I won't ask you to risk your life." I tell him, but he's already packing his bag and checking his weapon.

"Good thing I'm not doing it for you. We love Vanessa, Sebastian. I won't let you walk into some unknown situation if I could've helped save her. This is a family. It's what we do." He kisses Aurora, her hands clinging to his t-shirt desperately.

"Come back to me, Jason. I'm too young to be a widow." she says, and he smirks.

"Yes, princess. I promise." He gives her one last kiss on her temple before grabbing his bag and leaving the apartment.

"Please take care of him. I will reach out to Fortuna and send a team for extraction as soon as I can. They will transport him to the plane and back to Italy as soon as your doctor deems him stable to travel. Thank you, Rory." I tell her, and she hugs me tightly.

"Bring my girl back." She whispers, and I squeeze her tighter.

"I will."

twenty-eight

Vanessa

"HOW COULD you do this to your own daughter?!" I scream at my parents, and my father sneers.

"How could we? How could you! You left us with nothing, Vanessa! You had a duty to this family, and you ran away so selfishly! And all this time, you've been fucking the don of one of the wealthiest families in the fucking world and you didn't think for even a second to take care of your own family?" My father shouts, his tan skin turning red with anger.

"You are no fucking family of mine! You are the most disgusting people I've ever known, and I wish you were both fucking dead!" I yell back at him from the chair across from my sister, and he slaps me hard enough to make my ears ring.

"Ah ah ah, easy on the merchandise now. Once I

have Sebastian in my grasp, I don't care what you do to her, but until then, lay off her face." The man who brought me here says.

"I'm sorry, Luca. You're right. Why punish her when it would hurt so much more for her to watch this?" My father says as he grips Aria by her hair, tipping her head back.

She's barely conscious, one brow busted and bleeding, blood pouring from her lip, and bruises blooming under both eyes. I can't imagine what she's already endured. My sister is a fighter. Hell, she's the one who taught me how to defend myself. I know she put up a hell of a fight before they got her here. But what I can't fathom is why they would do something so horrific to their own child. Just to hurt me? Just to keep me from running? He tugs her hair harder, and she whimpers.

"Stop! Leave her alone!" I scream, tears springing to my eyes.

"Why? She is my property, I can do what I wish with her. She defies me just as you do, useless fucking women." My father spits back, and I sob.

"If you want to hurt someone, hurt me! Leave Aria alone!" I scream, but he hits her again. Her chair rocks slightly from the impact, her body slumping to one side.

"FUCKING MONSTER! I'LL KILL YOU!" I scream, pulling against my restraints so hard I'm sure my wrists will bleed, but I don't care. My sister is suffering.

"Calm down, sweetheart, you'll hurt yourself acting that way," Luca says, and I want him dead.

I want them all dead. Every single person who's ever made me feel insignificant, like a victim, like I don't count for more than a pawn in this game. I want to kill them all. My mother stands wordlessly behind my father, just as she always has. She may not be the one inflicting the pain this time, but she's not doing anything to stop it either. She's just as guilty as he is. They will die for this, and I will feel nothing when they do. Nothing but vindicated.

"When is he-" my father starts to say, but we're suddenly plunged into total darkness.

"Ah, it seems we've got company. Finally," Luca says, coming behind me and pressing his gun to my temple.

A door opens at the back of the warehouse, and no less than a dozen men enter, all looking confused.

"Luca, what's going on? Someone cut the power to the security feeds." One of them says, and Luca just laughs maniacally.

"Seems like daddy's angry." he says, and I shudder. He's insane.

The only light filters through one small window in the top corner of the empty space, but I can't see anything outside. There's no movement around us, no sound coming from outside. We're all just staring into the darkness, waiting for something to happen. Suddenly, the glass in the window shatters as a shot rings out, the sound of a body hitting the floor behind me echoing through the space. It happens twice more before Luca pulls me out of my seat, pushing his gun into my skull so hard I'm sure the barrel will imprint there.

"Come out, you fucking coward! You can pick off my men from the shadows, but you can't face me? Some fucking leader you are!" Luca shouts, his fist tightening in my hair as he shouts into the darkness.

The lights flicker back to life, and I squint against the sudden brightness. All is silent for several long moments before the front door opens, and my heart stalls in my chest. Sebastian steps into the space, looking as calm as the day he walked into my coffee shop for the very first time. He fills every inch of this room with his presence. Immediately, I want to run to him, but Luca's grip is too tight and I'd be dead before I made it two steps.

"Welcome, cousin. We've been waiting for you," Luca says, kissing my cheek again. I shudder against his touch as his grip loosens on my hair. "Oh, don't be shy now, baby. It's time for the big reveal."

"You wanted me here, Luca. I am here. You will not leave this building alive. None of you will. Unfortunate for you all really. You've convinced these men you are some kind of savior, and it will cost them their lives." Sebastian says, slipping his hands into his pockets so nonchalantly.

The men behind us shuffle uncomfortably, confused whispers spreading through the ranks.

"See, this is what happens when you try to buy loyalty instead of earning it, Luca. There is never a price worth someone's life. What I offer the men of Fortuna is not what you've given these men here. This is a perversion of our lifestyle, of our brotherhood." Sebastian fires back.

"You know nothing!" Luca barks, a whipped dog waiting to bite.

"Release her. She has nothing to do with whatever this scheme is you've cooked up." Sebastian replies, appearing far too casual for my comfort.

"Oh, but that's where you're wrong. Isn't he, Vanessa? You see, this is a family business here. Vanessa's parents and I have been planning this for so long, and all we needed was for her to worm her way into your bed. She played her part so well, didn't she?" Luca suggests, and rage burns hot under my skin. "She's a very convincing little whore. But the time for games is over. She's served her purpose, and she can be returned to her parents now."

"You expect me to believe any of the vile dribble that pours out of your mouth? Really, Luca? Not a fucking chance," Sebastian replies, and my heart clenches. He knows how much I love him.

"You don't have to believe me. She can tell you

herself, right, Ness?" Luca says, his face pressed so closely to mine.

"You tell him what I want to hear, or I will empty this magazine into your sister's chest, understand?" He whispers so softly only I can hear him, and I choke down a sob.

"My *family* is everything to me, Sebastian. I would do anything for them." I say, watching the darkness in his eyes churn.

"Anything?" He asks, his voice wrapping around my heart and warming me to my very core.

I pray he's remembered every single conversation we've ever had about the way I feel about the family I've created and the one I came from. That he can see the truth in my eyes from where he stands now.

"Ti amo," Sebastian says, and I remember the exact moment I heard those words from his lips for the first time.

"Anima mia," I reply, and he smirks that familiar smirk.

"What the fuck are you two talking about?" Luca says, jerking me back against his body.

"Vanessa, do me a favor?" Sebastian says, and my heart pounds in my chest.

"You're not calling any shots here, fucker!" Luca snaps back, releasing me and leveling his gun on Sebastian.

"Duck," he says, and before my mind can catch up with what he's asking, my body is already obeying.

I hit the ground in front of Luca and shots ring out again, the men behind us dropping one by one. The front door bursts open behind Sebastian, and I'm shocked beyond belief to see Enzo charging in behind Sebastian, an army of men at his back as they open fire throughout the space. I crawl towards Aria, covering her with my body to protect her from the bullets flying through the air as I try to loosen her restraints.

"What are you doing? You're ruining everything!" My father says, rearing back to punch me. Before he can, a loud shot echoes through the space and his body lurches forward, blood staining his shirt as his body quickly slumps forward. My mother screams, throwing herself on top of him as he bleeds out, the life draining from his eyes. I don't spare him a single second more of my time or energy. Instead, I focus all my attention on getting my sister out of the middle of this chaos.

Luca lunges for Sebastian, knocking his gun from his hand. Sebastian punches him in the jaw, causing Luca's head to jerk back violently. Seb pulls his knife from its sheath, slicing through the air at Luca as he jumps back. Enzo and the other men make quick work of rounding up all of Luca's men, killing those who wouldn't surrender and detaining the rest. We all watch this fight to the death unfold, knowing there is no other outcome but to let Sebastian end this uprising for good.

Luca dodges to the right, attempting to punch Sebastian low in the ribs, but Seb is so much quicker than him. He ducks lower, grabbing Luca by the throat and twisting him around until he's completely immobile.

"This family, this empire, belongs to me. You reached for what was never yours to take. Family is the one thing worth protecting. But you forgot that, Luca. I warned you it would be your demise. You should have listened." Sebastian draws his blade across Luca's throat, blood pouring down his shirt as his body falls to the floor.

Finally, this nightmare ends.

Somewhere in the scramble, I hear the sound of a slide racking. Turning, I see my mother pull a small pistol from her waist and point it straight at Sebastian. I never thought this is where my life would lead me, my sister barely breathing next to me, my father dead on the floor of some warehouse in the middle of a blood feud between a family we had no business meddling in. Yet here we are. This life is full of choices. And for once, mine are completely clear. Picking up the gun my father dropped when his body hit the floor, I level the barrel at my mother's head.

"If you touch him, you won't live to see tomorrow. That's a promise I have no hesitation in keeping, mother." I say, silence washing over the room.

I stand, not wavering for a moment in my convictions. I will kill her. I feel no reservation or cause for second guessing that decision. But enough blood has already been spilled here today because of stupid men, I don't need to add to it unnecessarily.

"You would never kill your own family, your own blood." My mother spits, and I straighten my spine. She will never change. She will perpetuate this vicious cycle for every one of my siblings until they're all nothing but shells of the people they were once meant to be.

"Sebastian is my family. And I will do anything it takes to protect him," I declare, and I see the exact moment she loses her sense of reality.

She lunges towards me, and I pull the trigger. I expect to feel...something. Sadness maybe? Or guilt? But all I feel is vindication and a sense of relief, knowing Sebastian is safe for the first time in so long.

A groan sounds behind me, and I drop to my knees, the gun clattering to the floor. A sob wracks my body as I survey the damage they've done to my sister. I can't imagine the internal injuries she's sustained or how long she's endured this torture.

"Aria? I'm right here. You're gonna be okay, I promise. We're going to get you to a doctor." Maybe I'm trying to convince myself more than her as I brush her curls out of her face. They're caked in blood and my stomach rolls, bile creeping up my throat.

"I've got her, Ness. Let me take her out," Enzo seems to materialize next to me, scooping her up gently.

"Be careful! Please, Enzo...don't..." I beg, and he looks at me knowingly, sympathy lacing his features.

"I promise I will take care of her. I will keep her safe." He vows, and I nod, letting them go.

"Vanessa?" I hear the voice I've been waiting what feels like an eternity to hear, even though it's only been a matter of hours.

Turning, I cross the space between us in seconds, jumping into his arms. He catches me with ease, kissing my chest, my arms, my face, any part of me he can reach.

"I'm so sorry, I let you walk right into the hands of my enemy. I could never be worthy of your forgiveness, but I will spend my life earning it." He holds me tightly to his chest, and I never want to leave this embrace.

"It's not something you have to earn. There's nothing to forgive, Seb. Our lives will be a constant state of someone reaching for the power you possess and us fighting back. And it's a fight I'm willing to be a part of every single time if it means I get to stand by your side, Sebastian. But maybe next time, let's not keep me in the dark about cousins trying to burn the family tree, okay? Next time someone tries to make a grab for the family jewels, try to keep me informed." I joke and he just laughs, burying his hands in my hair.

"I don't know what kind of deal I made with the devil to earn a woman like you, but I don't care. I love you, Vanessa." he says, crashing his lips against mine in a desperate kiss.

I could get lost in this moment, the world disappearing around us even though Sebastian's men are cleaning up bodies and evidence only a few feet away. All I can think about is how safe I feel wrapped in his arms, in his kiss. I'm sure a therapist could unpack something about that, but I'm gonna leave it alone. He makes me feel seen and understood for once in my life, and I won't ever give that up now that it's mine.

"Wait!" I say, pushing back from his chest. "Matteo?"

The look in Sebastian's eyes tells me all I need to know. The aftermath of this chaos will be a long road of recovery, but we will do it together. And that's what matters in the end.

"He was badly hurt. Rory is with him now, and some doctor Breaker brought in. I do not know his condition. He managed to escape the house with his life but... whether he will survive his injuries remains to be seen." he says, and my heart drops like lead.

"I don't know that I really want to know the answer to this but...my dog? My house? They're gone, aren't they?" I ask, burying my face in his chest.

"I don't know the extent of the damage to your house, but Breaker said it was very substantial. It will likely be a total loss. I am so sorry you've lost your memories there, Bambina. But if you choose it, we can rebuild it just as it was." He hooks a finger under my chin, forcing me to meet his eyes as a tear escapes over the edge of my lashes.

"And Doug?" I choke back a sob, not wanting to hear any more devastating news, but feeling like ripping the band-aid off all at once is really the best way to go.

"I wish I could give you an answer there, but I cannot. Matteo said he ran into the woods surrounding your home when they got out of the house. We haven't seen any sign of him. I'm so sorry, Vanessa." He wipes my tears, kissing my forehead gently and pulling me into him.

The thought of him wandering alone in the woods, scared and probably hurt, is more than I can handle. Sobs break through, pouring from my body in wave after wave. Adrenaline finally crashes in my system, and I feel unsteady on my feet. Fuck, if I pass out now in front of these men, I may never hear the end of it. I have to remain strong. Even though my body is begging for a moment's peace. My parents are dead, my sister is hanging in the balance, my life as I've known it has been blown to pieces, but I have to hold it together. A queen does not falter, after all.

"You refused to let me fall. Let me spend every breath I have left returning that vow. You will never stand alone again, Vanessa. I swear it on my life. Let me hold you up now." Sebastian whispers against my cheek, stroking my curls softly.

I lean into him, letting him support my weight as we

walk out of the warehouse and into the light of day. Somehow, the sun on my skin feels different than it did even yesterday. It feels like a new beginning, like the dawn of a new era for Fortuna Nera, for Sebastian, and for me. For now, I just want to find the doctor who is working on Matteo and my sister and feel some semblance of reassurance for the first time today.

twenty-nine

Sebastian

THE DRIVE back to Grovewood is silent, both of us lost in our thoughts as we process the events of the day. I can't stop touching her, my palm grazing her thigh, my thumb caressing the soft skin on the back of her hand.

"I'm sorry about your parents," I speak into the silence, and she just stares out the window.

"I'm not." She replies, not bothering to look my way but not letting my hand go either. "They deserved everything they got."

"I don't want this life to turn you into someone like me. Someone cold." I tell her, worried it may already be too late.

She looks at me for several long moments, and I glance between her and the road, doing my best to keep us on course. A small smile lifts the corner of her mouth, and I could melt into it.

"You keep me safe, I'll keep you warm. Deal?" She replies, and I laugh.

"Of course, Bambina. Keep me warm. For all the days of our lives." I tell her, kissing the back of her hand as I pull into the long driveway at Breaker and Rory's home.

"How the hell did Enzo get stateside so quickly?" She asks, and I scoff.

"Would you believe he was already on the way? He caught word of what Luca had planned and was on the first flight to us. He barely arrived in time to prevent an all out massacre." Seb shakes his head in near disbelief at the fortunate timing.

Their compound sits on acre after acre of beautiful low-country, their home nestled in the middle of it. Breaker's security is unlike anything I've ever seen, completely airtight. I've been trying to recruit him for years, even though I know he has no desire to work for the kind of enterprise I lead. So I will be happy with what I can get, accepting his help as often as he's comfortable offering it.

Rory stands at the front door, a nervous look on her face. Several cars are parked haphazardly in the circle driveway, and I hope Enzo has beaten us here with Vanessa's sister.

She rushes to Vanessa's door, pulling it open and wrapping her in a hug so tight, I'm not sure she can breathe. But Vanessa doesn't complain, she squeezes her back just as tightly. I give them both their reunion, meeting Enzo on the front steps. His expression is grave, and my fear for Matteo grows exponentially. Bracing myself to hear the worst, I gesture for him to go ahead.

"Matteo is stabilized. That doctor patched him up really well. He's going to have many scars, but he will survive this. Vanessa's sister is in surgery now. Most of the wounds to her face were superficial, just requiring simple stitching. But the injuries to her torso were far more severe. Boss, I've seen torture before. Hell, I've inflicted beatings like that myself. But for that to come from her own parents? Her spleen was ruptured. It was horrible." Enzo says, shaking his head. "On the other hand, it's very convenient that Breaker's compound is equipped with medical facilities that rival our own. Surprising, but useful."

"I would like to speak with this doctor. Hear for myself about the updates on Matteo's condition. I'm sure Vanessa will feel the same way about Aria. Shall we?" I suggest, reaching for Vanessa's hand.

"I have something I really think you're gonna want to see," Rory smiles a mischievous smile, and I quirk a brow at her.

She leads us inside, not bothering to stop in the living room where an older woman bearing a striking resemblance to her holds her son on the couch. I'm always so surprised by how normal they all find it when a group of mafia soldiers come marching through their living room, and they don't ask any questions.

"Break is in the basement as usual, and Sanaa is in the medical building next door. She hasn't sent word about your sister," Rory says quietly. Vanessa's face falls slightly, but I squeeze her against me. "But I promise you, Sanaa is the best surgeon we know. If there were anyone I wanted working on someone I love, it would be Sanaa. Aria is in the best hands. Matteo is recovering in the guest room if you want to see him. But I think there's someone who may want to see you first."

"Who else could possibly be more important?" I ask her, confused about who else she could be referring to.

A jingling sound echoes down the hallway, and Vanessa's eyes snap up, a gasp caught in her throat.

"Son of a bitch, you're kidding?!" I say, a smile breaking through for the first time today.

"Doug?!?" Vanessa squeals, dropping to the floor as he comes lumbering towards her.

He tackles her with his entire body weight as they both collapse to the ground. As he whines in excitement, she buries her face in his fur, sobbing and holding him closely.

"The prodigal son returns, huh? How the hell did you find him?" I ask, and Rory laughs.

"He actually found us. I brought Matteo back here to meet the doc, and you'll never guess who was sprawled on the deck next to the pool, panting and waiting to be let inside. He found his way to a safe haven, I suppose," Rory replies, and I'm dumbfounded.

"I thought I'd never see you again, my boy! I thought I'd lost you forever!" Vanessa cried, hugging his neck as he leans into her. "I promise I'll never let anything happen to you ever again, Dougy."

"Thank you, Aurora. We appreciate everything you've done, you and Breaker both. I am in your debt." I tell her, wrapping an arm around her shoulder.

"No, you aren't, Seb. This is a family. *You* are our family, whether you like it or not." She replies.

Shouting echoes from down the hall, Matteo's voice instantly recognizable. It sounds as though he's arguing with someone.

"You're gonna have to say something to him. He's been less than compliant." Rory says, rolling her eyes.

"I'll see what I can do." I laugh, stepping past the girls and walking towards his room.

"Take me home, I want to get out of here! She's a masochist, I swear to God! Get me the fuck out of here on the next fucking flight! I can't be here anymore!" Matteo shouts as I make my way into his room, leaning against the door frame.

Two of my men stand guard around his bed as he tries to remove his IV from his arm on the side of his body that isn't charred. His chest and right arm have been treated, cleaned, and wrapped in new bandages. I'm sure that was no walk in the park. Hopefully, the doctor gave him a decent amount of painkillers for that procedure.

"What are you screaming about in here? You're going to scare the women and children." I say, as calmly as possible. His eyes snap to the door, finding mine instantly.

"Oh, now you come back? After you've had all the fun?" His usual snarky tone retorts, but something is missing. He's in pain, I can tell.

"Who is a masochist, huh? What is all this you're yelling about?" I ask, and he shifts in the bed, scooting back and sitting up.

"That doctor. I swear to the gods, she's trying to kill me. She scrubbed half my fucking skin off. I felt every fucking second of it, too. And did she apologize? Not even once. Bitch." He looks away, pissed as hell with this doctor.

"Ah, so she's a woman, huh? That part I didn't know." I smirk, and he rolls his eyes. "She sounds very good at her job. I can't wait to meet her."

"I'd rather you just put a fucking bullet between my eyes now. It would definitely hurt less." He replies.

"You sound like a petulant child, brother. If I can be honest, I am grateful to her. I'm not sure what I would've done if your time on this Earth had come to an end. At the risk of sounding like I'm cheating on my woman, I love you, Matteo. You are indispensable to me. I will do all I can to ensure your recovery is as smooth and painless as possible. You've already given so much for Fortuna, it's about time you get something back for your trouble." I tell him, and he looks out the window, thinking over all I'm saying.

Regret for ever putting him in a situation like this weaves through my veins like poison. But he knows the risks of Fortuna, we all do. I know he would die for this Family, and Vanessa is a part of it now.

"I've never felt like I've given up anything to be with Fortuna Nera. This is my destiny. I chose this, and I have no regrets. I don't want you to think I feel like I'm owed anything for my service to the Family. I will always be grateful for this life I've been given." His gaze is far away, his eyes hollow with the memories of all the dreams I know he left behind. "Just maybe not tonight after that devil woman is done torturing me for her pleasure. Doctor, my ass. Dominatrix, maybe. She enjoys inflicting pain, I swear to the gods," Matteo says, and I can't help but laugh and roll my eyes at his bitching.

"I really can't wait to meet this woman." I reply and he sighs heavily.

"Must be talking about me," someone says, walking into the room behind us.

A petite woman with beautiful bronze skin stands at the foot of Matteo's bed. Her curly brown hair is pulled back in a ponytail, and her navy blue scrubs are stained with blood. She checks his IV lines, making sure nothing is kinked before hanging another bag and checking his pulse.

"Hello, Satan. Come to put me back on your torture table?" Matteo asks, and I snort out a laugh. Ridiculous.

"Very dramatic, Mr. Gallo. I've asked you numerous times if you want the pain medication. Unfortunately, some of the pain I can't prevent. That's the nature of severe burns. But I can take the edge off if you want to go to sleep. Maybe when you wake up, you'll be halfway to Italy." She shrugs, the lilt in her voice difficult to place, but I nod.

"She's right. You should take the deal. I can have you on a plane as soon as she gives me the green light, Teo. You can recover at home." I add, and he seems to be thinking it over.

He waits several moments before finally nodding. She draws up some kind of medicine in a vial from the side table, pushing it into his IV slowly. He winces for a moment before relaxing a little more, his head bobbing to one side as sleep pulls him under. Morphine is hard to fight in such a high dose.

"He'll be more comfortable now. As long as you keep the dressings clean and changed regularly, he's safe to transport whenever you're ready to go home. The girl will unfortunately take much longer to heal. I think it's going to be a few weeks before she's fit to travel anywhere. But she'll be okay in the long term, physically at least," Sanaa says, and I feel the most relief I've felt in days.

"Thank you. I don't know how I can possibly repay

you for your service today, doctor. We will commit every asset we can to aid in their recovery, mentally and physically." I tell her.

"Don't you know that's not how it works around here? We don't work in favors. It's just what we do. I'm glad I could help today. Maybe one day I'll need help and you'll be able to provide it," she holds out her hand, and I shake it gently.

"Anything I can do, just name it." I reply, leaving the room to find Vanessa.

She sits on the back porch, Doug sprawled at her feet, Rory by her side as they both smile. All I want is to spend the rest of my life keeping that smile on her face as often as I possibly can. If I'm honest, I don't want to spend another second longer than I have to apart from her. Even now, though I'm only feet away, I can feel the pull to her. Something is dragging my soul to hers, and I won't deny it, won't fight the feeling.

"Surprising, isn't it?" Breaker comes from somewhere behind me, standing shoulder to shoulder as we watch the women through the back window.

"To what do you refer?" I ask, knowing he's going to give me some nugget of wisdom. He always does. Though he and I are very close in age, his knowledge of relationships far outweighs mine.

"How quickly she becomes the axis everything else revolves around," he smirks, and I can't deny the truth he's speaking.

"It was quite unexpected, yes." I reply, thinking back to the first day she threw coffee in my face and called me a fucking bastard.

"Not to me. I saw this coming from the moment you two met." He claps me on the shoulder with a laugh, walking out onto the patio to join his wife.

Wife.

The word almost seems small compared to my love for Vanessa. Not that I take it lightly. It would be the highest honor I could ever impose on another person. Hell, I know I'd be honored to be her husband. It just seems so much smaller in comparison to the magnitude of our souls, long searching for their match in one another, finally finding peace. She is my home, my solace, my sanctuary from life's atrocities I so often must face. She keeps me centered when I stray too far from myself, something no one else has ever been able to do before her.

Following Breaker out into the cool afternoon air, I find myself taken aback by her beauty. Her face is marred by bruises, and I'm glad Luca paid with his life today. I wish I could bring him back and kill him slower for laying a finger on my woman. But she is still a vision of strength and elegance.

"Can we be done fighting dragons today? I need a nap," Vanessa says, reaching for me. I take her hand without hesitation, stopping behind her chair to drop a kiss on top of her head.

"Of course, Bambina. We can rest. And when we wake, it will be a new day for us, and a new chapter for Fortuna Nera. It's been a long time since they've had a queen, but I think it will be a welcome change." I smile down at her, and she looks panicked for only a moment before that familiar resolve overtakes her features.

There is nothing we cannot do together. I will spend my life building this empire, and she will rule by my side, the perfect confidante and partner. My lips collide with hers in a kiss that will echo through my bones for the rest of my life. I pay no attention to the audience around us, this moment is only ours.

"I have faced death and walked away. But you? You undo me completely, Vanessa. You are the most breath-taking thing I have ever had the privilege of surviving for."

epilogue

Vanessa

"WHY DON'T you just take them off?" Aria asks, rolling her eyes for the third time.

"Not a chance. They complete the outfit." I reply, adjusting my elbow length satin gloves for the hundredth time today.

"You obviously hate them." She laughs, and I can't deny it. I do hate them.

"Shhh, don't say that so loud. If you offend Rosetta on my wedding day, I'll have to kill you. And then what will all this time we've spent helping you recover have been for? Nothing, that's what." I smirk, adjusting them yet again.

"I don't think she likes me," Rory says, smoothing the front of her emerald green dress over her baby bump.

"I don't think she likes any of us," Aria laughs, tucking a stray curl back into her loose chignon.

"That's not true! She loves me," I shrug, lining my lips with a deep red lip pencil.

My ivory satin dress hugs every inch of my curves like it were painted on, the back dipping low on my spine and the train flaring out wide like a cape behind me. I feel undeniably sexy, but the girls are right, I hate these gloves. Slipping them from my fingers, I drag my hands down my hips, smoothing the fabric. I can't believe I'm here right now. This is a dream I never thought I would find, and I'm living it at this very moment.

Six months ago, we buried my parents. Sebastian offered to help my siblings start over in any way they wanted to, a far more generous offer than I would ever have extended. They could have a fresh start and get their education, pay off their debts, and finally be free from the world my parents kept them trapped in for so long. My oldest sister declined, refusing to even speak to me. But my brother seemed receptive to the help. He's young enough that he might not be too far gone to save from a dangerous path of self-destruction.

Aria spent three months recovering from her injuries before deciding she wanted to take a vacation and spend some time with me at the villa. We've toured half of Italy, seeing the most beautiful architecture and eating the most incredible food, spending all of our time healing our minds and bodies together as we planned this wedding. The bruises have faded, but her skin and mind still carry scars of the atrocities our parents committed against her. Now the day for only happiness is finally here.

"You look beautiful, baby sister." she says with a watery smile.

"I can't thank you enough for all of your help making this day so perfect. I couldn't do any of this without you." I squeeze her hand, and a tear rolls down her cheek.

"Don't you dare make me cry, asshole." Rory hands her a tissue, and she dabs under her eyes gently.

"Knock knock, are you ladies ready to go?" Enzo pokes his head in through the door frame, his jaw hanging open when he looks at me.

"Are you sure you're not willing to be my flower man? I mean, I really think you could pull it off." I tell him, and he rolls his eyes.

"Never gonna happen, regina mia. But you are a vision. Shall we?" He offers Rory his arm, guiding her through the labyrinth of halls in the villa until we reach the beautiful gardens he showed me several months ago.

When I envisioned the perfect place to stand in front of Sebastian and become his wife, this was the only place I could see in my mind. He hands her off to Breaker at the doors, and they make their way outside, sitting in the front row next to Rosetta. Matteo stands at the door, waiting for Aria. Through the open garden doors and flowing curtains, I can see Sebastian standing at the end of the aisle. He's facing away from me, his shoulders tensed and hands in his pockets.

"Ready to take a walk, sister?" Teo says, offering her his hand.

"I'm ready, are you?" She asks, looking back at me.

Some people may feel nervous on their wedding day, some may even have second thoughts. But I woke up this morning with the kind of peace of mind I didn't know was possible before today. I never thought this was the path I would walk in life, but this place feels like my home, these people like my family.

"I'll be right behind you," I reply, watching them walk up the short aisle and take their places on either side.

Taking a deep breath, I take the first step towards the rest of my life. The garden is full of all the people who love us most in this life, but all I can see is Sebastian. He turns to face me, his eyes dilating as he blows out a breath. I don't need to be a mind reader to know what he's thinking right now. He's imagining every way he can peel this beautiful dress off my body right this moment. God, I love that man. I take his hand, letting him help me up the few steps at the end of the aisle, and he gives me a wink before turning to the priest with a nod.

"Knock it off right now," I whisper, and he laughs softly.

"You started it," he says, brushing his thumb over the pulse point on my wrist.

"Promise you'll finish it?" I ask, quirking a brow.

"I just have a small prior commitment here, Bambina. Then I guarantee you, I'll finish it." He grins mischievously, and I swear I could fall for him all over again.

"If you two are done being disgusting, the rest of us are waiting." Matteo says drawing a few laughs from the crowd.

We listen to the priest talk for several minutes about love and fidelity, the importance of partnership and respect in marriage. All I can do is dive deep into Sebastian's dark eyes. We opted to pass on writing our own vows, knowing that everything we could possibly say to one another is only for the two of us to share. He slides the gold band onto my left hand when the priest prompts him to, a wide smile on his face. I follow the same motions, loving the look of the pristine gold band against his tattooed knuckles.

"In the name of the Father, and of the Son, and of the Holy Spirit, I now pronounce you..." the priest speaks, but Sebastian is already pulling me into him, crashing his lips against mine in a kiss full of so much devotion, I'm practically exploding from the inside out.

The world falls away as his lips glide across mine, his

tongue warring for control as he explores every inch of my mouth until I'm saturated in his taste, in his all-consuming presence. This kiss seems to go on forever, neither of us interested in breaking the connection.

"And now I think the rest of us will go inside so we don't have to watch any more of that," I hear Aria gag, and the garden clears out behind us, but I don't care.

Sebastian pulls my body flush against his, kissing me deeper, taking and demanding all I can possibly give. Everything I have is his anyway. He buries his hands in my hair, my flawless updo falling apart at his savagery.

"This dress is exquisite, my wife. I would hate to damage it. But your beauty has my control slipping more and more with each passing moment," he says, kissing a path down my neck, across my collarbone, and over my heart. He stops at the scar above my heart, the perfect *S* etched into my skin there, and places the softest kisses on top of it.

He wraps an arm around my waist, ushering me away from the center of the garden and into a more secluded area guarded on every side by tall, slender cypress trees lining the walkways. He pushes me into an alcove, my exposed shoulders scraping against the stone walls.

"I want to be inside you so badly it's causing me physical pain, Vanessa. But we don't have the time I need to worship your body the way you deserve to be worshipped. Hold your dress up," he says, dropping to his knees in front of me. He braces one of my heels against his shoulder, opening my core to him. "You were hiding this bare pussy underneath all of this beautiful wrapping just for me?"

The flat of his tongue swipes across my clit, and I suppress a scream. He licks and sucks my delicate flesh, feasting on me like I'm the remedy for hunger and he's fucking ravenous. My fingers slide into his hair, gripping the strands tightly as my climax builds. He nips at my clit and I explode, unintelligible sounds falling from my lips. Stars dance across my vision, my head swimming with waves of desire that flood my system every single time he touches me.

"We should really get to dinner," I pant, sliding my dress back down my hips and smoothing the fabric the best I can.

"No thanks, I already ate." He smirks, laughing to himself. "Turns out, you actually were on the menu."

I smack his shoulder, rolling my eyes. This will be the rest of my life, and the many after, doomed to live with this never-ending frat boy. I can't think of a better way to spend all my eternities.

acknowledgments

RMF. The realest motherfucker I've ever known. The man who always takes the time to see behind my mask. There are not enough words in existence to describe how grateful I am for you. So I'll borrow a few from Vessel, "You take the dark and carve me out a home…"
You are my sanctuary, my safe haven, my Eden in a world of chaos. There will never be enough time for me to express my devotion to you, but I will never stop trying. Everything I write is simply an ode to this great love.

Stephanie. Thank you for reading every book, cheering from my signing tables, and making me feel like what I do matters. Your support means more than I could ever explain. I hope this one didn't scare you away from all the rest.

Brittany Ashley. A selfless friend, an incredible wife and mother, and an inspiringly beautiful person inside and out. I'm so very grateful to know you, to learn from you, and to be on this journey of life with your support. Your kindness, your infinite support, and just *you* – it all means more than I can put into words. Thank you for being my friend.

Bobbi. I am infinitely appreciative that you took a chance with me and with this novel. Your hard work helped to shape it into the beautiful dark diamond that it is. I'm so very proud of you and I can't wait to see just how far this road leads you!

And Kammy. My original alpha baddie. You've been by my side since Jump Street. I will never have the words to explain what you mean to me and how knowing you has turned me into a better author, a better friend, and a better woman overall. I'm so thankful our paths crossed, and you stuck it out with me for all these years. You are the woman I aspire to be. I love you endlessly.

also by sage st. claire

THE GROVEWOOD INK SERIES

Follow these deliciously tattooed men in their pursuits to protect the women who capture their souls. True love and passion are never lacking in the South Carolina Low-Country. These intense alphas have met their matches in the fiery, headstrong women who win their hearts. Stroll down the streets of Grovewood, South Carolina and fall in love with the sprawling Oak Trees dripping in Spanish moss. Love, loss, pain, and pleasure all come together in this sleepy little town.

The Storms Between Us

A brother's best friend romance.

Stay With Me

A friends to lovers romance.

Tell Me No

An age-gap romance.

Yours To Keep

A fake dating romance.

Bring Me Back

A curvy queen romance

meet sage!

Sage St. Claire is the author behind the addictive Grovewood Ink series & the Fortuna Nera mafia series — a steamy, inked-up saga of tattoo artists, mended hearts, and love stories that burn as hot as the South Carolina streets.

Sage now writes from her home in Central Texas, where she lives with her own book husband, two kiddos, a rotating collection of houseplants, and far too many coffee mugs.

If you're into brooding artists, fiery banter, and chemistry that crackles off the page, you're exactly where you belong.

Join Sage's reader group for the latest news, book recommendations and plenty of spice, Sage's Sin & Ink Society!

facebook.com/SageStClaireAuthor
instagram.com/sagestclairebooks
goodreads.com/sagestclaire
tiktok.com/@sagestclairebooks
amazon.com/author/sagestclaire

www.ingramcontent.com/pod-product-compliance
Lightning Source LLC
LaVergne TN
LVHW100516110826
845146LV00002B/655
* 9 7 9 8 9 9 5 5 2 9 9 0 3 *